THE WATER WAS RED . . .

The boy's father grabbed at the air, trying to reach his son's hand but in a second his face was white with panic. The water gushed over him, encircling his face with red.

The boy fell backward as a sheet of ice broke out from under him. He crawled up quickly on his hands and knees. Then his father's head disappeared. The boy strained, he tried to reach out, but at that moment he saw a sight which made him shiver all over. Not from the cold, but from an infinite sickness which tore him apart inside.

Bodies of seals bobbed up through the thick red waves. There were hundreds of them, hideously bloated, floating, their eyes bulging . . .

Also by Frank Spiering from Jove

PRINCE JACK

BERSERKER

FRANK SPIERING

A JOVE BOOK

Acknowledgments

There were certain people without whom *Berserker* would not exist: Dr. Barry Zide of Bellevue Hospital, Eugene Bergmann of the American Museum of Natural History, and my enthusiastic and supportive editor, Bill Grose.

But most of all I was blest by the most brilliant of agents, Freya Manston, who initially encouraged me to write this book and whose faith in me was boundless.

First Jove edition published May 1981

First printing

Printed in the United States of America

Jove books are published by Jove Publications, Inc.,
200 Madison Avenue, New York, NY 10016

berserk(er), n. Grandson of the eight-handed Stark-adder and Alfhilde, had twelve sons who were famed for their wild frenzy in battle. Although they fought without armor, they were subject to seizures of diabolical fury, howling, foaming at the mouth and raving for blood and slaughter. They were expelled from Iceland for their unnatural acts in the year 1037.

—*Etymology translated from the Old Norse*

"Let no man awaken it, this same berserker rage."
　　　　　　　　　　　　　—Thomas Carlyle

PROLOGUE

6 A.M.
April 13, 1959
Greenland

Lanuk's eyes opened wide, his long lashes spreading, jutting up, as he swallowed against the lump in his throat. With his matted black hair chopped across his forehead in a sharp straight line and his father's huge sealskin jacket drooping down over his knees, he looked more like an elf than a boy of eleven.

"Angut Kagpog," his father called to him. The lean, half-naked man smiled. His lips minced into a great round grin as he rubbed his belly with his thick brown hand.

Lanuk had to look away. Squinting up, he saw that the sky looked like mountains of white snow with the dim sun shining through them. The stars had drifted together, faded, separated, and then continued to fade with a vapor, more like darkness, but with a translucency that cold brings.

"Angut Kagpog," his father called to him again.

He wanted him to see, *to learn.*

The boy forced himself to watch as his father tied the neck of the sledgedog with a leather strap. The dog whimpered and snarled as it was hoisted slowly up. The leather strap grew tighter, until it began choking the dog. The dog's feet kicked with fury as it fought to get free. Then as the knot around its neck doubled over into a wad and its feet swung to and fro above the ground, its tongue dropped out.

Finally it just hung there.

Lanuk hated seeing it. But according to his father,

there was no other way. The long sharp teeth of most sledgedogs were dulled by a stone or a file when they were puppies. But, as his father explained, this dog was already full grown. It was beautiful-looking with thick silver fur, a pointed snout and erect ears. But his mother had continually warned Lanuk not to pet him, as he was part wolf.

In a few moments the dog's eyes closed.

Quickly his father lowered him and pried apart his jaws with two skin lines. Now, while the dog was barely conscious, its mouth open and its tongue hanging out, his father began to pound down its teeth with a hammer.

Lanuk turned away. He could not watch. With each thud and crunch a chill shot through him.

Now the dog would no longer be able to eat frozen meat in winter, unless it was thawed out for him. He would be fed in a group with the other dogs and would have to gulp down his food with no time to chew it.

The meat would remain in his stomach several days, as it took that long to digest. This would be done purposely to give the dog the feeling he had just eaten.

The dog would be trained to work like the others. When harnessed to a sledge he would be guided by a whip. To Lanuk the whip seemed a brutal weapon. The Eskimos knew to a hair's breadth how to hit not only the particular dog, but the very part of the dog's body they wanted to reach.

Six to eight dogs would be harnessed in a pack. Lanuk recalled ruefully how often after a few hours' run the traces which were tied to the dogs' shoulders became so entangled that it was necessary to stop and clear them.

That was his job. Even though the weather might be severely cold, it had to be done with bare hands.

Sometimes he had worked until his hands had become frozen and raw.

If the trail lay across hummock ice and the sledge was heavily loaded, the dogs might toil and pull but the sledge would not move. His father would lend a hand, an encouraging yell would be given to the dogs—but the sledge would not move. A mound of snow would be removed in front of the runners. The sledge would inch forward. The dogs would howl with the strain—suddenly it would free itself. But often the whole thing would have to be done again and again every few feet.

Seal hunting was exhausting. It wore him out. There was no strength left to play or even to shout or laugh afterward. But according to his father, it was the best source of food the Eskimo had.

He knew that later this morning this beautiful dog would be harnessed with the rest and prodded by the sting of the whip. He would become a member of a fierce, snarling pack. Lanuk felt sorry for the dog as he listened to the hammer pounding and breaking its teeth. Finally the boy could take no more. He put his hands over his ears and ran back into the tent.

His mother sat by the fire preparing the fish he had caught for the morning meal. Lanuk huddled beside her.

She smiled at him and tousled his hair with the tips of her fingers, grinning and hugging him to her.

"Lanuk—*anâlurshe, anâlurshe,*" she murmured, trying to quiet the anxiety she sensed within him. Her eyes glowed with that special radiance that made him feel warm.

Lanuk loved her eyes. She was no longer as pretty as she had been when he was a small child, but in some ways she was more beautiful. Her deeply browned face was harshly wrinkled, especially around her cheeks and mouth, but her silky black hair fell unknotted down over her shoulders.

It was her eyes that he liked most. Their twinkling blue glint said to him that he was special.

The fish she cleaned were his. At midnight he had taken his kayak into the fjord and paddled in and out between the icebergs. He had used a spear and a net. It was a good time to fish, as the water was cooler and the fish rose toward the night sun's rays dancing across the surface. In less than an hour he had brought home a large catch of trout and halibut.

His mother had been pleased with the fish.

He dangled one foot within a pebble's width from the fire as he watched his mother slash them open with a knife. The flames rose up, throwing huge ominous shadows against the walls of the tent.

Above him the ceiling was hung with dozens of harpoons, their blades fashioned of narwhal tusk with a crude bone pick at each end for chipping holes in the ice. At the end of his bed lay two pairs of sandals made of polar bear skin which would enable his father and himself to walk noiselessly across the ice, advancing at the sound of a snorting seal, which meant that the animal was at a breathing hole. They would stop when the snorts ceased so that their footsteps could not be heard. Once again, when they heard a snort, they would rush to the hole and thrust their harpoons at the unsuspecting seal.

But he did not want to think of that now.

His mother's voice was soothing as her wrinkled hand smoothed his forehead. Softly she sang:

> *Ja-a ja-a ja-a ja-a*
> *Ha ja-a ja-a ja-a*
> *Haja-a ja-a ja-a ja-a . . .*

Suddenly his father burst through the flapskin opening of the tent.

"*Kamlikag*—" he pointed at Lanuk. His eyes flashed fiercely as he turned toward Lanuk's mother.

"*Utoq*—" he motioned, waving his arm as if
hurling a harpoon, "*Itsuartornuq.*"

"*Saluvara*," Lanuk's mother replied, shaking her
head.

His father was unhappy about the coat Lanuk was
wearing. He wanted him to have a sealskin jacket of
his own, one that fit him properly.

Lanuk's mother shook her head again. "*Saluvara*,"
she answered. She had not gotten around to making
one for him yet.

Finally his father dropped down to the edge of the
fire to wait for the food to be cooked.

His father looked very handsome in his soft caribou fur coat and his long hair tied back with gutskin.
He was one of the best hunters of the Netsilik tribe.
The other men had started out already, but his father
always hunted alone. He knew a special spot where
many seals waited beneath breathing holes in the ice.
It was a great distance and it would require several
hours to get there. It also meant that they would not
be returning home until very late.

It was warm in the hut and Lanuk was not eager to
get started.

Instead he would like to have stayed home and
played with his friends Tertaq and Inuteq or gone
kayak racing in and out between the icebergs.

Why was it so important to kill a hundred seals
before winter? It seemed wrong that it should be a
man's sole activity. Yet most Eskimo men had no
other purpose in their lives. Without the seals to
show their friends and family, they had no position.
The success of their hunting brought them importance. But to Lanuk, it seemed pointless.

His mother threw the fish on the grate below the
fire. They crackled almost immediately. Blisters of
heat began to bulge and pop beneath their skins.

The fish looked delicious.

His father was in a bad mood. He wanted to get

started. He did not want to wait. He sat staring into space, pretending to be patient, but marking time. Each day he was driven to face the challenge of using his skill against the seals who waited quietly beneath the ice and could easily escape capture.

His father, the hunter. As soon as they ate he would leap up and race outside to harness the dogs. He would yell at Lanuk to get moving.

Lanuk yawned. He felt warm and lazy in the tent. He leaned forward and kissed his mother's cheek, completely taking her by surprise.

She smiled down at him. Her blue eyes twinkled. Quietly she began humming the song, the one with no words.

11 A.M.

Lanuk and his father put on the sandals which would allow them to walk noiselessly across the ice. Slowly they crept forward, his father carrying the harpoon.

The trick was to find a breathing hole, to chop away a little of the ice and lower a string with a piece of bone tied to the end into the water beneath. Then they would wait for the first seal.

As soon as it rose to the surface to find the breathing hole, the piece of bone would jiggle. His father would stand, poised, until he saw the dark shape of the seal's head. Then he would hurl the harpoon at it with all his strength.

The air had become a blinding blur of sleet and frost. The boy's hands were numb with cold and he had to beat them against his sides.

Covering the narrow inlet was a sheet of thin ice. It was easily accessible, yet none of the other hunters had found the place. It was too far from camp.

The other men preferred to venture out a shorter distance so that it would not be so difficult to return home with their catch.

But there were more seals here, Lanuk's father insisted. And the fact that there were no hunters constantly coming and going made the seals less cautious.

The dogs had stopped barking and the sledge was left by a small hill of snow near the edge of the fjord. After the harnesses were untied the huskies had formed a circle, sitting just out of the wind.

Lanuk rubbed his eyes and glanced at his father's wide face. His expression was one of tense seriousness. He was doing what he had done all his life. It was a ritual which he had learned from his father, and his grandfather. It forced him to hide all feeling and emotion. His father had reminded him heatedly that it was not a game they were playing. Their lives depended on the day's catch.

Lanuk wished that his father might suddenly laugh, throw up his hands. Dance. But there was no happiness in his father's eyes. There was not even expectation or excitement.

It was as if each moment of wind which bit through their clothing was a reminder that he dare not relax. He had to earn the warmth that they would later enjoy in the tent. Lanuk remembered his father's eyes as he told him these things. They became very sharp and black. They would pierce out of his head. Then he would grit his teeth.

To sit lazily by the fire was not enough. One's worth had to be proven every moment, each day, he insisted. He would raise his arm and strike it forward again and again.

Lanuk watched as the end of the harpoon was

stuck into a clean section. His father began to chip carefully, picking away, until the chipping became easier.

There were seals beneath the ice, his father assured him. They were waiting. And as the harpoon chipped away Lanuk wished that one would suddenly give himself to them so that it would be all over. It was too cold and windy to be out there.

Lanuk buried his face in his hands. He wished that he were home in his tent. He wished that he were watching his mother flensing the fur from an animal with her sharp knife.

The wind suddenly slammed against his ears and cheeks. His eyes watered into a blur. Slowly the numbness in his hands was growing into sharp pains which stung the insides of his arms.

There was no question that he and his father were alone. There were no specks in the distance which might have been other hunters or sledges. There was only the pathless ice and snow.

"Lanuk!" his father yelled at him, "Lanuk!" hurriedly gesturing for him to back away from the hole he was chopping. With that his father jammed the harpoon's point into the ice. It stuck and then wobbled a second. His father pulled it out.

The ice cracked, buckling, and then a spurt of water shot up.

Lanuk blinked his eyes. He was not certain what he was seeing. The water was red.

He looked around him. Through patches where the wind ceased he saw that the ice was beginning to break and crumble.

Suddenly his father yanked him, pulling him by the hand. He dropped the harpoon. He flung him back across the ice.

The water below rippled. The soft ice crunched down. Then opened up.

He felt his father's hand lunge for him, touching his leg.

Lanuk grabbed for the harpoon but it was out of reach. He grabbed for his father.

But the ice suddenly shifted.

His father was struggling, trying to rise up out of the water, desperately trying to grab onto the ice with his arms and his shoulders, but his caribou skin coat was soaked.

Lanuk stretched toward him bracing his feet. His father grabbed at the air, trying to reach his hand, but in a second his face was white with panic. The water gushed over him, encircling his face with red.

Lanuk fell backward as a sheet of ice broke out from under him. He crawled up quickly on his hands and knees. Then his father's head disappeared.

Lanuk strained, he tried to reach out, but at that moment he saw a sight which made him shiver all over. Not from the cold, but from an infinite sickness which tore him apart inside. He almost threw up.

Bodies of seals bobbed up through the thick red waves. There were hundreds of them, hideously bloated, floating, their eyes bulging.

5 P.M.

Lanuk felt a burning in his chest. His feet shuffled forward but it was only the cold which kept him going. If it had not been for the bitter wind he would have stopped, unable to walk any farther.

He kept seeing his father . . .

Then there were the dead seals and the ocean of

bloody water seeping up through the jags of ice until he closed his eyes as hard as he could, wanting to be lost in the darkness inside his head.

He had to get home to tell his mother what had happened. He had seen his father sink into the water. He had watched him drown. There was nothing he could do but wait, hoping that his face might reappear.

But the ice and water had closed over him.

Lanuk had stood there in panic. Time went by, hours. He kept peering into the water until the smell of the seals and the blood filled his mouth. His stomach began to churn. He threw up. And then he cried, bent over, sobbing uncontrollably, his arms and legs limp.

It was terrible to be there. He wished his father would reappear, suddenly emerging, smiling. That would have made it all easy to understand. But the wind bit through him, burning his face and ears. And the smell of the dead seals grew worse.

That was when he finally turned away. He felt as if he had broken a link with his father forever. Yet each step had to be taken to get away from there.

Lanuk felt dead, as if part of him were frozen in the snow and would never awaken. A dull listlessness seized his arms and legs. But he had to keep moving.

He had left the dogs and the sledge behind. Not because he wanted to, but because he did not want to stop. He was afraid to stop.

His father would never again take him hunting. There would be no sound of his voice, no great hearty grin. It would be a memory. And yet, as these impressions flooded in on him, he could not cry.

Later he would cry. He would hold himself in his mother's arms and the tears would burn through his eyes, choking up into his mouth.

For the first time he realized that he really loved

his father. There had always been affection, but there had also been a distance between them. At times it was as if he were not his father's son, but someone else who had different ideas, different feelings. But his father had been a kind, gentle man. Beneath the rough exterior of the hunter, his father had cared for him.

The feelings were the most painful he had ever known. They choked up inside him, filling his mind with fears. Suddenly he was afraid of everything. But what about his mother?

As the pain continued to throb up through him, he gritted his teeth. It all seemed so pointless. Yet it was also as unavoidable as the dog's teeth being hammered and broken. There were laws. They had no meaning and yet men lived and died.

He wished that he did not have to watch his mother's face when he let her know. Perhaps he would be spared. In some way, perhaps he would be delivered from seeing the awful sickness which he felt, reflected suddenly in her eyes, from hearing her choke with agony, from hearing her screams . . .

His mouth was dry. His sealskin jacket hung heavy around his shoulders. Although the sun was no longer shining, he still wore his wooden snow goggles.

In the distance the clouds flowed into banks of gray. Violet shadows moved behind them. He imagined that their shapes resembled animals chasing each other. He saw a bear catching up to a seal. There were great whales and musk oxen rolling in waves a hairline above the horizon of ice craters which shone glistening beside the fjord. But he could not enjoy any of it. He was too afraid.

Afraid of what? He laughed to himself. And then he shivered. He *was*. He really was . . .

He squinted, peering across the ice at the horizon line. With each step he could feel the ice rock slightly beneath his feet.

It bothered him that no dogs ran out to meet him. Normally they would begin to bay when he was within a mile of the huts.

With each step he grew nearer, yet he saw no signs of activity. In the distance there were several reclining objects which he recognized as the shapes of weather-beaten kayaks pulled up along the beach.

But even if the men were still out hunting, the women should have been in front of their huts preparing food for the evening meal. The small children should have been running through the camp, the little girls with their dolls, the boys imitating the spirits of the tribe, pretending to hunt polar bear.

But there were no shapes moving. There was no sound except the wind. He heard no voices laughing, no shouts. The silence was unbearable.

They were waiting. That was it. They were waiting for him. He could have eagerly rushed forward and shouted, *"Ignatu lasuqua!"* With his eyes streaming tears he could have yelled that his father was no more. He had drowned beneath the ice.

Or he could say nothing until they asked him where the sledge was? The dogs?

But he could not wait for that. He would tell them in his own way when he got there.

He would announce to them the details of how brave his father had been, how resourceful, how good and kind and wonderful, all the things he remembered about his father.

But what about the seals? they would ask. Why were they all dead?

As his feet moved, Lanuk's stomach throbbed. His ribs and chest ached until his insides seemed to roll up on themselves. He took deep breaths as his feet walked on their own.

Approaching the clearing of huts, he kept his head down. He did not want them to see his expression, to take away any part of him until he had a chance to

tell what had happened. Then they could feel sorry
and sad, then they could probe his mind to find out
what he felt.

He continued to look at his feet, not wanting to
raise his eyes to see his tribesmen.

At the edge of the clearing he took a final breath
and stopped. For a second he saw their faces staring
at him, wondering. Then he looked up.

It was a blur. It was red and there were bloody
waves and bloated seals with popping eyes. But they
weren't seals.

He began to howl, he could not stop himself.
"Aja! Aja!" he yelled. A voice came out of him, not
his own. His father's! *"Aja! Aja!"*

He tore at the air with his hands and feet, leaping
and kicking, until finally he fell on his back. The
tears rolled out of his eyes.

Through the grass he glimpsed the bleeding bodies
that lay beneath the flapping skins of the huts. He
knew them. He had known them all his life.

Then he leaped up. He ran. He raced into his hut.
But his mother did not hear him enter. Her poor face
and hands would feel him in his thoughts. But she
had no eyes. She was naked, propped in a corner,
her face practically gone. He reached for her arms,
to hug her, to enfold her in himself, as her blood
poured over him.

TWENTY YEARS
LATER

3 A.M.
September 8, 1979

For hours the endless fury of rampaging snow had howled downward in consuming white sheets as if fueled by an inferno, until the clearing was finally hemmed in, cut off on all sides by the bleak, unyielding wilderness. Through the early morning darkness, several hundred yards beyond the long jet runway, two tiny headlight beams loomed haltingly across the cascading drifts of shifting ice. Four thin well-worn tires spun, attempted to dig in, to adhere, to propel the Volvo pickup truck toward the lonely freight hangar. It was a treacherous journey. Several times a surge of wind seemed to nearly lift the truck off its axles. Yet with a final burst it managed to free itself, to fight its way forward across the final stretch of plunging ice.

The truck slid to a stop. Blinding snow swept over his neck and shoulders and the screaming wind pounded against his face as Knud Ebbersen urged his thick, muscular body out from behind the steering wheel. Impatiently his watery blue eyes glared at the enormous wooden crate standing in front of the hangar entrance. Across its pine slat sidings were visible the slashed markings:

N. W. Rasmussen
American Museum of Natural History
New York, N. Y.
Berserker Statue
Weight 400 Pounds

Why had it been taken out of the hangar and left in the snow? It should have been loaded hours before in the S.A.S. DC-8 waiting on the field. It angered him that Sven Jensen's ground crew had become so negligent.

Knud hurried inside the dimly lighted hangar and grabbed for the telephone. Repeatedly jabbing the red intercom button at its base, he paused, listening.

But there was no answer. Perhaps the phone line had been knocked out by the storm.

Cursing to himself, he slammed down the receiver. The DC-8 would be taking off in less than an hour. As head dispatcher it would be his neck if the crate was not on board.

The prospect of the relentless pelting snow enraged him as he headed toward the tow motor. His mind reeled with antagonism. Sven's ground crew had let him down. Starting the engine, he lowered the long blades into position, jamming down the floor pedal.

Through the shadows of the hangar he drove out into the torrent of freezing wind, his face blistering with pain. As he angled the steel blades under the platform supporting the wooden crate, it wobbled a second. He pulled up on the lift lever. The twin blades lifted easily. He flung the tow motor into reverse, raising the crate up, up, backing out of the wind, swinging it into the protection of the cavernous hangar.

Reving up the tow motor's engine, he slid the wooden crate onto the huge scales. He watched as the long black indicator rose, hovering, finally jiggling back and forth beneath the numerals 398. That *was* what it weighed. The statue inside must be hollow, he thought to himself. Jotting the figure on the manifest sheet he climbed down from the tow motor seat.

Now the crate would have to be loaded onto the plane.

He gripped his hands together tightly, attempting to force circulation back into his fingers, then he blew on them, hoping the white exhaust from his mouth might hasten the warming process. But it was cold. Much too cold to be standing idly in an unheated freight hangar.

No. He refused. He wasn't going to load it himself. Not in this weather. It wasn't his job.

Hugging his arms to his sides, he raced back outside. He would find that son of a bitch Sven Jensen. That was for sure. He was probably inside the terminal, leisurely sipping coffee.

Knud climbed back into his Volvo pickup truck. As the wind howled in fury around him, he quickly slammed the door, flicking the ignition key to start the engine. But there was no contact. He tried it again. Still nothing. In sudden irritation he twisted the key on, off, on again, flooring the accelerator, hurriedly twisting the key on again. Still nothing.

For several seconds Knud leaned back helplessly, his stomach churning. He was too far from the terminal building to walk. Now what?

He shoved open the door, cursing violently to himself as he climbed out of the truck. Pounding his hands against his chest, he gritted his teeth to ward off the cold. Sven's negligence had caused him real trouble. Deep down he was beginning to hate him. But as he strode back into the hangar he instantly halted. In amazement he stared at the wooden crate. It no longer rested on the scales. It was standing on the floor beside the blades of the tow motor.

"Sven? Sven?" he shouted into the lurking shadows at the rear of the hangar. "Sven?"

He listened intently. But there was no response.

At that moment he was seized by a feeling of fierce loneliness. And then a sound echoed. The clipped, recurrent movement of a heavy door slapping open and shut, open and shut. At the same

moment he experienced an intermittent gust of freezing air swirling against his body from the darkness at
the other end of the hangar.

"Sven!" he shouted again.

He gritted his teeth. That must be it. While he was
outside in the truck, Sven or one of his men must
have slipped the crate off the scales and then hurriedly escaped through the rear door. *But why?*

He felt a sudden chill as he laughed to himself
crazily. All right. He could take a joke. He would
load the crate himself. But they would pay. He
would show them. He'd get even for this.

He hoisted himself back up onto the seat of the
tow motor. Flicking on the engine he eased the
blades forward slipping them under the wooden crate.
He pulled up on the lift gear. The blades strained to
rise as the tow motor's wheels dug in, rearing back
against the load.

Something was wrong. The crate seemed to be
stuck.

Desperately he yanked the lift gear with all his
might. The edge of the crate gave way, lifting a few
inches. Suddenly he felt a shot of air whip by his
face as the hydraulic chain curled up, snapping in
half. The crate fell forward, toppling over onto the
scales with a thundering crash.

For a split second Knud was worried that the
hollow statue inside might have shattered. Then with
alarm he noticed the scale. The long black indicator
flew past six hundred, seven hundred, past a thousand pounds. He could not believe his eyes. It hurtled upward wildly, hovering finally beneath the
numerals *1,237.*

He stared aghast at the pine sidings of the huge
packing case. Was this another of the ground crew's
jokes? Had they somehow jimmied the scale? No.
They couldn't have had time. Perhaps he had misread

it before. But it couldn't weigh that much. Not one thousand two hundred and thirty seven pounds!

Knud jumped down from the tow motor. Grabbing a crowbar, he was about to claw open the wooden slats when he heard a faint rustling inside the crate. He hesitated, his heart fluttering with mounting anxiety. Finally he ripped back one of the slats, peering in. What he saw filled him with panic. *There was an eye—a single eye staring out at him.*

And then the lights went out in the hangar.

Knud backed up quickly, flicking on his belt flashlight, wanting to get out of there. What he saw almost made him faint. The thin glow beamed against a mountain of heaving black fur. Knud screamed, his eyes throbbing with disbelief.

Instantly there was a roar which seemed to shake the walls of the hangar. He tried to pound it with the crowbar—something—*it had him by the arm*, pulling him in—he yanked backward. There was a splintering sound as a shower of wooden slats fell loose at his feet. His arm was gone—he felt it—the roots catching the cold wind. "Aaahg!" Knud cried, whirling in horrible pain, as four rows of teeth tore into his throat. His lips bulged forth, spitting fitfully, sputtering. He fell backward, choking, gurgling for breath, as the spurting geyser of his own blood gushed up into his face.

4 A.M.

Austere icy crags towered over the vague outline of the unlighted building which resembled a long two-story factory supporting a dormant spiny smoke-

stack in the center. Above the building's concrete
and glass facade shuddered a thin, hand-lettered sign:
Søndre-Strømfjord Airport. When Sven Jensen and
his two crew members emerged from it onto the jet
runway, they spotted a large wooden crate standing
next to the DC-8. Sven hurriedly directed his men to
lower the plane's hydraulic lift. Carefully the huge
crate was tilted up to the doorsill and loaded by
conveyor belt into the belly of the aircraft.

Within minutes the four Pratt and Whitney en-
gines began to shiver, emitting a stream of exhaust
which radiated across the runway in silken pulsating
furrows. Ten sand-packed wheels cracked loose from
their shocks and the DC-8 began to taxi forward. As
the plane's speed increased, the pilot stared up through
his cockpit window at the falling blanket of impenetrable snow. Two thousand feet from the end of the
runway he pulled back on the steering column and
the plane roared upward, heading east to avoid the
towering ice cap at the west end of the field.

There was no visibility and yet at a ninety degree
angle the huge jetliner groaned relentlessly higher,
buffeted by massive deepening crosswinds, higher
still until it hurtled upward at two hundred miles per
hour. A dark bluish mist poured eerily across the
plane's wings. But there was no sunlight. Where the
sun should have appeared, there were only swirling
bands of encircling white vapor. And then the pilot
saw it. A dark object plummeting toward him across
the murky sky. He immediately suspected it was
another plane. He braced himself, attempting to bank
the plane to the right. Fear gripped him as he yanked
back on the steering column, anticipating a collision.
But at the last instant the object unfurled its mighty
wings and veered away. He stared at it in astonishment. It was a gigantic black falcon, its eyes flashing with the color of emeralds.

As he watched the enormous bird, the pilot's

clenched hands froze around the steering column.
For several seconds the bird savagely dived in hurtling swoops. It seemed intent on attacking the plane.
Yet each time it veered away at the last second.
Then it let out a harsh echoing scream, wailing
frantically. Clapping its wings, it spun upward. Its
great body began to shimmer, radiating an incredible
red glow. Suddenly it caught fire, blazing with a
molten, diamondlike incandescence, blanking out the
sky as it rolled through glowing rivers of crimson
and violet and diappeared high into the heavens.

Later that morning two Danish workmen found a
bloody arm near the empty freight hangar. Just inside
the hangar entrance they discovered a mass of broken flesh. Shreds of clothing hung from clawed legs.
A detached head lay a yard or so from the mutilated
torso. Most of the face had been ripped away but the
eyes were open and staring.

In a short while the remains were identified as
Knud Ebbersen. A search was begun for the wild
beast, perhaps a wolf or a bear which, unnoticed
during the storm, must have descended from the
surrounding wilderness.

PART ONE
New York City

1

Miranda Reichert whirled to the melody of *La Valse* as the lights of a dozen penthouses smiled like jewels through her open window. It was the happiest day of her life. She had been given a principal role in the new Balanchine ballet premiering in October.

Mr. B. had taken her by the hands, looked into her eyes with that wonderful imperious face, spoken in a deep somber voice and told her that he wanted her, she was ready.

She would have the same chance he had given to Gelsey Kirkland and Suzanne Farrell. All the years of class, her father's dreams, her own burning hopes would be answered, all of it. The feeling excited her so much that she could not stand still, she had to run, to lift her feet and her legs, spin, laugh. It was a beautiful night. A perfectly beautiful night. She would never be as young or as happy. She did a jeté winding around to a pirouette, pleading with her hands as if to an invisible partner, take me, take me away, then she spun out, the tempo building. She loved Ravel. She loved Balanchine. She loved what was happening to her heart. She felt it flutter and ascend. And as she leapt and spun and whirled through the barrenness of her empty apartment, she imagined an audience sitting watching her, in their red velvet seats, their eyes fixed, entranced, as she ran and leapt and tore across the stage with violet and blue lights fondly caressing her dreams, her expectations.

After Balanchine told her, she had wept. She

could not eat. The memory of it made her want to run to the park, to embrace and kiss the trees, to find a path where there was no one. It was almost too much to feel so important, yet she did not feel important as if there were other people anywhere. For the first time she was alone in her private world, a mad, insane, wonderful world. Finally, she was a *dancer*.

As she whirled across her apartment, the intercom buzzed with a monotonous wail. Miranda pressed the button marked ''Talk.'' ''Hello. Who is it?'' The faint, shaky voice of her boyfriend was barely audible. ''It's Mark . . . do you—want—me to come—up?''

Did she want Mark to come up? To intrude upon the spell that had overwhelmed her? Quickly she glanced around the kitchen. The sink filled with two days of dirty dishes and the enormous brown paper bags of garbage piled next to the stove met her eyes. ''I'll be right down!'' she shouted out of breath, without bothering to press the adjoining button marked ''Door'' to let him in. She was certain that the night outside was warm. He could wait. The thought of telling him what had happened delighted her. She could picture his eyes floating with amazement.

Heading into the bathroom she checked her makeup, giving her artificial lashes a flick up just to prove that she was not wearing too much green eye shadow. Finally satisfied with herself, she turned and whirled toward the door. She would leave the lights on. She wanted the rooms to stay exactly as they were. When she returned it would be magic all over again.

It was her first week living alone on Manhattan's west side and as she opened the heavy door and then wrenched it shut behind her she took an extra moment to make sure it was double-bolted. The short L-shaped hallway with its grimy brown walls was an infuriating contrast to the special world within. Next to the elevator was a mail chute with a crusted bronze slot for depositing letters. Someone had pasted a series of United Nations posters on the walls in an attempt to make them seem less forbidding. An elderly woman teaching a child to dance was captioned, "Do your children get special help if they are gifted or handicapped?" Next to it a smiling child clutching a ball of cotton candy swung happily from a tree, while opposite it a color photograph of a child in a garden filled with daisies read, "Do *your* children live in a healthy environment?" Crossing the hall Miranda pressed the button for the elevator and patiently watched the ancient indicator above methodically flashing numbers as it rose the twelve floors to where she stood. The elevator door rolled open. With her head thrown back she was laughing as she stepped in. She did not notice the drop of three feet.

Her legs went out from under her, even though she landed on one knee. A sharp pain flared up toward her ribs. The knee was bruised, broken, oh God, she hoped not. But when she tried to stand up she felt for her foot, the other one, the left foot. She noticed it was wedged between the edge of the elevator floor and the cement shaft wall.

She screamed, fighting with the air, howling, please help me, shouting for someone, anyone to come. The door stayed open for several seconds, then slowly began to close with Miranda praying, begging that the elevator would not move as she stretched up frantically trying to reach the "Open" button on the dash above her head. She continued to shout, to scream for help as at that instant a lady on the eighteenth floor rang for the elevator to ascend.

The door slapped shut. There was another pause, a sickening deathlike silence, and then with a lurch the elevator jumped up drawing her in, scraping against the bone of Miranda's calf, mangling the flesh, vessels and nerves, sucking her foot down deeper, finally, hideously, snapping it off and almost pulling the other leg in, as she fell back clawing pitifully at the walls, her agonized howls reverberating throughout the shaft.

A siren shrieked across the night, followed by the grunting gear-mauling belch of a fire truck reeling around a corner, roaring into the maelstrom of traffic past the canopied entrance, squealing down the block where finally only its echo was felt as it abandoned the towering apartment buildings and powered its way up Riverside Drive. Milton Reichert, summoned by her staggering boyfriend, held the head of his beloved nineteen-year-old daughter in his arms, tears rolling from his eyes, as outside the glass doors leading to the lobby two ambulance attendants debated where to deliver the girl, to which hospital, uptown or across to the east side.

"We can get her to Roosevelt in minutes."

"They don't have the facilities—"

"Part of her leg and foot is still in the shaft," the older, more masculine-looking attendant muttered.

"I'll find it," his partner replied.

In the brightly lighted darkness a crowd of strangers had gathered, looking in at the middle-aged man, his torso shaking with grief, but especially at the blanket-wrapped form on the wheeled stretcher. Suddenly Milton Reichert let out a moan. He could not keep it inside—the pain was so terrible that he stood up, wringing his hands, babbling and bawling like a baby.

"What is it? What happened?" questioned a shivering black lady, an inmate from the nursing home next door.

"Her leg got caught in the elevator," snorted a surly doorman from across the street who had been watching the scene for several minutes.

"The elevators in all these buildings oughta be shut down," she slurred. "They don't work right. I almost caught ma foot in one last week."

As Milton Reichert watched, the older attendant made up his mind. Decisively he and his partner strode into the lobby and began to wheel the stretcher out toward the ambulance double-parked on the street.

Milton Reichert looked up, his face swollen red, his eyes sinking with puffiness. "Where are you— where are you—" he gestured, helpless, unable to speak the words "taking her."

"Bellevue," the older attendant said. "That's where the best doc is."

All eyes were on the bearded young surgeon from the University of Copenhagen Hospital. Still alert, there was an incredible handsomeness about him that was hypnotic. At first one might have concluded it was his jaw, intense and sinewy, the cheeks and earlobes finely sculptured beneath sliver spikes of close-cropped, coal-black hair. But it was his eyes, seeming to stare into infinite space, which drew more avid attention as they focused on the most delicate of objects with absolute control. He could have been the dream of most doctors, or in another role, perhaps the ideal of any man who had ever found himself pitted against the inscrutable challenge of violence and death. A magnetic aura radiated from his assuredness, his lack of hesitancy to take the chance which might prove to be the one hope for success. And always it was a desperate chance, arrived at by his supple resourcefulness. As he braced his right arm against his body to avoid the slightest quiver, with the smallest of forceps he imperceptibly sutured the vein leading from the leg into the foot.

The zoom lens on the closed-circuit television camera attached to the overhead microscope revealed each twist of the seventy micron needle as he allowed it to wiggle its way in and out, finally freeing itself enough to curl the suture so he could knot it. The young surgeon took a breath. He had been working without hesitation for seven straight hours and he purposely blinked his intense dark eyes several times to remove any blur of an image which might slide between his vision and the slim vibrating vessel magnified four and a half times beneath the glass of his eyeloop. The micro forceps felt dead and for a second unresponsive in his hand, which is why he bent his fingers ever so slightly to permit the circulation to trickle back into the tips of his index finger and thumb. Letting go of the microscopic needle, he straightened up, finally giving in to the unmerciful throb of his strained back muscles.

Few of the one hundred and twenty-two residents seated in the steeply banked, spotlight-washed amphitheater knew his name, but several of the women sat forward in their seats, completely enraptured by the sensitive lines of his mouth contrasting with his dark bold features. He did not look Scandinavian; they pictured Scandinavians as being blond. And when he spoke to either the female anesthetist or his fellow surgeon Bill DeCormier, his English was almost American. But those that did know him or had seen his former work were well aware that Christian Bangsted was one of the most brilliant young micro surgeons on the face of the earth. He had studied with some of the most famous men alive and had come to them not only because he had chosen to, but as a gift.

Bending over again, the young surgeon tapped the floor pedal to allow the zoom lens to focus on the ending of an almost invisible motor nerve. It trailed off slightly, vaguely, yet he sensed it was only millimeters away from the nerve ending leading up from the foot. He nodded to Bill DeCormier. Perhaps the distance was right, he had to make certain, but there was no way to tell.

With the micro forceps he reached for a second needle, its eye threaded with transparent nylon suture. Delicately slipping it into the tip of the nerve ending, he threaded it through. Then he reached with the very point of the needle until he was confident that it had pierced the severed nerve, sewing the two ends together as Bill held them back with the tiny forceps to avoid possibility of overlapping.

The young micro surgeon smiled. ''I hope this is the motor nerve,'' he gestured with the forceps.

Bill's nervous laugh broke the tension. ''We'll find out when they wake us up in the morning.''

''You mean you are able to sleep?''

''Not as much as I did when I was in medical school.''

The scrub nurse had turned on the radio and soft music poured into the operating room. The melody was familiar ''Lucy in the Sky with Diamonds,'' and for a second Bill let himself go, humming the refrain.

A rush rod had been shoved up through the center of Miranda Reichert's tibia and her foot was held extended by a pulley. The young surgeon continued to check the alterial line on the transducer to make certain she was not going into shock, as he worked steadily reconstructing and suturing the two-inch gap where her leg had once connected to her ankle. It was apparent that she was an attractive girl, which is why he asked that the meshed skin graft be taken from her buttocks so she could still wear a bathing suit. But whether or not she would ever walk on her left foot was questionable. It depended on the stress she put on it. The bone would have to strengthen and that could only come from her attempting to walk.

But the foot, the ankle, the leg would look the

same. The meshed skin graft would cover the scar-
ring.

The dial on the monitor at the side of the operating table indicated that her blood pressure was steady,
between 40 and 50 cc's, enough to keep up urinary
output. The voice of a commentator broke over the
radio.

*Last night nineteen-year-old Miranda Reichert, a
dancer with the New York City Ballet, suffered the
loss of her foot as the result of a tragic elevator
accident on Manhattan's west side . . .*

The scrub nurse hastened toward the radio, reaching to turn down the volume, but not before the
commentator uttered,

*Bellevue Hospital's micro surgery team is at this
moment working fervently to reconnect the severed
foot to the leg . . .*

As the young surgeon reached toward the exposed
artery with his micro forceps, he murmured out of
the side of his mouth, "Are you working *fervently*?"

"Hell no," Bill chugged, "I'm fuckin' worn out."

"Dr. Bangsted, do you feel that the operation
will be successful?"

"Will Miranda's foot heal?"

"Will she be able to walk?"

A rush of reporters rudely cornered the handsome
dark-haired young doctor in the reception room. Christian tried to draw back as flashbulbs ignited from all
directions. Television cameras loomed down on him.
Alarmed, he turned to Bill, "What is this?"

Bill managed a quick shrug as he was elbowed out
of the way. "It's a Cinderella story. You're Prince
Charming."

A smartly dressed woman shoved forward, "Dr.
Bangsted, do you feel that micro surgery is the
most advanced form of medicine in the world today?"

Christian cleared his throat, aimiably trying to

appease her. "No, it's not new. It's been around for several years."

"Who did you study with?"

"Dr. Erhardt Friedlander, the foremost surgeon in the field. He's a genius."

"You're a genius," the smartly dressed woman coyly smiled.

"Will she be able to walk again?" another reporter burst in.

"That depends on the bone—the tibia—how it heals—how quickly she puts pressure on it."

"What about the other bone—what's it called—"

"The fibula."

"What about the fibula?"

"It does not matter as much."

"Dr. Bangsted, you're from Denmark. You don't look Danish."

He shook his head. "I'm not."

"Where do you come from?"

At that point he felt Bill tugging at his arm. "I'm going out for a beer."

"Wait a minute, get me out of this!" Christian pleaded.

"You're the genius," Bill smiled mischievously as Christian helplessly watched him disappear out through the double doors leading to the street.

More voices piled at him.

"Dr. Bangsted, is it true that the secret of micro surgery is a thread that can't be seen?"

"Dr. Bangsted—"

"Dr. Bangsted, where *are* you from?"

"Are you married?"

Christian fumbled his way back into the privacy of the Reconstructive Surgery Department. The metal doors sucked him in and with gradually deepening relief he sensed the silence beyond. No one else was lingering to speak with him. No one waited hyper-intensely to pick his thoughts.

Sunlight victoriously drenched the hanging drapes of the reception room with its brown plastic couches leading into a complex of cell-like offices, each furnished with ugly plaster lamps and huddled desks arranged atop a crossword of shag carpet. Danish modern furniture. The thought tickled him. *Det Laegevidenskabelige Hovedomrade*, that is what he was. One of the Medical Faculty encased in a chamber of Danish modern furniture. It made him laugh as he thought of it, but it hurt the muscles of his face too much to laugh.

He was tired, too tired to come up with any more decisions, to make up answers, to listen to questions. Explain what? What more could he tell them about needles and transparent sutures and micro incisions. But they were hungry. Suddenly they had seized on the subject like a voracious mouth coveting each ritualistic detail, and their readers were hungry. The Hoffman apparatus, a rod piercing through the bone, supporting the foot while it healed—he had offered to show them how it worked, promised to give them photographs of transplanted arms and legs. "I never throw anything away." That made them laugh. Why did they laugh? Was it out of sensitivity or fear for themselves? Or were they haphazardly letting him know that he was in the circus business— *fresh freaks and oddities, step right up*.

Fingers of exhaustion crept across his eyelids, his head was beginning to ache. Is that why he had come to America? To be a celebrity? Everybody in America wanted to be a celebrity, why not him?

He laughed as he shook his head derisively.

Passing the conference room occupied by a man in a baggy suede sport jacket sitting alone, he noticed that the man's eyes were red from weeping. He was a large, heavyset man, obviously in his late fifties, with tufts of white hair strewing from his temples.

Immediately Christian knew that the man was waiting for him. "Dr. Bangsted?"

"Yes."

"I'm Milton Reichert."

"Your daughter—" Christian pointed back toward the main corridor of the hospital from where he had come.

The man nodded. "She's only nineteen. I never should have let her live by herself. Do you know what it is to have a daughter, Dr. Bangsted? To see her lying there helpless, so alone, and know that I can't help? I helped her since she was a little girl. I gave her dance lessons—she wanted to dance more than anything . . . I gave her dance lessons . . ." He suddenly sobbed.

Christian felt exasperation well up inside him, exasperation at himself because he had nothing left to say, he had said it all. "I think she'll be all right," he finally said.

Then Reichert peered straight at him. He looked at him as if he were God. "Will she be able to dance?"

Christian stopped dead. Staring at the middle-aged man, he felt as if he should manufacture an answer, something to let himself out of answering at all. The question seemed so illogical, so amazingly incoherent. The girl's foot was connected to her leg only by a series of threads. It was the kind of thoughtless question a reporter might ask.

After a second's hesitation he decided to give him the truth. "I don't know." Christian shook his head. "With foot surgery we don't know if it even works. With a hand—I mean I had a case last week where I transplanted a toe onto a thumb—it is easier."

"But you did your best." Reichert seemed desperately intent on prying from him some form of reassurance that his daughter would be returned intact. A lie would do, some mental panacea that would soothe his immediate anguish. Couldn't he at least come up with that?

Christian let out a choked sigh, "I don't even know that. I think so."

"Well, what the hell are you playing in there, games?" Reichert's eyes popped out at him, crackling with intimidation.

"Sometimes . . . it's like a game. I try something new. That's all. That's all I do."

"It's immoral!" Reichert shrieked. "Doctors heal people! They make people whole!"

Christian gaped at him. It was the final surprise. Reporters could prod him for answers but this man was challenging his whole life. He felt sorry for him. Disgusted and sorry.

"I wish," Christian began, "I wish I could tell you—that your daughter will walk, will dance, will be exactly as she was. I wish I could tell you that I could perform miracles . . ." He sank down into a couch exhaustedly closing his eyes.

"Well then, what is it you do, Dr. Bangsted!"

With that a thought came over him and Christian began to laugh. In the darkness of his mind he remembered his grandfather. His grandfather had been the shaman of his tribe. He had been able to perform miracles. At that moment he wished he were his grandfather.

2

Navarana Rosing-Porsild strode through the dim corridors of the Museum of Natural History, her handmade, jeweled sandals slipping soundlessly against the black marble floors. There was a subtle pride about her, a regal essence to her walk. She held her shoulders high, her head poised, her long black flowing hair carressed tightly in a bun. She was a sensitive young woman, uncommonly lovely. Yet there was a tension about her lips and throat, an efficient stalwartness in her manner that might have put off even the most confident, secure man from summoning the courage to encounter her glance, to stare evenly into her dark brooding eyes. She could have been an athlete, her body possessed that kind of discipline. But not a modern athlete. Instead there was a classicism about her, as if she had run in marathons many centuries before, thrown a discus, hurled a javelin, or even been exalted as a symbol of what woman in her mind's eye, then rigidly cloistered and considered unequal to man, knew in her fondest dreams she could one day become.

As Navarana's long perfect legs moved silently forward she glanced at the walls covered with great scowling masks, feathered lances, harpoon heads and glittering knives edged with shark's teeth. Soon the galleries would echo with a hubbub of milling spectators, with eager schoolchildren researching class projects and camera-laden tourists from other cities. But at the moment it was quiet, the way she most enjoyed it. The front doors had not yet opened.

She made rapid notations on a small yellow pad of various changes that had to be made. The rehanging of special ceremonial masks. She would order a row of pin spotlights shining down from above to be refocused. She passed painted caribou skins depicting the battle between the Eskimos and their Viking invaders, scenes of tortured human bodies twisting and dying, the frightening impressions of a slaughter which had occurred a thousand years before. It was an awesome collection. The exhibit she had designed was so authentic that it filled her with intense pleasure. And yet Dr. Rasmussen had insisted that she inspect one more statue which had just arrived from Greenland.

She had been resentful at first. She disliked Rasmussen's interference. He was a giant in the field, respected throughout the world, yet as head of the department he ceremoniously flaunted his enormous influence, regarding the primitive artifacts which she had collected with almost a blasé coldness. There was a constant threatening distance between them. He was dispassionate and aloof, and yet she knew more about the Eskimos and their traditions than he would ever know. She had been raised in Greenland, brought up in the ways of her ancestors, inundated with their folklore, their legends.

Then when she was eleven her parents had moved to Egedesminde. Her father had taken a job working in the fisheries and her mother had enrolled her in the local Danish school. Yet she had wanted more than to raise a family and settle down along the shores of Disko Bay. At eighteen she had won a scholarship to Roskilde University near Copenhagen where she had studied anthropology. When the opportunity to come to the United States presented itself, she had welcomed it with enthusiasm.

But working for a man such as Dr. Rasmussen was a terrible disappointment. He was manipulative, constantly treating her as if she were a child. He seemed involved solely with his own image as the all-guiding, all-knowing intellectual-in-charge. In other areas such as warmth and understanding he failed miserably.

The exhibit needed nothing, she was convinced of it. The relics it contained told the story of her people. What more did Rasmussen want?

And now this statue. What would it add? A statue of what?

Indirect lighting pouring from the tops of the heavy marble pillars reflected against her high copper cheekbones, fixing her mouth into a look of expectancy as Navarana walked through the door marked *No Admittance*. She felt an immediate damp chill. And then an odor, a harsh putrid stench, assaulted her nostrils. It was sickening. The gray receiving room violently contrasted to the intricately designed galleries beyond. It was littered with refuse. Everywhere there were heaps of dirt, sections of discarded displays waiting to be broken up and burned, rusted metal tools, twisted shanks of black electrical wire and ladders, brooms, shovels, even traces of sharp shattered glass strewn across the floor so that she had to be careful where she walked.

But it was the fetid stench which most disturbed her. It was overpowering. Her stomach churned as her eyes desperately scanned the walls and the floor.

The huge wooden crate from Greenland had been left intact, in the center of the room, exactly as it had been shipped. She suddenly gasped, noticing the scrawled letters on the side of the wooden slats. The word *Berserker*. Her heart leapt, then raced forward, pounding. She knew the word. She still remembered it from vague, distant dreams. Yet she had forgotten most of the primitive legends. At least she had tried to. They had been told to her in another world, another life.

She felt light-headed as she envisioned campfires, the members of her family clad in gutskin robes, her grandmother's deep troubled eyes as she related the ancient stories, chaotic tales satiated with images of barbaric violence, and above all, the dark features of the *Berserker*, part beast, part human. Its supernatural presence had once overwhelmed her innocent mind with unbearable spasms of dread. She had been but a quivering infant crouched beside her grandmother's knee listening to the old woman's labored sighs, her grandmother's tense singing voice mingling with the screams of the night and the lost lonely cry of the arctic wind. Over the years Navarana had managed to blot out the hateful nightmares, the spectre of the raging beast descending from the frozen wilderness.

But some memories had never left her. At times in the early morning hours she still awakened screaming in breathless terror, clutching for her grandmother's knee, begging the old woman to stop telling the stories, to protect her from the monster . . .

Navarana forced a smile to her lips. The stories had been told to her so long ago. But she was grown up now.

As she stood there in the cold gray room the smell continued to trouble her. The awful odor was coming from the packing case. She was certain of it. Yet according to the markings on its wooden sides, it contained only a statue. Weight four hundred pounds.

She hesitated. Her first impulse was to call for a workman to help her unpack it. The smell coming from inside the wooden crate was nauseating. She tried to resist it, but it was vile. It took every bit of effort to stop herself from vomiting.

Yet she felt drawn in, mesmerized, as the suggestion of something alive inside the packing case egged at her imagination.

She was intensely bothered by the feeling that it

might be a cat or dog, trapped, some form of animal, rotting.

Navarana spied a hammer lying on the floor. With uneasy fingers she began pulling away the wooden slats, twisting them loose, her neck and arms beginning to tremble—*and then something moved inside the crate.*

Her breath stopped. Could she have imagined it?

Summoning all of her remaining courage, she pried free another wooden slat, then another, as if a frenzy had enveloped her hands. Suddenly she dropped the hammer.

The plaster figure of the *Berserker* leered out of the packing case. It seemed almost as if it were alive. It was as her grandmother had described, as she had always imagined it, the revolting tissue of its crumbling features swollen in a death mask of hideous rage, the mouth a venomous crawling gash slashing downward, twisting the neck and curved, sabre-shaped ears into hulking scarred mounds. But there was something else. Something that was not part of any statue. A turgid trickle of blood, fresh blood, dripped in a dried foaming mass from its white lips.

It was abominable. She was sorry that she had pried open the wooden packing case. It brought back too many frightening memories. Her hands were wet with perspiration. She wanted to get out of there, more than anything in the world. She felt sick, weak. She wanted to run.

And then its mouth opened. She couldn't believe it. It couldn't be happening! Suddenly the thing seemed to pulsate. Hundreds of veins tore across its deformed features, beads of moisture sprung from its hideous snout . . . and there was fur . . . black fur shifting across its neck . . . bristling down its ghastly body!

It was a statue, Navarana screamed to herself, a statue!

You know who I am. It's voice rocketed through her, encasing her mind, entrapping it. The eyes, the four hideous orbs descended as its massive head bent forward. *You know who I am, Navarana.* Slowly it opened its jaws, revealing endless rows of jutting jagged teeth. Its taloned feet stretched toward the edge of its pedestal.

She wasn't imagining it! Its horrible claw slashed out at her!

Navarana sank backward, tripping over something, losing her balance, falling to the littered floor, trying to slide away. She felt its sickening belly looming over her, its horrendous jowls dripping blood and clots of green bile onto her face. And then a sensation gripped her, wrenching across her body as if she were being choked, more like a force than anything physical. She clutched her neck fearfully, gasping for breath, tears riddling her eyes. She squirmed in frenzy, fighting for her life. *It's not you that I want,* it screamed through her. But it couldn't have come out of her. The words were not hers! Desperately she grappled, trying to free her neck, her throat as its roar clawed upward through her stomach, *I must have him! The leader of your tribe!*

His gray hair parted up the middle caught the glow of the fluorescent arc lamp over his shoulder as Dr. Nils Rasmussen leaned closer to the yellow oak desk. He was a scientist, a Nobel Prize winner, distinguished looking, imbued with the special magnetism of someone whose struggle for worldly reputation had been rewarded. He sighed deeply as he shuffled through the pile of papers comprising the museum's yearly budget, aimlessly reaching across the desk for more matches to relight his pipe. And then he heard a woman's scream, a terrible spell-binding shriek. Followed by the sounds of frantic rustling in the hallway outside.

His heart almost stopped. In alarm, Rasmussen swiveled around in his red leather chair. "Who . . . who's there?"

There was the long drawn-out sound of sobbing, pathetic and uncontrollable. And then Navarana burst through the door of his office, her face frozen, a look of storming panic in her eyes. "Come! . . . Come!" her stricken lips twisted in a trembling mass. She was beside herself. She pointed to the hallway behind her.

"Navarana!" he exclaimed.

Tears gushing from her eyes, she clutched his arm, shrieking, "Please!" She yanked at him, trying to pull him out of the chair.

"What's the matter!"

"Oh, please!"

Quickly he rose. "But what is it!" Her terror confounded him. "Now come, come, Navarana— pull yourself together—please tell me . . ."

With spasmodic gestures she continued pointing toward the long curving hallway.

Reluctantly he followed her out of the office, aroused by the feeling something terrible had happened. She hurried him down the corridor, around a turn densely bordered by collections of animal bones, beads, copper utensils, unable to speak, to summon a rush of words to explain, as she dragged him down the four flights of stairs to the basement. He let himself go, giving in, unable to resist the urgency raging inside her. Suddenly he, too, had become afraid, afraid of whatever it was she wanted him to confront.

Quickly she led him through the darkened galleries, past the rows of heathen masks and ceremonial costumes, the feathered lances and stark, jagged harpoons which glittered ominously. Through the door marked *No Admittance*, into the gray cluttered receiving room.

And then instantly she howled in inconsolable dread, letting out a torrent of tears. "It's changed back," she murmured, choking with sobs.

In the center of the room stood a startling figure, an artist's conception of something strange and terrible, the rigid plaster depiction of a monstrous beast. It was loathsome looking with a massive sloping head and slashing rows of incredible teeth. Where the eyes would have been there were great gaping hollows. Was this what had caused her to break down? This statue? "It's very realistic," Rasmussen commented.

"You don't understand . . ." she trembled, her face stricken. "It was alive! I saw it!"

"You what?"

"You've got to believe me!"

"Is this a joke?"

"Oh God . . . oh God . . ." Her eyes blazed with tears, as she shuddered all over. "Ship it back!"

"But I can't. I don't want to."

"Please! You must—you must! It spoke to me . . ."

"I see." He smiled uneasily, staring at the features of the horrid shape which had obviously overwhelmed her imagination. Something inside her had snapped. He wanted to say something to quiet her. Finally he shrugged. "It's not real, Navarana. It's a statue . . . you imagined it . . ."

"No . . . No!" she shrieked, tears overcoming her body as she sobbed uncontrollably. "You—you don't understand—you don't . . ."

"Of course," he nodded, touching her shoulders, wanting to comfort her. She was like a child who had just awakened from an awful nightmare. "Of course . . . I want to . . . I do . . ."

3

The decaying three-story shell of the Jefferson Theater gaped out at Fourteenth Street as if it were an immense haunted house. Ironically some trendy entrepreneur might have looked upon it as *the* place to show vintage horror movies; the atmosphere was perfect. Yet at another time, in another world, famed actors strode its stage. Such names as Maurice Barrymore, Richard Mansfield and Ellen Terry now merely tugged at the imagination, their presences forgotten, as all that remained was the broken edifice where they had once expressed their art, a gray abandoned hulk with a painted *For Sale or Rent* sign creeping over the marquee. There could have been more. There could have been some sort of plaque welded into the structure granting it the respect it was due. But the New York City Historical Society had chosen other sites to remember, firehouses and banks and the brownstone two blocks away where Theodore Roosevelt had lived from 1889 to 1892.

On both sides of the Jefferson Theater neglected buildings exposed their ruined interiors behind crusty somber-looking windows clouded by the filth of decades. There was a used furniture outlet selling shabby battered furniture in a long vacant hall which had once been a fashionable nightclub. The faded emblem *Gaslight Cafe* had never been removed from the door. Beside it was a liquor store protected by bulletproof glass, where service was summoned by ringing a bell. A pint of cheap liquor was slid into a boxlike contraption, while a surly bullet-headed sales-

man waited behind the sheet of glass carefully counting, making certain that the money offered added up
to the purchase price before the bottle was delivered.
Next to it a shop selling secondhand garments for
women was lodged on the ground floor of a building
bearing the chipped letters *Italian Labor Center*, in
the doorway of which an aging wino, with saliva
dripping from his jaws, agonizingly attempting to
vomit. On the filthy brick walls surrounding him
were pasted color posters of film stars from movies
of the past: Edward G. Robinson in *Nightmare*,
Tyrone Power and Maureen O'Hara in *The Black
Swan*, Bela Lugosi in *Dracula*.

Weaving anxiously, the tall delicate brunette in
the silver terry-cloth jumpsuit made her unsteady
way along the ashcan-cluttered sidewalk. Perhaps
she was dazed or strung out on dope, but under the
bleary gaze of the men who sat and knelt in the
rancid doorways of the sleazy shops, she epitomized
everything they could ever want. Yet none of them
had enough money to afford her, so they hungrily
stared at her white thighs cut just above the cheeks
of her buttocks by the shimmering outfit, they ogled
the soft flesh of her behind which flagrantly wagged
at them.

Her breasts were large and pressed against the
silver terry-cloth fabric which, if she had been wearing a brassiere, might have held them into jutting
points but instead allowed them to sag voluptuously
so that they fell forward, her flopping brown nipples
clearly outlined and suggestive. She had the unre-
strained looks of a girl in her early twenties, with
exhausted eyes, long satin black hair and a puffy
sensuous face, stark white, with skin as thin as
paper, as if she had not been out of an apartment in
weeks. It was only the grimy sordidness of the dilap-
idated record and appliance stores, the Chinese and
Puerto Rican food stands and the burned-out shells

of a dozen surrounding rooming houses which emphasized the fact that she was too young and pretty to be there.

"Want a date?" she slurred at a man dressed in an unfashionable brown business suit who quickly shuffled by her.

She stopped, as if she were lost for a moment. She licked her lips, squinting with the uncertain, dazed eyes of someone prematurely born into a world of sudden sunlight or recently let out of a hospital.

"Want a date?" she squeezed out a smile at a young blond-haired man in a white turtleneck sweater. Obviously a visitor from another city, his pants were too tight, cuffed too short, so that his bright yellow socks glared above his black shoes. He was titilated. Momentarily he hesitated, as if the look in her eyes conveyed that the world that second might have reversed itself, that *she really was* innocently asking him to join her for a drink, followed by a passionate rendezvous in a quiet bed, that it was prompted solely by his good looks, and that scantily clad women did suggest such things.

Then he leaned backward. Immediately he saw that her greeting required more on his part than a desire to accept her into his bed, that she longed for the money in his pocket before she would be willing to respond with a semblance of routine dull mechanicalism. As he hurried away in embarrassment several of the men in the doorways laughed.

The young woman continued west on Fourteenth Street. The clip-clop of her sandals made her legs appear to shiver in the streaming sunlight. Near the subway entrance she passed a clump of hookers who eyed her suspiciously. They had not seen her before and immediately she posed a threat to their business, being so young, while they looked dreadfully tired and unwholesome, with teeth missing and inflamed dark splotches covering the skin of their necks and arms.

The incessant traffic of horns and buses passing by gave the street a wrenching, ugly feeling. The girl in the terry-cloth jumpsuit ignored the glares of the women as she staggered forward. The angle of her walk became more unsteady as the unwieldy pressure of the street sounds pounded at her. Her oval face and bloodshot eyes suggested intense inner pain.

"Want a date?"

Another prospective customer passed her by. It was an endless morning and she had not eaten in two days. A residue of gin was caked on her mouth and she continued to try to lick it off. Her thick mane of hair was disheveled as if it had never been combed, yet there was an animal presence about her that was unbelievably alluring. It was as if she had fallen on hard times after being evicted from a much more sumptuous way of life.

One man followed her. He was small, very thin, almost skeletonlike. His gaze never left the contours of her pulsating thighs as she sauntered up the steps to Union Square. When she got to the grassy area he quickly closed in. At last, near a park bench, placing his hands on her shoulders, he enfolded her and spun her toward him.

Her eyes suddenly glowed, she seemed so happy and thrilled to see him. "Larry!" she giggled with pleasure. But there was no joy on his face. He stared at her intently as he slipped a small capsule from his fingers into her right hand. Its tiny yellow beads glistened. Immediately she pressed it into her dry mouth and swallowed.

"How's it going?" he asked.

"Great, honey. I'll be back—I'll be home—I will in a little while," she murmured, breathing heavily through her teeth.

He gave her a reassuring pat on the buttocks, followed by a long intense squeeze high up on her right thigh. His hand lingered for a second over her thick wide crotch, then he walked away.

She sat down on the bench, rubbing her legs for a second, trying to relax as she waited for the capsule to take effect. She wished that she could have downed it with a gulp of water; that way it would have dissolved faster. The pit of her stomach pitched angrily as pangs of hunger stripped her insides. She should eat something; she wished she had the appetite. She felt terrible as she closed her eyes.

She had wanted to become an actress. Every time she went to the movies she still dreamed of when she was a little girl watching all those beautiful women on the screen, wondering what it took to get up there. But Larry was good to her. He never beat her up and he let her have downers whenever she needed them. In return she gave him all her money because he reminded her of Ben. It was almost two years ago, yet she and Ben had never been divorced. He was still caring for her baby in North Carolina. And she wrote him letters telling him how well she was doing, how any day now she was going to make it. But in a small town they didn't understand how difficult it was. No one ever understood. How she survived in New York, the memory of the things she had to do when she first got there made her nauseated and afraid. She had seen a man purposely pushed out of a window at a party. *No—she had promised herself never to think of that. Never.* God, she didn't want to think about anything. She shrunk down into the bench.

Quickly she tried to remember Ben, his gruff voice. He had a warm heart but he used to beat her up sometimes when he got drunk. That was a problem she had with men, something she had never understood. Except that somehow it turned them on.

At least now she felt safe. Larry assured her that everything would be all right, and she believed him. No one would hurt her.

It felt warm in the park. Soon someone would approach her so that she could get some more money. As soon as she made fifty dollars Larry would be kind and sweet to her. She needed Larry desperately.

The pill had not begun to work, at least she didn't feel the cool fizz up her skin, turning everything off around her. She'd just sit there a few more minutes until she went quiet inside, then she'd be able to let her feelings float. Just float. That's what she needed. To float on a plastic raft in the middle of nowhere, covered by the white sea, feel nothing, remember nothing, just go away, far, far, where there were no more sounds, no more people.

"Millie?" The moment she heard the sound of her name her jaw hardened. She shut her eyes as tight as she could, shuddering as a chill swept over her body. The downer wouldn't help now, not even a dozen of them. She felt hot tears surge against the insides of her throat. The terrible party roared back, the image of the man flying out the window—*Coburg*—the name that haunted her nightmares.

Her eyes watered as she glimpsed the cold limp hands of Myron Brenner, his face icy, his thin lips smiling. Quickly she thought of Larry. Where was he? Why wasn't he there?

"Please—I promise. I won't tell anybody," she pleaded.

Myron smiled. "We've looked for you everywhere—Mr. Coburg has a man who wants to put you in a movie."

The waters of the Hudson River were dirty brown slicks with streaks of white light oozing across them, mixing down as if they were oil paints. Flapping wings which might have been sea gulls if seen from a closer view scattered in the distance beneath the luxury towers of the gigantic apartment buildings on the opposite shore. Before him the rows of boats, oblong, square and round, painted brown, green, red, stood empty. But the one boat Bill DeCormier could not take his eyes off sat resolutely in the river, halfway to the New Jersey shore.

He never had any intention of going out for a beer, that had been an excuse. When he left the mob of reporters converging around Christian, he had picked up a pair of binoculars at his apartment and then walked steadily across Thirty-fourth Street until he got to Tenth Avenue. From there he had taken a bus up the forty-five blocks to the Seventy-ninth Street boat basin. In his mind there was a thought continuing to fester. It had curled its way in while he was staring at the silent body of Miranda Reichert and it kept charging at his senses until he could no longer control it. He *had* to get uptown, he had to see it over again, even though seeing it made him furious inside, tore at his heart with hooks so sharp and vile that he felt as if he were a creature other than a man, some form of reptile that slunk out of the shadows.

If he had been a munitions expert he could have blown it out of the water, but that would have inadvertently murdered both of them. Besides, he was not a killer. But he wanted to strike back, to finish the evil force which had so impregnated his brain that he could no longer think. He would have screamed out, but immediately all eyes would have taken him for a lunatic, yet he felt worse than any lunatic. He felt less and less like a man.

The gigantic two-hundred-foot Feadship yacht appeared to be constructed in several sections with triple cabins and shirtless men bobbing up and down bending over, polishing, refinishing the deck. They worked for one man, one hideous creature who had

floated to his eyes. She was so young. So fucking stupid and young.

Yet what could he do? It was her life. She was no longer under twenty-one. But had she chosen to do this, or was it a weakness in her character? Perhaps *she simply could not resist*. That's what bothered him. That she might end up a tramp, going nowhere after he was finished with her. Did she really believe that she was using *him*? She could not have been in love, that idea was out of the question. No. She must actually have thought she was using him. But why? Did the success, what he could do for her career, mean so much? Were they worth her life? It was her life at stake—Bill shook his head again and again pounding his fist into the top of the railing, trying to hold back the anger.

Then as he looked again through the binoculars he saw her on deck for an instant, it looked like her, wearing a purple robe. She flashed in and out of a doorway, then vanished in front of his gaze.

At that moment near the large Texaco sign at the end of one of the docks a speedboat shot out. There were two men inside and Bill saw a girl, her black hair blowing in and out of the spray. She was wearing a tight silver outfit, her legs bare, and she seemed to be struggling with one of the men.

Through the binoculars Bill saw the other man pick up a dark object, it looked like a wrench, and slam it across her face. As blood poured out her nostrils she fell backward. Within seconds the speedboat drifted up to the ramp of the *Cyclops*. The two men dragged the girl out of the boat, her head flopping back as they prodded her forward toward the yacht. The deckhands did not turn or take notice, but continued working as the two men carried her onto the deck. She sank for a second but they grabbed her forcefully, pulling her into a cabin.

Bill lowered the binoculars. His first impulse was

to find a policeman. Or should he phone the nearest precinct? What should he say? That he saw a girl in silver clothing being beaten and forced aboard a ship?

When Sergeant Joseph A. McDuffie of the New York Police Department's Harbor Unit received the message from headquarters over his ship-to-shore radio he was scanning the waters of Randall's Island for abandoned automobiles. Most of the harbor patrol units had been eliminated due to a recent budget appropriation cut, and even though he was the nearest officer on duty it took him almost an hour to get to the Seventy-ninth Street boat basin. Gliding at a speed of five miles per hour he piloted the blue and white fifty-two-foot steel launch tightly up to the hull of the *Cyclops*. A white cresting wave hit up between the two boats and it took another few seconds to even out the space between them. The red-faced deckhand, his face and arms splattered with freckles, stared over the railing.

"Any problems on board?" McDuffie called up, glancing over the ship's streamlined body.

"No—no problems," the man answered.

"Who's the owner?"

"Mr. Coburg."

"Is he on board?"

"No. He'll be back tonight."

McDuffie cocked his head in the direction of the main cabins. "We got word an assault took place—"

"Who made the complaint?" The brawny deckhand lowered his chin.

At that moment a girl with pouting lips and iridescent green eyes appeared on deck in a purple beach robe. For a moment McDuffie was distracted by her sheet of blond hair, her shy, almost embarrassed expression. Then he glanced self-consciously back toward the red-haired man.

"A doctor—from Bellevue."

The blond's green eyes wavered, focusing on the police sergeant. "Who?" she asked faintly.

"Some doctor—DeCormier—he swore to the complaint."

The blond's frightened eyes drew back.

"Nothing happened here," the deckhand reassured him. "But if you want to wait until Mr. Coburg comes back—"

"No, no, that's okay. Thanks—" McDuffie waved as he pulled the police launch away from the side of the yacht. Circling, he headed back down the Hudson dismissing the complaint in his head. After all, he could not board the vessel unless he had proof of assault. But a more threatening political reason stopped him from proceeding any further.

His frowsy rain-soaked overcoat slopping against him, an old man, with a face sinking into deep cavernous cheeks isolated by gaping, almost frozen solid eyes, stumbled down the steps of the Spring Street subway station out of the rain. He wore a ragged orange stocking cap which buried his ears so that the most predominant feature was his lips to which a green funguslike film seemed to adhere. Nizzy Stefansson leaned toward the microphone, gesturing for him to stop, but he shuffled through the yellow gate marked *G-1 No Admission* without looking back. Then she recognized him; she had seen him every night for the past week. He slept in the tunnels.

She could have stopped the disheveled old man, it was against the law for him to be there, yet she knew that he would wander on to the next tunnel and the next until he was able to slip by someone looking the other way. Was it her job to police everyone who came and went? If he had no other place to go and wanted to sleep in the tunnels, let him. He was not doing anyone any harm.

Fortunately there was no one around or her job might have been in jeopardy. Not that she cared. Nizzy hated her job.

There was a roar, she could hear it in the distance, a roar which never ended day or night, then a burst of steel on steel overwhelmed by a squealing scream as the express train to Lefferts Boulevard tore by at seventy miles per hour. The ten-inch pillars bracing the ancient rafters shuddered as if the weight of the entire street above would come crashing down. A sudden frantic gush of air was quieted by a gradual seeping silence. It was a cold impersonal thing, a subway train rushing by with no intention of stopping. But in New York City there were many cold impersonal things.

Inside the modern box-shaped glass token booth with the huge "M" painted on one corner, Nizzy finished reading the *Daily News* from back to front for the third time, its black ink soiling the ends of her worn fingers. Detectives and uniformed police were searching Bedford Stuyvesant for two young gunmen who had killed an off-duty cop in a shoot-out on a busy street. Senator Edward Kennedy called the nation's response to his potential presidential candidacy heartening. While another article described how President Carter's administration would publish a new set of wage-price guidelines by the end of the month. None of it mattered to Nizzy however, as the only reason she had read all of it, each article at least twice, was desperately, futilely to try to stay awake.

It made her cringe as she thought of how she would spend the rest of the night in this subterranean world of dark tunnels and caves, but she always experienced that feeling early in her shift. Her eye was caught by a slimy brown substance which appeared to hang creeping through the cracks of the white tiles next to her. Tremulously, she admitted to herself that she had guessed right all along. At first she had thought that even though the rush hour had long passed, the dimly lighted atmosphere still stank with the stale fumes of perspiration. But now she knew that what she smelled was human excrement.

It was an awful place. In fact, her assignment in this particular change booth of the Eighth Avenue local was the most depressing she had ever experienced.

On the wall near the turnstiles, in red paint, were sprayed grotesque infantile scrawlings—the shape of a woman's breast with clots of blood dripping from the nipple, a man's penis at least three feet long and the words ''Eat Me!'' While above it a printed sign posted in every subway station politely ordered ''No Smoking, No Spitting, No Littering Please. Sanitary Code Section 216.''

Outside torrents of rain poured down and there were floods reported along the tracks tying up trains in both directions. Around midnight she had sold tokens to seven or eight drunks and a few tired-looking workers from the lofts in the area on their way home. Since then she had been totally alone. It was a long, endless, empty night, one more in a vague succession of long, endless, empty nights. And she was trapped, chained to it, feeling nothing, wanting for it to be over. Glimpsing the ticking hand of her watch, she noted that it was only minutes after one a.m. For seven more hours she would have to sit imprisoned in that glass booth.

Then she looked across the tracks. A huge brown

rat was heaving over one of the rails, so fat he could hardly move. Shuddering, Nizzy looked away.

Glancing at the pile of subway tokens in front of her, she wished that she had not been so eager to work for the city. She could hear the rain dripping down into the tunnels and the sound of it made her even more depressed. A few minutes before it had rushed in rivers through the sidewalk gratings, but now there was only a monotonous flow, matched by an occasional express train shooting by, rattling through her eardrums.

Sometimes in her sleep she would hear the trains tear by and would awaken crying aloud. What was happening to her? Was she becoming a machine, handing out tokens all night into the early morning. Was she no longer a person? Was she becoming a thing? Each day she was beginning to feel more lost, more trapped, until something inside of her, a voice, had started screaming out, "No, this is not you. It is someone else doing these things. No, no, please, I know it's not me. Please. It can't be."

She glanced back at the tracks, hoping that the rat was gone.

She could no longer see its eyes.

Six years. She had come to New York when she was twenty and immediately joined her sister in an apartment in Flushing. But now she hated New York. She missed the quiet silences of the land where she had grown up. She yearned for the rivers and the fishing, the long summer nights and the cold biting air of the forests. But someday she would travel; she had made up her mind. In the Sunday section of the *Daily News* there were trips offered to Florida and the Caribbean. She would go there. But she had to save enough money and that was becoming difficult. Perhaps she could wait it out another year working in the token booth, then fly to Puerto Rico or the

Virgin Islands. The thought of it was all she lived for.

She wished that another customer would come by, just a face, even someone drunk and incoherent. She was beginning to feel encased in her cage in the dark. The tube of fluorescent glow running the length of the platform was all the lighting there was except for a luminous clock, its hour hand pointing to "6". If only it *were* six—a.m. or p.m. She could not leave, could not close up even though she wanted to more than anything. Perhaps in a few hours there would be people coming up from the trains to go to work. In four hours it would be five o'clock. There were always people going to work at five o'clock. She closed her eyes wondering about the old man in the orange stocking cap who had slipped by her through the gate. Would he crawl under the ledge of the platform into the dark three-foot area where the electric cables were hidden? Or edge himself along the ramp of the tunnel wall, burrowing into one of the hollows between the signal lights? Perhaps he would climb into a space above where the trains went by. But what if he lost his balance and rolled unexpectedly onto the tracks . . .

She moaned deeply, allowing sleep to overcome her. She had liked working uptown at Seventy-second Street and Central Park West . . . the air in the mornings was filled . . . with perfume and men's after-shave . . .

She awoke with a start. The naked fluorescence crackled, sputtered, went out, then on again. Where was the rat? She could see its eyes. But was she dreaming?

The rain must have caused a power failure. She blinked quickly back to consciousness.

Something had awakened her. Something she could not make out. Another train had ripped by, shaking the rafters and there were odd sounds in the darkness. Deep down along the tunnel she heard a scraping noise. There must be workmen moving along the tracks to her station. But why were they repairing tracks in this kind of weather? The rain must be gushing down on them through the gratings. It was not until the last moment that she was aware of a terrible crashing up the stairs.

· It was the old man, he was running toward her without the orange stocking cap, coat flopping, his eyes and nose white as a skull. And then she saw something which made her blood freeze.

It was enormous, covered with slime as if it had come up from under the tracks, wearing a huge steel helmet—*wielding a gigantic stone axe!* She looked for the face—the face—

Nizzy shrieked as the huge figure charged after the old man. Yet part of her must be dreaming. *Part of her must still be dreaming! It was at least twelve feet tall!* The old man stretched his hands at her, hollering, his face twisted, screaming for help, but she could not help, she tried to move but she fell backwards—

With a sudden whoosh of the axe the old man's head was gone, lopped off, his bloody torso sinking—

Nizzy ducked behind the change counter, knocking tokens everywhere, squealing, holding her eyes with her hands. It was worse than a nightmare. Worse! But she had been sleeping, now she was wide awake, her heart pounding, rolling up into her breast. What she imagined, the thought of it horrifying, terrible—*It was after her!*

She crouched there seconds, then she heard it, felt it as the earth cracked open. With a rippling sound, a shower of pelting glass drenched her eyes, she was cut, bleeding. She wailed, her heart buckling as she gasped up into the black empty void beaming down at her—the face—where was it—where was it! The mountainous axe hurtling at the booth—her legs giving way, falling off the stool, fumbling on her arms, clutching the key out of her pocket—to unlock the door, pounding it open screaming, crying inside as that instant the stone axe split the booth in two, exploding the spot where she had been sitting into pieces.

She crawled, hands and knees frantically quivering, for a second trying to find a corner to bury herself, feeling something warm, moist, a pocket of urine and what looked like rat fur gathered in a drain under her hand. She choked, yanking back the feeling of vomiting, letting out a pitiful shriek as she got up. She tore under a turnstile—down the platform—there was an exit at the other end—but the figure crashed after her—its shadow in front of her—almost on top of her! She grabbed for the gate—it was locked! She howled, saliva flowing through her lips as she leapt onto the tracks—afraid of the electrified rails—her breathing almost stopped—hopping over the steel runners, pulling herself up, scratching her legs as she wrenched onto the platform ledge—wanting to get up, to run, but her legs would not hold her anymore, she fell on her knees, howling, scrambling for the yellow banister bracing the stairway to the street, hoping to fight her way up, her thighs sagging, as she felt the axe rising over her head—*oh God*—she screamed!

Had to move her legs—had to move—but luckily she could, she could, she was faster, more agile than she imagined—as a child she had run from bears—suddenly she was out in the dark street—but the terror in her throat bleared her eyes—she howled, howled, howled—someone please! Help! Someone please!—racing, screaming past deserted warehouses floating in blurs of hanging shapes, hooks, mounting scales, huge lightless windows, her hair dragging her back, her legs moving faster than they ever had as her feet slipped, too late she tried to regain her balance—she rolled head over heels like a ball.

"Hellpp—" she yelled, mud and slime filling her mouth—oh God—she looked up—a block ahead were the bright lights of a main throroughfare—Canal Street—*it was so close*—her knees and her feet jumped up at the same time, tearing toward it, shooting out her arms as if her grasping hands could get there closer.

But she fell—*she fell*. Something cracked up her knee. Rolling sideways, sliding down under a narrow ledge of one of the warehouse platforms, cowering, her whole body rattled with fright. "Oh God—oh God—oh God—" she whimpered as the huge shadow drew over her. The smell of its disgusting flesh forced her nostrils to expand in agony as she stared up into the blank blackness where its face should have been.

"Oh God, please," she begged. "Please—" Slowly it lifted the massive stone axe. "Oh God—oh God—" She tried to curl deeper under the platform. Then suddenly the axe roared down.

5

"She's an Eskimo." Bill DeCormier gazed across the two Styrofoam cups of coffee at Christian Bangsted's startled face. It was seven a.m. and the cafeteria jostled with interns and nurses scooping down breakfast, the arid atmosphere congested with the smoke from their cigarettes. Christian tried to keep his eyes off the gradually depleting stack of plastic food trays and the lifeless blue wall where the typed food menu was posted. The morning special was a combination of watery scrambled eggs, charred strips of bacon and wet soggy piles of greasy home fries. It was not appetizing, more like concentration camp food, and Christian, even though he was uncomfortably hungry, could do no more than cope with a cup of coffee. Bill went on. "There are no wounds but there is possible intraabdominal perforation. Some signs of cellulitis."

"What does it have to do with me?" Christian replied somewhat defensively, although he knew the course of Bill's twisting ironic humor.

"I thought you liked Eskimos."

That was it. Bill wanted to get a rise out of him. Instead Christian nodded with a smile.

"She's assigned to you," Bill continued.

"That was your doing."

"I like Eskimos. I saw an Eskimo documentary once—they stood around in their fur coats waiting to fight a polar bear with their knives and harpoons."

Bill's cockiness rankled him. Perhaps it was helped by the incessant bank of cigarette smoke and the uneatable food. Normally Bill would have ranted about how brilliantly the Yankees had played the night before.

"You do not like Eskimos. You are prejudiced against them."

Bill groaned. "I thought I was a liberal. Could you have sensed a part of me that I've kept hidden from myself?"

"Not only that, you secretly support the polar bear movement. Did you ever fight a polar bear—armed with only a dull pocket knife?"

He shook his head. "Did you?"

"Many times," Christian said with a straight face. "A polar bear can be vicious, cruel, and you have to hold him around the neck like this." He stood up, demonstrating with a sweep of his arm as if grabbing the imaginary jaw of a towering beast.

Bill shook his head. "What do you do if he tries to bite you?"

Christian gestured. "You kick him in the balls." With that he plopped back into the chair.

"Then you eat him?"

"Only the Danes eat polar bear."

"What do Eskimos eat?"

"Whale."

Bill choked for a second as if he were about to become sick.

"There's smoked whale blubber, frozen whale blubber, steamed whale blubber, whale blubber soup, baked whale blubber, roast whale blubber—have you had enough?"

"You grew up on that?"

"No," Christian shook his head. "I hated it."

Bill chuckled as Christian beamed, his dark intelligent eyes bright, an expression of burning honesty crossing his face.

"Well, that's why she's assigned to you."

"Who?"

"The Eskimo lady. She's in intensive care. She just lies there staring."

"Was she in a fight with a bear?"

"The police think it was a gang. The subway token booth where she was working was wrecked. They found the decapitated head of a man on the steps of the platform."

Christian winced. "I'll never get used to what goes on in this city."

"According to the admittance chart she has a funny name—something like Missy or Mitty—"

"Do you think she speaks English?"

"Talk to her in Eskimo."

Christian grinned, shaking his head. "I don't speak it anymore."

* * *

The woman's dark hollow eyes stared up from the bed. She choked spasmodically, attempting to breathe in. Her waxen yellow skin was discolored by the broken damaged veins beneath, melting into her stringy white hair surrounding her face. It was still raining outside and the dull gray of the atmosphere was punctured by the bright fluorescent ceiling.

"I am Dr. Bangsted," Christian began, focusing only on her eyes, trying to make some contact with the fleeting light which shone from them. "I am an Eskimo—from the Netsilik tribe—from Greenland— near Umanak."

The woman's eyes failed to respond, remaining glassy and opaque. The preliminary diagnosis had been unable to determine the cause of her symptoms. Yet her body was riddled with disease. Her arms and legs had swollen to three times their size and her face was a grotesque mass of red blotches and caked dried blood, some of which the attending nurses had attempted to sponge away.

"I work here at the hospital—" He paused, hoping for a glint of life, some look of recognition to rush up into her face. He wished he had brought her flowers, anything to relieve the feeling of astringency and death in the room. "I want to talk to you. It's very important." Still no response. The eyes could see him. They focused on him when he moved. And the lips, although horribly bruised, could form phrases, but they uttered no sound, no explanation that might unravel the riddle of her condition. Suddenly he felt angry that he could not reach her.

She *was* an Eskimo. There was no doubt in his mind about the Indianlike features . . . he had treated many such women at the hospital in Suddertoppen where he had first learned about medicine.

Then he tried something. He began muttering words that he had not repeated in years, phrases he had not used since he was a child living in a hut covered with sealskins on a terrain of glittering snow. *"Anâlurshe . . . Anâlurshe . . ."* He began gesturing, picturing faces with his hands, concepts which as a boy he had understood, *"Inua tarneq . . . tamalrutiga . . ."* Then he pointed to himself and back to her, "Iglorik." But there was no response. Nothing. Finally he stopped gesturing and requested simply that she speak to him, *"Ogoloqati ginairuma galuar pavkit."*

But the woman did not stir. She gave no sign of recognition. The eyes were all that remained of her Eskimo identity and Christian clung to their expression as he spoke in the modern language of an American doctor. "You were found in the street near the subway station. Do you remember what happened?" If she had any inkling of the circumstances which had brought her there, it was buried beneath those eyes. Christian wanted to reach her. More than anything.

He looked up. Bill was at the door, quickly motioning to him. Rising, he left the room. In the hallway Bill confided, "Her sister-in-law is here. Did you get anywhere?"

Christian shook his head. "She's conscious, but she won't speak. I want to make one last try." Hesitant for a second, Bill finally nodded.

Christian reentered the room. For a long moment he stared at the wall opposite, then began chanting.

> *Aja-ja, aja-ja-ja . . .*
> *aja-ja, aja-ja-ja—Hoi! Hoi!*
> *aja-ja, aja-ja . . .*

The string of syllables sounded foreign, so long ago had he left the culture of the *Kalatdlit Nunat*, the land of the people. But a feeling of urgency gnawed at him, mingling with a strange uneasiness. There

was something about her swollen face and distorted
purple body that he remembered.

There was no air in the room, yet Christian did
not have the energy to reach across to the window
and shove it up. Call it laziness or inertia, something
had infected his being, his arms and legs felt as if
they were strapped with leather, his head burned
with a slow deadening pain. He was certain that a
shower in the stall across the hallway would free
him; he could practically feel the warm foaming jets
stabbing at his skin. But to indulge in the experience
meant that he would have to crawl laboriously to his
feet. He wished that some giant pair of hands would
reach down and settle him underneath the shooting
spurts of water. Why couldn't there have been a
button near his bed that he could push to slide into a
cool soft pool?

He creased the edge of his beard beneath his nose,
smoothing the cracks cutting into his lips. Then he
flopped over and lay sprawling in his green scrub
shirt and scrub pants watching the hands of the
clock. Even though he had been awake for twenty
hours he could not sleep. It was intensely hot and he
lay soaked in perspiration, causing his clothes to
stick uncomfortably to his shoulders and back. It
was impossible to relax when he was on call. Luckily
the resident orthopedist, Wally Freundlich, who occupied the bed next to his had decided to sleep on a
chair downstairs in the TV room. Christian yawned
and stretched. He felt hemmed in by the white walls
of the tiny cubicle, the unusable white desk and the
banged-up dresser pushed against the tiny window.
But soon it would be over. He would be off duty in
two hours.

The room assigned to him in the doctors' residence had no air conditioning, but a small fan often
made it almost bearable. But today was excruciating.

Since he had come to New York he had never felt so wrung out. He wondered about the men who worked in the streets, spending their days in a pit shoveling rocks or swinging a pick. How did they stand it? Men and women were constantly being forced to perform tasks beyond their endurance. To survive depended upon a relentless momentum. All his life he had been aware of what it cost, the terrible demands of making it through the day—a night—a year—a lifetime.

But was there some other way? Could there be a utopia somewhere created for people to live in with no stress, no strain, no inner battles? Could man have been different once, before he allowed himself to be tyrannized by difficulties?

He would like to have been in a boat fishing. That was a feeling he had never forgotten, gazing into the water at another world, another landscape. Someday he would have the time to locate that child in himself, to explore who that child might have been.

The cardiac arrest monitor on his belt beeped. After the second beep, he pushed the button on the side. The female operator's high-pitched voice lingered through the static. "Code seven hundred."

Christian leapt out of bed. He fumbled into his blue Adidas without tying the laces. His first thought was the Eskimo woman. Charging out of the room, he headed for the elevator, envisioning her lying there surrounded by the respirator team and the anesthesiologist—they were shining a light in her eyes—the pupils were dilated and nonreactive . . .

Christian pressed the elevator button "Down." The elevator door opened. He got on and jammed the button for the main floor. What seemed like several minutes rode by him before the empty green elevator stopped and the doors opened. He tore down the dimly lighted corridor into the main building.

The lobby was filled with patients waiting to be

admitted. Beside the reception desk a small boy sitting in a plastic chair was howling. The boy had dimpled cheeks and curling black hair. Christian rang for the elevator as he caught a glimpse of the stolid-faced woman sitting next to the child, indifferently letting him bawl. Finally the child stood up and angrily stamped around her until the woman murmured something to him in Spanish.

The elevator doors opened and Christian got in.

The elevator slid up slowly to the seventh floor. Christian shot through the doors the second they opened and ran around the corner down the wide hall, heading toward the women's quarters. A half-dozen frightened-looking patients stared out of their rooms through the curtains as he hurried past them. He caught glimpses of their faces, which seemed especially old-looking and tired, as he raced for the room at the end.

A crowd of nurses, residents and interns swarmed around the woman, working feverishly as she lay sprawled on the bare bed, her feet draped over the edge of the sheet. Bill DeCormier was bending over her. "What caused it?" Christian muttered. Bill shook his head.

Suddenly there was a series of ear-splitting croaks from the woman's swollen body as two of the cardiac interns began pounding heavily on her chest. A nurse was handing a long needle with a syringe toward one of them. The voices of the supervisory nurse and her assistant joined in—

"Fourth bicarb—"

"Fifth Eppie—"

"You want another Eppie?"

Christian glanced at the machine by the woman's feet. The cardiogram showed a flat line. The interns continued to pound her chest. More needles were injected into her body. There were no spontaneous pulses. At one point she developed a slow rhythm.

Atropine was administered to speed it up, but it was no good. The code did not work.

At last the supervisory nurse signaled for the room to be sealed off so that the women patients in the hallway would not be aware of the decision. The door was closed. They were alone in the room. The senior resident, who had taken charge, murmured in a dry voice, "We may as well stop now—it's all over." Christian was about to ask the cause of death but the senior resident, looking up from the lifeless body, anticipated him. "Severe liver damage. No platelets. We'll have to wait for the coroner's report."

With that the cardiogram machine was disconnected and the door to the room was flung open. The residents and nurses quickly filed out, leaving Christian alone, staring at the woman's body.

Finally he turned away, slipping out of the room.

He did not see the woman open her eyes.

As she watched him move away down the hall, she laughed, or what seemed to be a laugh gurgled out of her throat. Then the grotesque blue lips parted and a voice snarled out, "You'll die—with every member of your race—until I'm free."

6

Bill's apartment stretched long with odd-shaped hallways turning into a maze of narrow bedrooms. The living room shelves were piled high with copies of the *New York Times Magazine* encircling an elaborate modern stereo system, crowded by slouching piles of records strewn across the severely scratched parquet floors. Near the window a red earthenware pot comforted the remains of a dead avocado plant, and there were other plants which looked like they were either dead or in the process of dying lining the windowsill next to the radiator. The entire apartment was badly in need of being cleaned, repainted or having some form of living order reestablished. Perhaps it was out of embarrassment that Bill had never invited him there before.

It was a shame he had permitted it to get so run down. It could have been a great apartment. Christian wished that he could afford such a place instead of the railroad flat he shared with two other surgeons in Greenwich Village. Bill lived alone except for an occasional houseguest from the nurses' residence or the accidental lady he managed to inveigle up from one of the local bars along Third Avenue. Yet in the year they had worked together Christian had never known him to have a steady girl friend. He was good looking, with robust features, rust-colored brown hair and narrow expressive eyes, the kind of looks which were popular with American girls, or in fact, girls anywhere. But it was obvious Bill shunned close relationships, preferring instead to party, drinking himself into oblivion five nights a week. Perhaps he did it to relax from the intense work schedule or to ward off the letdown, the gnawing grip of loneliness which seized him at the end of the workday. But Christian sensed it was due to some deeper problem which he could not allow himself to discuss. Sensing some inner disturbance, he had never commented, not even in jest, when Bill showed up at the hospital hung over, his eyes blemished with deep red crevices.

Bill and he preserved a distance between them, an invisible private boundary over which neither of them would allow the other to trespass. It was a front, as if there were some secret Bill was hiding behind a barrage of stinging quips and enthusiastic jibes, and Christian was expected to do the same, never to venture into those areas which close friends might discuss. As a result it was not a real friendship, they shared the work. Admissions of self-doubt, fear or inadequecy were forbidden subjects. In their place was a superficial camaraderie. What it came down to was that Christian had never wanted to get close enough to Bill to really know what was troubling him. And something told him his caution was well founded, that it was better that way.

As Christian settled back into the plush forest-green sofa, Bill put on a Joni Mitchell album, one of several Joni Mitchell albums at his feet, this one with a photo of her basking on a rock near the waters of the Pacific. Christian closed his eyes. He could not erase the image of the Eskimo woman.

What troubled him was the way she had died. Blood poisoning. Yet there were no wounds on the body and no evidence of intraabdominal perforation. There had been cellulitis but the cause was unclear, even though the coroner had agreed to run tests.

None of it made any sense.

In a second Bill was there offering him a beer in a tall highball glass. "I'll be right back. I've been wearing these shit-stained clothes for the last forty-eight hours." He rumpled through his soiled jeans and checkered shirt, turning down the stereo, heading into the bedroom.

Christian liked the sound of Joni Mitchell's voice. He was not thirsty so he set the glass of beer on the coffee table next to his knee. Across the room was a tinted photograph of a girl with a mane of blond hair and wide, amazed-looking eyes. She was obviously very young, very innocent and very appealing. Christian gazed at her a long moment before yelling to Bill in the bedroom, "Who is she?"

"Who is who?" came the muffled answer.

"The girl in the photograph."

"Who?"

It was obvious Bill could not hear him.

"The girl in the photograph," Christian repeated in a much louder voice.

There was a sudden tingling from the wall phone in the alcove next to the kitchen. Bill raced in, grabbing it.

"Hello . . ." Bill paused. "I'm alone except for a friend."

Christian was momentarily startled; he could not imagine who it was. He had no idea that Bill was that close to anyone, so close that he should feel it necessary to explain he was not alone.

"I'll talk to you later—I'm just going out." Bill's voice was hurried, wanting to get off the phone. Then Christian saw his expression change. Whoever was on the line seemed to be telling him things he did not want to hear. Bill's eyes grew dark and anxious, his face glowered. "Look—I'm not lying, I wouldn't lie about something like that—I saw it happen!" he spit into the receiver, gritting his teeth, half turning away to hide his expression, murmuring, attempting to channel his words so that only the caller on the other end of the line could hear them. "She had black hair . . . she was wearing a silver outfit . . . I saw them hit her . . ." Christian glanced at the girl in the photograph. Her face had a wonderfully innocent smile that shone back at him as though something about his presence, perhaps the fact he was an Eskimo, astonished her. After the day's events he had begun to feel his Eskimo ancestry more strongly than usual. Yet she trusted him. He fantasized that she might be English, with those wonderfully fresh looks and lips formed as if she were about to say, "Hi, love. I see you—and I love what I see."

Suddenly Bill shouted. "Look Neville—I don't

want to hear about that son of a bitch! He's scum,
okay? *I don't know what you're doing with him.*"
He hesitated, then his voice became shrill. "I'm not
your father or mother—don't grab out for me when
you're in trouble . . . I know . . . I know . . . I
know, honey," Bill argued, "but you're a grown
woman, goddamn it! Please stop!" Bill rocked forward. Then his voice became very quiet. "I wish
you wouldn't call me."

After a second, Bill hung up the phone. He stood
stiffly, unable to move.

Christian broke the silence. "Who's that?" He
pointed to the photograph of the girl.

Bill glanced at the wall as if he were in a daze.

"She's beautiful. I'd like to meet her," Christian
went on.

Bill's face went dead. He stared at Christian but
there was no longer any life in his eyes. With that he
turned. Christian could not be certain whether his
comment triggered them off, scissoring across the
crest of what he was feeling, but there were tears in
Bill's eyes.

7

The exploding pulse of loud disco music spilled
out into Sixth Avenue as Christian pulled Bill out of
the path of a fleeting blue van. The sidewalk throbbed
with people, making it a problem to move forward
except in pockets formed by the crowd as it surged
against them, pushing, encircling, thrusting itself in
and out. To make Christian more uncomfortable, in
the three bars from which they had fled, Bill had

thrown down martinis until his face was as white as
a sheet. Weaving unsteadily, bumping into people,
several times he had almost fallen into the street
before Christian could grab him.

They had not eaten. Bill refused to eat. The gin
had gone to his head, causing him to slobber as he
attempted to light a cigarette. His eyes watered, his
head sinking so low at times that it took enormous
effort for him to straighten his shoulders to see
where he was going. It had started with the phone
call back in his apartment. Bill had poured himself a
drink and that had begun it. His easygoing attitude
disappeared as if his self-confidence had been un-
dermined. At times he would babble with rage but
what he said was incongruous, in snatches, unable to
form a complete thought. *He hated her, he wanted
to kill her.* But he loved her. She was all he loved.
She was all he cared about—*but he had to finish that
fucking son of a bitch,* he had to get him! He would
sob, then burst out laughing. No, he would shake his
head. No, he did not want to hurt anybody. He had a
brilliant career ahead of him. He did not want to hurt
anyone.

Christian stopped himself from asking who the
woman was. In the months they had worked together
he did not remember Bill having spoken of anyone
he cared about that much. Her name was Neville,
that he had overheard during the phone call. Obviously she was the girl whose photograph was on the
wall, someone he had fallen in love with, who had
left him for another man. And she had gotten to Bill.
The things she said had driven him crazy. Over and
over Christian observed the tangled inner conversation. The hate, then self-hate, then justification, as if
he were a child arguing with himself, trying to get
out of doing something, but tumbling back in, head
over heels. As Christian glanced into a store window

he saw his face reflected, dark with exhaustion. He wanted to leave, to go home, to forget about Bill.

"C'mon, let's go," Christian said finally.

Bill turned on him. "Aren't you having a great time?"

"We've had enough to drink—"

"I haven't had enough," Bill angrily shot back. His hand shook and his eyes kept closing out of focus. He stumbled up the street, becoming more and more intense, his head down, as if at any moment he was about to collapse.

The sky was like ink, the moon having disappeared behind heavy clouds, but the bright streetlights glanced fiercely off the yellow cabs racing past them in a flurry. Approaching were two black girls in rhinestone shorts cut up very high and very tight. Their oily legs glistened.

"Hey baby," Bill grabbed the thigh of one of them. She swung around as Christian cut in quickly, trying to save Bill from being knocked cold. There was anger in her eyes. At that moment Christian realized that the two women were together, without men, and were intent on remaining that way.

But Bill was blocking them from moving through the crowd.

"He's sorry," Christian quickly reassured the tall girl.

"No I'm—not," Bill butted in, slurring his words. "I'd love—love to get you—to get into you baby," Bill leered at her, trying to stroke her, grabbing at her blouse.

Christian pulled Bill away, but he lurched forward tearing back at her. "No one gets into you but your buddy here. Right? Right, bitch?" Bill spit out. The two girls shrank. "You don't even know what a man's dick feels like inside of you—right? You don't have any idea . . . how great it is to have a man come inside of you . . ."

"Hey man," the girl flared at Christian, "you'd better not let him touch her." Her hand was already inside the beaded purse hanging from her wrist, groping for something. Christian sensed what she was after. "I'll cut out his tongue," her eyes menaced.

"But I want her—*I want her*," Bill shouted as Christian began dragging him up the street. Then suddenly Bill laughed, hardly able to stand up. "I thought you wanted her, buddy . . . the short one," he roared. But Christian wasn't laughing. More and more he felt queasy inside. "Pigs . . . all of them are pigs . . ." Bill muttered.

On Tenth Street they passed a dimly lighted bar with a large front window. "I want to go in there," Bill prodded, tearing away from Christian's grasp.

Christian desperately reached for him, "C'mon, let's get a cab. It's late."

Bill stormed, "I want to go in!" Before Christian could stop him he was through the open door.

The bar was filled with a dozen or so men, well dressed in suits and ties. But the bartender saw Bill coming, he shook his head, he wouldn't serve him. "I want a drink . . . a dry Beefeater . . . a mar-rr-tini . . ." Bill slid out the words as he grabbed for the edge of the bar, almost sinking to his knees.

The bartender defiantly shook his head. No way was he going to serve him.

"Look—look you—" Bill glared, gesturing with his fist. "I come—I come in here a lot."

"I never saw you before," the bartender stood his ground, staring him out. Then he motioned to Christian to hang on to him, to get him back out into the street.

"C'mon, Bill," Christian grabbed his arm, trying to spin him around. But as he did, he had the feeling of being watched by someone, something outside. A despicable, unnerving sensation seized him. He peered through the large front window as Bill's arms shot up, grappling with him, attempting to shove him. And then Christian *saw it*. Hovering in the shadows, caught between two buildings halfway up the street, a dark, sullen figure, towering, amorphous, with a fur helmet and huge horns jutting up—

Through a mist of light two infernal gaping hollows raged in at him—*Christian trembled*—

Bill pounded him back. "Let me alone. I want a drink!" Yanking him to one side, Christian glanced again through the front window.

The figure was gone. Perhaps he had had too much to drink.

At that second Bill shoved him, as if suddenly overcome by a frenzy. "I want a drink—goddamn it." Several of the customers drifted away in loose bunches as Christian saw the bartender tense up. He was smaller than Bill's six-foot frame, but obviously ready for him. Suddenly Bill spotted a man at the end of the bar. "You—you bastard!" he slurred, angrily curling his fist.

The man spun around. He was dark and graying with glittering white teeth and no smile.

Bill's eyes glazed over as if something spun off in his head. He lurched forward a second, then tore down the bar swinging with all his might, howling, "You're gonna leave her alone!" The man arched back a step just as Bill hit him in the face. The man fell backward, knocking glasses everywhere.

Christian was stupified as he raced forward, trying to grab Bill's arms.

Suddenly there were other men and Christian was trying to drag Bill away. The others joined in as the bartender leapt over the bar with a wrench in his hand. With one arm he pinned back Bill's shoulders while the other aimed for an angle to smash him in the side of the head. Christian grabbed for the wrench, pleading, "He's drunk." Bill's fists were flying.

Christian grabbed him by the waist, hoping to yank him toward the door.

"No! Let me go!" Bill screamed. Then someone hit Bill in the mouth and he went down. There was blood on his lips but he wouldn't stop, he got up, then fell, his fists hurling out at everyone. Finally the bartender managed to power the wrench down, pounding it into his right ear. Bill wailed, trying to get up. He sobbed, "I want to kill him! I've got to . . . ."

Yanking frantically at the one-ton cement block to which it was chained, the bulbous unlighted buoy which the Coast Guard irreverently referred to as "a nun in a can" dragged ominously through the shallow black waters of New York Harbor. Though the surface appeared calm, the tides beneath fetched and crawled in a restless monotony. Bits of bright autumn moon were reflected in flowing patches, rippling and falling over a shimmering silvery substance outlined by the shadowy reef below. As if it were already taken over by some form of virulent marine life, the body bobbled up between the buoy and the sixty-five-foot tug.

It was approaching two a.m. when Chief Petty Officer Max Grissom found her and immediately reported over the bubbling radio to the commander-in-charge at Gouvernor's Island. He had come back from patrolling the area near the Military Ocean Terminal at Bayonne. The three spotlights atop the boat cabin had stretched over the lifeless shape, spotting it in a twelve-foot stretch of water.

"She could have been here for hours . . . maybe longer," he conveyed over the radio.

All that remained of her silver terry-cloth jumpsuit were snatches of broken fabric still bound together by dangling threads infested with tentaclelike reeds from the slimy depths. The face hung inert like a shell of white dissolving children's paste, while her thighs had been unmercifully battered, battered beyond recognition, the flesh chewed and shredded by the rocks off Ellis Island. Part of one arm was missing, shorn from the shoulder, Grissom guessed, by the propeller blades of a passing freighter.

As he lowered a net into the water he whistled to himself, summoning up any tune which came to mind. He could not help but wonder about her, where she had come from? Why she ended up this way? But these were things he was not to know.

Eight hundred miles from North Carolina, from Ben and her baby, no one would beat her up again. Her colorless glassy eyes stared up as he lifted her on deck, those same eyes which had once seen a man murdered.

8

Christian had not moved from the brown solid-backed wooden chair for over an hour. He felt uneasy inside, a fluttery unstable sensation more like fear than weariness. It made his head ache and his mind whirl through caverns of thoughtlessness as if none of it mattered, the room, the time of morning, the fact that he had not eaten. Except he heard nothing. That troubled him. Occasionally an officer wearing a dusky blue shirt and dark pants would enter from one of the cages in back—followed by the whirring sound of cell doors snapping shut—take his seat at the desk in the middle of the room, pensively bury himself in several flipping pages attached to a clipboard, then leave. Without carrying guns, the officers appeared to have ultimate power over everyone coming and going.

The air was stale in the receiving room, trapped into a sordid clamminess as if the walls were perspiring. There were no air-conditioning ducts, yet the yellow tile seemed to hold everything back, insulating the world within, an ugly neon world of frozen furniture shapes, devoid of prison atmosphere except for the barred windows surrounding him.

It could have been the waiting room of a down-and-out dentist's office, even though there were no magazines. Nothing about the place was threatening. In fact the atmosphere induced one to blank out from reality, sitting, waiting, not aware of what might be occurring in the cells beyond. The police had brought Bill to the place and booked him, turning him over to the correction officer in charge. He was fingerprinted. They asked him his name, address, age, place of birth, where he was employed. Had he ever been arrested before? Misdemeanors? Felonies? Had he ever been convicted for assaulting anyone? Total strangers in bars? They led him away, no longer drunk, staring down at the floor, his right ear swathed in bandages. It was so efficient, a system which had no interest in motives, enforcing cold ruthless procedures.

The one touch of humanity was three tiny green plants on the windowsill. They seemed out of place amidst the starkness, the routine, the lack of warmth. Day or night was the same in that room and he felt sorry for Bill. That is why he had been unable to leave.

The door to his left opened. A young woman with straight blond hair falling down past her shoulders to the middle of her back stared in. She seemed completely unsure of where she was, as she edged inside, closing the door, her tight-fitting blue jeans clinging below a purple sweatshirt. Christian recognized her immediately. He had seen her face only a few hours before in Bill's apartment. It was the girl in the photograph.

She could have been no more than twenty or twenty-one, wearing no makeup, yet with healthy blossoming features as if she had spent her life on a farm, rolling in grass, feeding cows, chickens, not like the average New Yorker. The soft vulnerable green eyes darted, afraid, as she crossed the room.

"Yes, ma'am," the guard looked up.

She began to speak, then lost her breath. She tried again, clearing her throat, "I'm—I'm—I'm William DeCormier's sister. He called me . . . on the phone."

As she settled forward over the desk, letting her saddlebag purse fall from her shoulder, Christian sat up straight in surprise. *This was the girl.* The girl Bill loved—and hated—and wanted to kill in his fit of drunken stupor. *His sister.*

"You want to bail him out?"

She nodded, half there.

The guard shuffled through the brace of papers pinched to the clipboard, finally halting, pulling out one of the sheets. "That's twelve hundred dollars."

She reached into the saddlebag purse and rolled out a wad of bills bound by a rubber band. With long white fingers she began counting the money, finally handing it to the guard who stamped a yellow form and gave it to her.

She stood solemnly at the desk as he disappeared back into the cages. Finally she moved away, her eyes flitting an instant as they met Christian's, obviously uncertain as to who he was, a person such as she waiting for the release of someone jailed inside, or part of the establishment in which her brother was kept. Obviously desiring to gaze out of the room, she headed toward the windows.

But she must have felt his stare. After a second she glanced back, her green eyes rising to the walls, the overhead banks of light, near him, to the cages in back, then nervously out again at the street.

Christian got up from the hard wooden chair and walked toward her. He felt uneasy himself as if he were loath to reveal who he was. Finally he cleared his throat. "I'm Christian Bangsted. I'm a friend of your brother." She turned and there was fear and unhappiness in her face. "He was drunk. He had a fight," Christian went on. "But he's all right."

"Why did they lock him up?" she gestured toward the cages.

"He—he flew into a rage—hit a man—a total stranger. The alcohol—I don't know what caused it."

"He shouldn't drink." She looked away.

"There was nothing I could do. I grabbed him—" Christian shook his head, feeling helpless, uncomfortable.

"I came here as soon as I could," she said faintly. And there was something tragic about her, something overpowering.

Whatever had attracted him to her photograph now swept through him. He reached for her hand, feeling it clutch his in return as if she wanted him to be there, for a second, not to leave. "I know he will be glad to see you," he said quietly.

"I don't think so," she replied in a voice so empty of emotion that it tugged at him.

"He was talking about you—"

"What did he say?"

"A lot of things. They didn't make much sense. I've worked with him at the hospital for almost a year. I saw your picture in his apartment. He never told me that he had a sister," Christian laughed, trying to relax.

She looked up, her features softening. Her green eyes were beautiful. "I don't think he wants anyone to know," she said shrilly.

"Why?"

She stared directly into his eyes, letting go of his hand. "Ask him."

In a moment the rear door opened and Bill came out, stood there, face to face with them. His tall frame shook with indignation. He seemed disturbed inside, more disturbed than he was before. "Neville—" his voice broke.

She hastened toward him but he turned on her, suddenly defiant. *"Goddamn it!"*

"What's the matter?" she stopped, choking back.

"The money to bail me out!"

She bit her lip, brushing back a thin lock of hair crowding her face.

"Coburg! Right?" he demanded.

She paused, intimidated, as if dangling from an invisible string, then reached out for him.

Christian watched the two of them. It was her telephone call that had started it, had pitched him into wild despair. Now he clung to her, burying himself in her trembling arms as if he were a child desperate to be forgiven.

As he left the detention center, Christian saw a black limousine parked at the curb. The windows were too dark to tell if anyone was inside.

The tiny nurse stared through her wire-rimmed glasses over the counter at him.

"How did it happen?" Christian asked.

"They don't know. I talked to a young Irish policeman—he said they found her shoved down a grating on one of those streets off Canal." The nurse shook her head. "He said they weren't able to make an identification, but I saw her. The eyes, the hair, the face—exactly like the one they brought in yesterday."

"Like mine?" Christian peered across at her.

"Oh no, Dr. Bangsted," she giggled, embarrassed. "You're much more handsome than that."

"Than what?"

"Than an Eskimo."

Christian did not attempt to rumble through her mind any further. As he stood in the doorway of the emergency room glaring at the white walls he regretted, after leaving Bill, having returned to the hospital. But there seemed no point in going home. He would have had to rush through a shower to be back on duty by five a.m. Instead, he intended to sleep for a half hour in the residents' quarters, but now that idea would have to be put off.

"She's in room 482," the nurse babbled on. "There's no room for her in intensive care."

Christian retreated toward the elevator. He felt a tingling sensation crowd over his body. No sleep, no decent food in almost two days. He dreaded to think what they would be serving for breakfast in the cafeteria. His mouth felt burned through like worn rubber and his tongue smarted, seared at the ends. At that moment he would have enjoyed consuming a thick raw steak smothered in onions. Beside him was a kicked-in and broken vending machine. He flipped a quarter into the slot and forced the bar down for Fig Newtons. A tiny package fell out onto the metal tray. Swooping it up he peeled back the cellophane wrapper and bit into the driest, most unappetizing morsel he could imagine. It made his teeth hurt as he spat it out, bunching up and throwing the rest of the package in the adjoining trash bin. Closing his eyelids he rocked forward.

Again he poked the elevator button hard several times in succession as the doors opened and he got in. He shoved the "close" button, the elevator chugging, taking its time, lifting upward, clicking as it reached the second, the third, finally, endlessly, the floors sinking past him. The doors opened on "4".

He passed down the dim hallway. The wards to his left were quiet, bathed in greenish overhead lamps that cast eerie abstract shadows onto the white-sheeted curtains hung at night to provide some privacy behind the panes of floor-to-ceiling glass. On the right just ahead was room 482, the door white, closed. He reached for the knob. At that moment the lights went out in the hospital.

In the pitch dark, Christian felt for the knob, turning it, pushing in the door. He wished that he had a flashlight. As long as he could remember, he had never known the lights to go out in the hospital.

Taking a few steps inside, he stared toward where the bed should be. He hesitated, waiting for his eyes to grow accustomed to the blackness. Then he heard a low intense growl.

He backed up, feeling for the doorknob as a rush of panic choked over him. Whatever it was—he wished he could see—he felt it move, he heard it scratching across the floor.

Backing up, he let out a scream. Suddenly he turned, falling, as whatever it was came after him—crouching—he could barely make it out. He ran into the edge of the door, slipping past it, regaining his balance, running, flying down the hallway. Then he heard it rattling behind him. The patients in the wards were shouting in confusion in the darkness, yet through it he heard it—felt it—*it touched his arm*—

With a rush of speed he turned a corner, banging into a wall. He could not see, falling. Dazed for a second, he groped hurriedly along the wall. The cold tile gripped his body as he rose, until he felt a doorknob above his ear—he remembered—it was the door to an office. Quickly he turned the knob, then rolled inside, slamming the door shut with his feet.

Now he was all right. In the darkness his heart raced. He was imagining. He had to be. It was

madness! No reason to run. Then he heard it—
scraping at the door. He crunched his teeth. Suddenly with a surge of air the door crashed down on
top of him. He hunched back, sliding away on his
hands.

He held his breath, clinging to the darkness before
he heard it again. It was crawling toward him.

Reaching up he felt something metal attached to
the wall. He felt the round shape of a tank, a handle.
He ripped it down, squeezing the handle of the fire
extinguisher with all his might, shooting it in the
direction of the sound.

At that moment the lights poured on. Inches away,
kneeling on all fours, was a woman in a white robe.
Her face was hideously bloated, covered with a
scarlike tissue. The flesh was erupting from her arms
and legs as if it were being burned away—she seemed
to be covered with blood and yet it wasn't blood but
a black tarlike substance that hissed.

She stared at him, opening the flaps of her eyes, if
one could call them eyes. Suddenly that awful morning came back to him—his father sinking beneath
the ice—bloated carcasses floating up, swelling in a
sea of blood—eyes of mutilated seals, blood red and
bulging—*those same eyes.*

Christian let out a wail, shielding his face with his
hands, shuddering, crawling to his feet. He lurched
forward out of the room, not wanting to look back.
Who was she? Where did she come from?

The woman that morning. Dying.

And now this. It frightened him.

An Eskimo woman, the nurse had said.

As he reeled down the hallway a sense of insur-
mountable panic crept over him. He yearned to be
back out on the street, to hide somewhere in the
darkness, to run, to get away.

But from what?

PART TWO

October

9

The tall reporter leaned over the green metal guard-rail braced by the side of the bed and ran his bony fingers along the two feet of knotted rope attached to the pulley supporting Miranda Reichert's leg. He gave the rope a slight tug. "Does that hurt, Miranda? You didn't feel it, did you?"

"That must be the artery. Look. You can't see the thread," another man pointed.

"It's microscopic."

"How does it hold the leg together?"

"What's that meshed cloth, doctor?" asked the tall imposing woman in the gray and white flecked tweed jacket. She wore a continuous smile, the long tight lines of her cheeks and chin disclosing a deter-mined, almost obsessive involvement with her work. Christian remembered her clipped, probing questions from three weeks before. She had stood out among the horde of reporters that turbulent morning he had walked exhausted from the operating room into a labyrinth of flashbulbs and television cameras. She had descended upon him wanting to know every-thing, where he had come from, if he were married, how he *felt*. He had felt tired, worn out, empty inside, and not up to fulfilling her demands for more explicit details about his life. Perhaps he should have let her know that he felt she was rude and irritating. Instead he had remained patient, controlled, answer-ing her questions. He recalled she was from one of the wire services. "It's not cloth. It's grafted skin

95

run through a meshing machine which stretches it four times the normal size."

"Where does the skin come from?"

"From another part of her body."

The woman gave him a look of open-mouthed shock. "Which part?"

Christian chose not to answer the question. There was no point in embarrassing Miranda. He took the woman's timid hand, "Here, touch it if you want," guiding it over the soft dried-blood area where the foot was joined to the leg.

"That's amazing!" she responded. "It doesn't feel like skin."

The six other reporters edged closer, each of them eager to touch the same soft pulpy gap of flesh.

"Imagine, there's nothing there but threads and tissue!" the woman exclaimed.

"How do you feel, Miranda?" a middle-aged reporter asked kindly.

Miranda Reichert stared up at him and her thin colorless face formed a strange dazzling smile. "Fine."

"But doesn't it get lonely lying here all day?"

"Sometimes. But I've prayed to God and I just—" She clenched her front teeth together, dropping her voice.

"Just *what*?"

"I just know I'll be able to dance as soon as it heals."

"But that could take quite awhile."

"I know—I know I'll have to learn to walk all over," she laughed cheerfully. "But I'll be able to dance! Right, doctor?" She glanced sideways at Christian.

Immediately the reporters jotted down her words as Christian watched over them, experiencing a churning current of astonishment, unable to speak. It was obvious what Miranda was doing. She was not going to give up her dream without a fight. And Christian admired her. In no way did he want to see that dream wrested away from her. Eventually it might force her to put enough stress on the leg to cause the bone to knit.

"I think I can feel it—" Miranda hurried on.

"Feel what?" one of the reporters asked excitedly.

"My foot."

With that Christian drew back from the bed. A slight haze had taken over his brain, but he knew it would pass as soon as he was alone in the hallway outside. "I have to get back to my office," he said gently.

"Well, thank you, doctor."

"Thank *you*," the chorus of reporters came back at him.

As he headed for the door, Christian sensed them recirculating themselves around the bed, ready to pour more questions at Miranda, eager for her even more astonishing answers.

"Dr. Bangsted?" The lady from the wire service had followed him into the corridor.

Christian continued walking. "Yes."

"Did she really feel something?"

Christian immediately pictured his comments reprinted in a newspaper, a newspaper being read by Miranda Reichert. He knew that whatever he said would either raise her hopes or depress them completely. And yet this woman wanted him to commit himself in a way that could only incite within his patient irreversible panic. "I think she will be all right," he replied as he stepped into the elevator.

The woman followed. "But what did she feel?" she prodded.

It was an embarrassing question, made even more distressing by the fact that he would have given anything not to have had to answer it. He wished he had withdrawn from the reporters and their questions minutes before.

"I saw the nerves cut," he began as the elevator dropped.

"You mean she's imagining it?" the woman egged him on.

"I wish I could give you a more specific answer."

"But you can, Dr. Bangsted. You *know* the answer."

What was the answer she wanted? That Miranda was deceiving herself, that she felt nothing? Would she be happy if between them they managed to destroy the hopes of a young girl for whom there was only a slight chance of ever walking? But if he lied she would ask someone else.

As Christian left the elevator she followed him out. "She may feel something. The stump of the nerve ending could be giving her a false impression. It is not a sensation in her foot," he admitted, moving toward the reception area.

"Are you sure?"

"Perhaps it is the nerve along the pathway of the leg."

"You're very diplomatic, Dr. Bangsted. You mean she can't discriminate between one sensation and another?"

Christian shrugged. "I wish I could give you the exact terminology."

"What *is* the terminology?"

"It's sometimes . . . sometimes it's called a phantom sensation."

The woman continued to follow him. "You mean she may never again feel anything in her right foot?"

"I didn't say that," he snapped, reaching his office.

"But you don't sound overly optimistic."

Christian turned on her, partially in anger, but making an effort to reason as cautiously as possible.

He repeated one of the phrases he had learned at a recent seminar on handling the press. "As a micro surgeon, I do things similar to other micro surgeons . . . when done properly they can have positive results."

"Then you're not the only genius on the staff?" the woman laughed.

"I never said I was."

"I'd love to do a piece . . ." Her words rushed on. "A personality feature . . . about you . . . an Eskimo boy growing up to become a modern miracle worker . . . leaving his tribe . . . a modern medicine man. Would you let me do it?"

"Perhaps. I don't know."

"It would really be a trendy story."

"If you say so."

"Can we have a drink sometime at my apartment?"

"Sometime . . . maybe," Christian replied cooly, cherishing one thought, to get away from her—as he saw the hand-scrawled message taped over the dial of his phone.

Call Neville DeCormier 533-8130. Urgent.

The roof of the Waterside Plaza pool was a towering skylight through which the late morning sun fell, making the white walls shine. Beside it, the F.D.R. Drive roared past the East River. With frenetic gestures Andre Picard supervised the setup of several filtered spotlights, turning them on, allowing them to blaze, turning them off, while along the pool's edge a restless Doberman stalked back and forth, its neck held firmly by a four-foot chain.

> *Oh . . . it's love that makes me want you . . .*
> *Oh . . . love shows me ways to taunt you . . .*
> *Oh . . . it's love that makes me feel so . . .*
> *feel so . . . feel so . . .*

* * *

Neville slid into the bikini, taking one final sip of her coffee. It was humid in the dressing room and she was trying not to perspire. She dabbed her face and arms with a pink sponge and then finished putting mineral oil on her thighs and calves. The loud disco music boomed in her ears.

> *Oh . . . it's love that makes me want you . . .*
> *Oh . . . it's love that makes me want you . . .*

Staring at herself in the mirror she did not like what she saw. The bikini bottom was too tight. The night before she had eaten pasta and drunk three glasses of wine. She felt drained by the heat, the city, the airlessness of the atmosphere.

> *Oh . . . it's love that makes me, takes me,*
> *makes me . . .*

Gloria, Andre's makeup lady, covered her glistening skin with droplets of water from a plastic bottle. Fortunately, Neville still had the tan she had gotten a month before in the Bahamas. Swaying her hips to the music, she stretched her arms, allowing herself a half-yawn. She had awakened at nine but was still tired. With a shot of spray Gloria moistened her tumbling blond hair, combing it through so it would look as if she had just climbed out of the pool. Tossing her head rapidly, letting the water fly, Neville blinked her green eyes, giving the mirror an unexpected if exaggerated grin. At last she was ready.

> *Oh . . . it's love that makes me love you . . .*
> *Oh . . .*

The high-heeled Jordache shoes bit into her feet as she walked from the dressing room into the circle of strobe lights. The sound of the stereo became muted, partially drowned out by the traffic outside.

"Neville, I see you haven't been working lately. Too bad. You haven't been taking care of yourself!" Andre shouted.

That was what he always said. Especially at the beginning of a shoot. It was intended to keep her off balance, to make her feel insecure so he could more easily manipulate her.

"I've been performing," she shouted back.

"You have a contract. It would be a pity if Mark Barry wasn't happy."

But he would be happy. As always, he would be delighted with her. Both of them knew that.

She stood up in the light, feeling her body stiffen as Gloria worked with the spray bottle on her voluptuous legs, her shoulders—loosening the top of the bikini, pinching it together with a safety pin. Two more sessions and her modeling career would be over. Not that it had been much of a career until Dana Michael Coburg came along.

Andre took a Polaroid shot, continuing to try to bait her. "Are you happy in your new career? I think we should all have a new career," his pampered Bavarian accent crackled as he waited for the print to develop. The warm thing about him, Neville thought, was that no matter who you were he tried to make you feel as if you were ten years old. He showed the result of his camera work to an assistant who murmured something back at him. Finally Andre signaled, "Okay."

Neville was blinded by the electric flash of a strobe light, then another, and another as she moved, spun, turned, Andre shouting, "More sophisticated . . . not too much smile . . . now more . . . spin a little bit . . . move a little . . . let your head up . . . look away a little bit . . . inch to your left, darling." Andre's nervousness, combined with his thick guttural accent, created a terrific tension. He had missed his calling. He should have been directing movies, dark depressing German psychological movies. He was not happy. He wanted her to try it all over again. "All right, this time move a little more . . . walk across there. Get it walking. Turn your shoulders out . . ." Again and again she repeated her movements. "Spin a little bit . . . look away a little bit . . . let your head come up . . . relax." She hesitated a second as he readjusted a light.

His enormous brown eyebrows furrowed as he scrutinized her face. "Now let's try the dog—" Immediately the trainer leaned over to loose the Doberman from its leash. This was the disturbing part, Andre's little excursion into tough chic. Painfully aware of his slipping role in the world of model photography, he was desperate to keep up with the Mike Reinhardts and the Amelio Ricuccis. But allowing the dog's jaws to pull at her thigh frightened her.

Again the strobe lights flashed as she felt the teeth of the Doberman on her leg, straining, the sharp, incredibly lethal teeth. The dog's eyes narrowed. She tried not to move, but pretended she was dashing forward. The music poured into her brain. The flashing lights on both sides and above the camera charged at her face as the lens iris blinked through a hole in the center.

"Now project the fear—" Andre ordered, obviously enjoying himself. "More fear—terror—walk forward—in terror—not too much—"

At that moment Gloria burst in. "There's a Dr. Bangsted on the phone—"

Neville pulled away from the dog, rushing to stop the session. "I've got to talk to him!"

As Christian stood waiting, Neville's face swept past him, her cascading blond hair like sunshine.

"Hello, Christian—" Loud music throbbing in the background crashed over her voice.

"Hello."

"Is this Christian Bangsted?"

"Yes—hello."

"I'm sorry but I'm right in the middle of a shoot."

"A shoot?"

"I'm doing a modeling job. I wanted to get to you. That switchboard had me transferred to every extension in the hospital. Thanks for calling me back. Can we have a drink somewhere later?"

"Maybe. Where?"

"I'll be on the west side. At the Top of the Sixes?"

"I get off at seven."

"I'll see you then."

The phone clicked dead before he had a chance to ask why.

10

There was fear and pain in her face as if she were a child unsure of where to go next. It was not a beautiful face, at least for the first moment or so you watched it, then something happened to the nose and mouth, a girl-woman sprung out, the lips curled, the hair and eyelashes took you in. She was the kind of girl he might have fantasized about, but never approached even if they were in the same room with hundreds of people. Physically, they were opposites. Perhaps that was the reason. He had once heard the phrase "opposites attract," but were they truly ever at home with each other? Wasn't there always the pulling toward other backgrounds, other lives? Or was it an inner shyness that gripped him whenever he was with someone he idealized? Could that have been what made him feel uncertain and nervous? It was as if he had wanted to see her, but when the moment came he was agitated, almost unwilling to experience it. Or was it the longing, the longing— for what?

But perhaps it was because their backgrounds had been so different. Again he concentrated on that possibility. That made sense. She was white-skinned, golden, as if she had walked off a beach somewhere. He was dark, intense, with taut arms and extremely muscular legs. She had grown up with parents who raised her as every normal middle-class child in America was raised, while he had been orphaned and adopted by strangers in another world. He tried to picture what she would be like staring up at him from a pillow, embracing his neck, pulling him down, kissing him with flashes of passion and tender expectancy. Christian desired her more and more. He would have liked to have told her so.

"I wanted to be a singer. That's why I came to New York." She poked at the wooden bowl filled to the brim with potato chips. "But it's not easy . . ."

"I'll bet," he agreed.

"There are so many people you have to go through—besides agents and record companies."

"When did you come here?" he asked.

"A year ago. Bill and I were born and raised in a town near Green Bay, Wisconsin. I used to perform when I was in high school—at dances—I even sang with the school band. Bill used to brag about me to his friends. It made me feel great. You know how it is—or maybe you don't." She laughed self-consciously.

Christian chuckled, eager for her to go on.

"Bill went east after he got out of college. He kept writing to me—kept encouraging me—so finally," she smiled, "I took the plunge."

"How are you doing—as a singer?"

"I have a deal—I just made it with a small record company, but that doesn't mean much."

"But isn't that a great victory?"

She shook her head. "Not really. It takes so much more. Promotion and money and people believing in you—getting behind you and nightclub dates if you can get them. If you can't—you model."

"You hate it—modeling?"

"It's like pretending you're a doll for eight hours with people shouting orders at you. Sometimes I want to scream, 'Forget the whole thing. I'm going back home and settle down where there's people—*real* people with families and dogs and cats.' "

"But the next day it's all right."

"Sometimes. Sometimes I wonder if it will ever be all right." The corners of her mouth dipped and Christian felt sorry for her. The silence inside, behind the wall of even greater silence, was a quality she shared with her brother. He wanted to help her, to reach out for her—he had wanted to from the first moment at the detention center—and obviously she sensed his response. She had begun to relax.

"*Neville*. That's an uncommon name," he remarked.

"My father wanted another son."

"Oh."

"I imagine you were surprised when you heard from me."

"No, I knew you'd call."

She laughed, shocked by his brashness. "You're very nice, you know."

"I have a bedside manner."

"I imagine that you're pretty good *in* bed, too," she glowed at him coyly.

"No one's ever chased me out."

"I saw you on television—I thought you were wonderful. That girl—Miranda—"

An image of a leg hanging from a pulley shot through him. "Miranda Reichert," he said.

"Will she be all right?"

He nodded. "I think so."

"That was a horrible accident."

"Yes."

"But what you said to the reporters—" She smiled, as a whiff of the most exotic perfume he had ever encountered seductively, mysteriously blew across at him. "You looked so tired."

"I hadn't slept in twenty-four hours. Fridays and Mondays are the worst. They all come in. People pushed in front of subways, chain saw accidents. Faces disfigured . . . but Bill must have told you."

"No. I hardly ever see him. It's like we grew up together all our lives—and now he can't stand to be near me."

"But he cares for you."

Quickly she changed the subject. "I've read the articles about you in the newspaper. What is it like to have come through three cultures?"

"What do you mean?"

"You were born in Greenland. You were adopted by a Danish doctor and his wife. And now you're here."

"You must have read everything."

"It sounds exciting. I'm surprised you haven't started your book."

"My book?"

"Everybody in America writes a book."

"Most of it happened when I was very young. I remember some of it—some of it I've forgotten."

"Did you used to live in an igloo?"

"No. In a hut—covered with sealskins."

"I don't think I could stand that. You must have frozen."

"My mother built a fire. My father hunted. And besides, it's not always cold. During the summer in the southern part the temperature goes above twenty-eight degrees.''

''That's not very warm.'' She feigned a shiver as if she could feel a frigid wind blowing through her thin yellow blouse.

''That is twenty-eight degrees centigrade. It would be over eighty here.''

Her eyes were warm staring back at him and he felt comfortable as if she belonged with him. He wished that he had known her a long time, known all about her. But instead he knew nothing, except that she lived with some man.

''I wish—'' She lowered her eyes, obviously troubled by something, perhaps the feeling that he could not accept her—she must have seen it in his face. ''I wish that life were simple.''

Now it was coming. He sensed it. The reason for the *urgent* at the end of her message. Christian settled back, waiting. His eyes caught the eighteenth-century engravings on the wooden paneled walls. Pictures of fox hunts and men marching. He would have liked a plate of hors d'oeuvres from the steaming chafing dish near the bustling, cacophonic bar but he felt no compunction about not crossing the blue plaid carpet to sample them. It was the cocktail hour, yet the table by the window he had picked was quiet, left alone, except for the people milling on stools nearby. Nefarious, rhythmless strains of music poured from speakers in the ceiling.

''Do you know who Dana Michael Coburg is?''

''No,'' Christian shook his head, balancing the straw from his margarita on the ends of his index and middle fingers. If he had even wanted to look away, her expression was so intense, so uncompromising, that he would have been forced back into the blazing depths of her eyes.

''When he was fourteen he inherited five hundred million dollars.'' The magnitude of such an enor-

mous amount of wealth made her voice tremble.
"You see—that's why Bill has to keep his mouth
shut."

"I don't understand. He's extremely wealthy—"
He frowned, puzzled.

"In this country money buys everyone."

"*But Bill has to keep his mouth shut?*" He sat
forward, unable to grasp the point she was trying to
make.

"He hates Dana."

"Dana? Dana Coburg—" He remembered quickly.

"Bill filed a complaint with the police. He said
that he saw a woman with dark hair being beaten and
forced aboard Dana's yacht."

Christian felt a sting of surprise. "Bill did that?"
But he still did not understand. "Was he certain? I
mean—he really saw it?"

"I don't know why he was even there. I asked
him the other night—he kept saying over and over
that he saw it. That he was not lying. That he had
not made it up."

"What did the police do?"

"Nothing. What could they do?" She brushed
back a shock of hair with her fingers. "The harbor
patrol came out. Then they went away. They didn't
search the boat."

"Well . . . I still don't understand." Christian
gazed at her in bewilderment.

"Afterward Dana was furious." Her eyes narrowed,
a hint of fog catching in her throat. Her hands began
to shake as she clasped them together. "He threatened all kinds of things . . . I promised that I would
talk to Bill." Her voice broke as her lingering eyes
reached out to him, desperately, as if she were trapped
in some ordeal from which he alone could help her
escape. "I'm afraid what Dana might do."

"*What Dana might do*? I don't understand. There are laws."

She laughed unhappily, her expression switching back and forth from a small town girl to a sophisticated New Yorker. "The people Dana *owns* make the laws. His uncle was the governor of this state. His grandfather founded the nation's largest bank. And he—"

"He what?"

She wavered, weighing her words, for a second unsure of what to reveal. "He finances other things." She let it trail off, then fearfully picked up her thought again. "Do you know much about international politics?"

"I listen to the eleven o'clock news."

"When a country has a revolution—when a gang of terrorists takes over—do you know how they get guns and armaments? Do you know where the money comes from?"

Christian shook his head. He had no idea, but he now found the conversation fascinating.

"Usually, it's American dollars. It comes from banks, from investors—"

"From Dana Michael Coburg."

"That's as much as I know." She shook her head quickly, but he guessed that she knew more, much more. And for the first time it began to bother him as he suspected faintly, somewhere back in his brain, that he was about to be employed to perform some function in the whole scheme. That was why she had wanted to see him. To use him to protect her brother from this man!

He looked down at the patches of green trees which he recognized as Central Park, looking as if it were a gigantic floor mat bounded by a stretch of silver buildings and the distant white waters of the reservoir. Clustering on all sides were shapes of buildings in the process of being constructed, some of them half-finished, others with the bare outline of girders, the skeletal shapes of huge cranes stretching up from their foundations as if they were lofty arms grasping at the thirty-nine stories where he sat. One building stood out with its copper roof in the shape of a pinnacle beside an awesome sheet of smoky glass at least sixty stories high. "So what you're saying is that he has no allegiance to anyone, anywhere."

"Men like that don't have to answer for their actions."

He gazed across the table at her with a mingling of amazement and admiration. To be so young and have such an incisive view of corruption. Christian smoothed his thick black hair, his dark eyes glancing down at Fifth Avenue. The next obvious question was how could *she* be involved with someone like that? It bothered him as he watched the cluttered lines of traffic moving under him like toy cars.

"If he wants to, he can exercise the power of life and death over millions of people."

"Over you?"

"He knows everyone who matters—that's the way it is in this city—it makes no difference how good you are, how talented . . ." She laughed carelessly as if she would have liked to possess some of that power, and Christian realized from that moment on what he was dealing with. It had so merged with and taken over her vision of reality that she believed no one was safe without it. "That's why I want you to talk to Bill . . . to reason with him," she went on.

Christian felt reluctance stiffen inside him. He could not decide whether she was telling him what she truly believed or whether it was a conspiracy. That all of the feelings of intimate interest and the soft promising looks fleeting across her eyes had been intended to ensnare him into being an instrument to caution Bill, to advise him to shut up.

"No," he shook his head.

"No?" She stared at him, quickly disturbed.

"No. I'm not doing what either you—*or Coburg*—wants."

"What do you mean?" Her eyes sprung open wide.

"Your brother and I are friends. I can't . . ."

"But I'm afraid what Dana might do!" she repeated.

"How do I know?"

She reached across the table and grasped his hand. "I want . . . I want to be with you," she said, with eyes melting into a hundred different shades of green, passing through him so that he could hardly sit still.

"No," he shook his head, starting to get up from the chair.

"Please—" she pleaded, her body stirring toward him.

"I can't," he repeated.

11

The white clay head of the man rested on a block of wood in front of her. Navarana huddled in the shadows of the dimly lighted studio critically studying its smooth features. Shifting forward on the stool, she curled her shapely legs up under the rungs. Although the thick lips and the perfectly proportioned lines of the sculpted face were well designed, they portrayed no emotion. Dipping a tiny artist's brush into the murky liquid mound on the palette beside her, she carefully applied a second coat of black acrylic paint to darken the eyebrows. The mannequin's expression was almost lifelike, yet the eyes would remain hollow. It was museum policy that only animals should have glass eyes.

When the man's face was finished the next step would be to add the torso, the arms and legs clad in soft caribou skins with an ornamental ribbon of beads encircling the shoulders and coat hem, festive fox-fur leggings and thick seal-hide moccasins. Once the six-foot plaster and clay figure was costumed it would assume its role in the recreated village as a member of an Eskimo wedding party.

Sulfuric fumes from the liquid rubber molds near-by, in which more heads were being formed, swept unpleasantly past her nostrils as she rose from her stool and headed toward the sink. Turning on the faucet, a blast of water rushed out. Her almond-hued eyes peered listlessly through the black windows beside her. The hours of the evening had slunk by, yet she had barely noticed, so preoccupied had she been with her work.

By now she was alone in the offices of the muse-um. The cleaning women, the janitors had left for the night. Yet being alone did not threaten her. Hungrily she clung to the hollow silence, the protec-tive privacy.

While she bathed the paintbrush in soap and hot water, the creeping darkness made the silken luster of her long black hair invisible. The hot water stung her fingers. She listened to the silence as it swam against her.

And then she heard a sound which made her stiffen.

It was totally unexpected, at first like a sudden whoosh of air, succeeded by a banging crash, the thundering roar of two immense doors clanging open, echoing with a deafening clamor, resounding through the empty hallways, pounding up from the galleries below.

She gripped her hands together until the nails

almost poked through the flesh of her perspiring palms as she desperately listened, knowing in her heart that she hadn't imagined it. What could it be? An image flitted through her mind, a hideous face leering out at her, a network of raw veins slashing across its deformed features, its venomous mouth dripping saliva . . . fresh blood . . .

The tension was unbearable as she turned abruptly from the sink. Should she leave the security of her office? No, she couldn't. She didn't want to.

She shivered all over as a sickening sensation drove uncontrollably into her heart.

Hesitantly, Navarana started out of the office, her heart leaping as her steps quickened down the hushed winding hallway. Finding the stairs in the dim light, she hurriedly descended them into the overpowering darkness, through the cryptlike rooms, into the pitch-black galleries, her feet slapping across the marble floors. She was out of breath when at last she glimpsed the archway illuminated by a red *Exit* sign, the flat gray door marked *No Admittance*. She flung it open, switching on a flood of downward-pouring light. The receiving room was still in disarray, with litter everywhere.

A scream rose up inside her, a shriek of wrenching dismay.

The pedestal stood bare, empty.

She turned back toward the gallery entrance. And then she saw the great metal doors to the basement lobby standing open.

They had been pounded open! The thing was out there!

She hurried into the lobby, her steps charged with anxiety. As she passed the front security booth she saw that the guard was not inside. But nothing could stop her. Not her fears, not anything. She noticed that the emergency exit door was ajar. Without hesitation she rushed through it.

It took a moment for her eyes to focus under the yellow glow of the overhead fluorescent lights. A windswept green banner fluttered from a stanchion imbedded into the side of the New York Historical Society on the opposite corner. She stared across the trash-littered museum grounds, through the spiked wrought-iron fence leading to the empty street. Less than a hundred feet from where she stood, behind a row of unoccupied charter buses, was the entrance to Central Park.

The park seemed to drop down in a slope behind a low stone wall so that only the top half of its dark trees were visible. She gasped as she saw an enormous shadow emerge from behind one of the parked charter buses. She watched it creep through the darkness and slip down behind the low wall.

At that instant Navarana experienced more than fear. But dread, a rootless gagging thrust that stole down her chest until she felt what seemed like a cold metal stake jabbing across her lungs. She couldn't stand it anymore. Headlong, she raced across the street with no idea except to follow the hideous shape which had curled waiting inside her thoughts.

Pulling herself to the top of the low wall, Navarana crawled over. Losing her balance, she rolled down the short grassy slope. She got up quickly, running forward several yards, lost for a moment, searching for a pathway through the shrubs and twisted branches.

And then she heard a sudden clatter of laughter, followed by applause.

In the distance, half-hidden by the dark woods, there were rows of lights hanging from high, naked platforms. She heard more laughter, more applause. Reaching the top of a hill she spied something which made her halt in dismay. A large audience was seated, watching a play in the open air of the Delacorte Theater. The actors on stage were in ancient dress.

As an artificial mist rose into the darkness, their voices roared over the PA system:

> "Awak'd you not with this sore agony?"
> "No, no, my dream was lengthen'd after life . . .
> O! then began the tempest of my soul . . . I pass'd, methought, the melancholy flood with that grim ferryman which poets write of . . . unto the kingdom of perpetual night . . ."

A man lay on a bed in a dungeonlike room. He spoke to two other men with shadowy faces.

It was Shakespeare. *The audience was watching Shakespeare.*

Navarana spied a small building crouched adjacent to the nearest corner of the amphitheater. There was a thin, waiflike woman in a flowered green dress standing beside it, glancing nervously into the darkness. As Navarana approached she saw that the young white face had premature wrinkles of concern about the mouth. The woman accosted her in swift, worried tones. "Did you see a little boy and a little girl with blond hair—about this size?" She gestured in the vicinity of her slim waist. "Stephen was wearing trousers with light green suspenders and Jennifer had on a bright red jumpsuit . . ." The woman's frightened voice rushed on. "I went in to use the ladies' room—they were playing—when I came out they were gone!"

"No . . . no . . . I'm sorry. I didn't see them." Navarana shook her head.

The woman gave her an apprehensive, fleeting glance and then broke away, hurrying around the front of the amphitheater toward the surrounding trees and bushes on the other side.

There were stone steps leading up a hill which looked over the theater. Navarana began climbing them, thinking to herself how terrible it would be to lose a child, as the actors' voices pounded to a crescendo over the PA system:

"What! Shall we stab him as he sleeps?"

"No . . . he'll say 'twas done cowardly when he wakes . . ."

"When he wakes! Why fool, he shall never wake till the judgment day!"

The stone steps crept toward a long, stark, silhouetted mound overgrown with trees and bushes. It was darker there, lofting above the city. Yet the distant lights of apartment buildings lining the park shone radiantly. As Navarana climbed haphazardly higher, she glanced past the audience seated below, the stage crowded with actors, the black lake cutting across a grassy area dimly lighted by lampposts. But where she stood the lights had burned out. It was a lost, forsaken area. Above her beckoned a cold, luminescent moon. Through the dense undergrowth surrounding the steps there was even greater darkness. At the top of the hill brooded the outline of an abandoned stone fort which had been a lookout during the Revolutionary War and which now served as a weather station with spiny instruments swirling from its towers. It was surrounded by steep, carved walls careening down a high cliff toward the thick black lake below.

And then, from the top of the hill, Navarana heard a child's voice.

"Look—look at the castle, Jennifer."

There was a laugh, a tiny soft laugh, as if another child were exploring as well.

Navarana hurried her steps:

"Look, Jennifer," the child wailed. Then there was a shriek. Followed by a sudden cry, a muffled sob of bewilderment.

Navarana leapt upward, rushing to the top of the hill. But when she got there the two children had vanished.

Blatant, ugly crusts of graffiti were smeared across the neglected stone walls. Harsh obscenities leered

out at her in jabs of multicolored chalk and garish
streaks of spray paint. There were barred windows
high up, straddling the battlements and empty gun
towers. Yet there was no sign of an entrance. The
ancient fort appeared to be boarded up, lifeless. It
was an eerie sight in a world of high-rise apartment
buildings, hurtling taxicabs, glaring strobe lights and
ear-shattering, highly-intensified sound.

And then she heard a child crying. The sound cut
across her heart. Navarana's dark eyes desperately
scanned the graffiti-covered walls. The sound seemed
to be coming from somewhere inside.

Frantically Navarana ran around the building to
the other side. There was a stone ballustrade, a
guardrail imbedded with warning signs. But there
was no entrance. She stretched across the guard-rail,
fighting to keep her balance, craning her neck, desperately peering down over the edge toward the
black lake. The crying sounds seemed to be coming
from below. There appeared to be a curvature, a
hollow opening, illuminated by the moonlight, halfway down the rocky cliff. It was too far to crawl,
too steep and hazardous.

And then she heard a thin, agonized shriek. She
had to get down there.

Lowering her head she squirmed under the guard-
rail, onto the stone ballustrade, hastily crawling on
her knees toward a low ridge of rock. As her fears
overtook her she slid her leg over the edge of the
cliff, her feet stabbing at the darkness, fighting to
find a foothold as a clatter of surging applause rose
from the unsuspecting audience below. She found a
crease in the rock, slowly slipping her body downward, clutching the naked walls with her fingers,
gouging her nails into each crack that she found.
Inch by inch, she let herself slide a little, after each
minute slide grabbing again onto the rocky surface,
catching herself, holding her weight up by digging

her fingers in with all their strength. Lower and lower she let herself slide, the children's pathetic sobbing ringing in her ears, her heart thundering mercilessly, afraid to breathe, to allow herself the slightest unsettling stir which might cause her to lose her balance. She stretched her leg down as far as it would go, groping for support, her fingers raw, the tips torn, beginning to bleed. She clenched her teeth together, fighting back the pain as her arms scraped across a jagged layer of sharp protruding rock.

Then she slipped. She hung helplessly for a moment, her legs dangling. She managed to grip on, to edge lower. Her feet touched the curvature, the hollow center. She eased herself down until she felt confident enough to allow her full weight onto the soles of her feet, until she was able to crouch down and slip between the rocks.

Wedging herself inside the narrow tunnel she could hear a child still crying, somewhere near her. And then she heard a small voice, *"Please—please don't!"* Followed by a sudden gasping scream!

Immediately she was confronted by a wave of fierce, damp air and an awful stench which viciously assaulted her nostrils. The tunnel was dark, almost pitch black except for the moonlight. She noticed objects on the floor. A piece of scarf. A torn trouser leg. And then her eyes fixed on a fragment of red cloth—as the woman's troubled voice came back to her. "Jennifer had on a bright red jumpsuit . . ."

The child's screams had increased, bellowing into shuddering wails.

Navarana drove her way in further, gripping at the sides of the walls, pushing herself deeper through the dark tunnel.

She touched something soft, porous; it was caked all around her, it came loose in her hands. In utter horror she realized what it was. A chunk of human flesh attached to a sheet of loose hanging skin.

Pieces of something crushed beneath her knees. In the streaks of moonlight she discovered that she was crawling through a charnel house of putrifying organs.

Gagging, about to vomit, she felt her way to what appeared to be a center of light pouring from windows high above. There were bones on the floor everywhere.

And then she saw it.

Directly in front of her, the huge form bristling with thick black fur, the hideous snout dripping with foam, and the eyes, the horrible gaping sockets—

Near its talons lay the disemboweled body of a little girl, her silken entrails ripped loose and strewn over her face. As the enormous jaws dropped, chomping into the little boy's chest, an explosion of blood spurted across the venomous crawling lips.

Navarana let out a hoarse scream. She could no longer hold it back—

The creature glared up at her.

Suddenly it rose, dropping the mutilated body of the small boy from its mouth. Its moist lips seethed with incredible rage.

I wanted you to follow me. Now do you see? the snarling voice rattled through her.

Navarana sank back in terror.

At that moment the immense ghastly form seemed to shudder forward with laughter. *"You're helpless, Navarana . . . you cannot stop me . . . no one will believe you . . . I'm leaving you . . . but this time you won't follow, will you?"*

With that it leapt suddenly upward in triumph, straight up, its massive sloping head and shoulders crashing through the barred windows above, sending down a barrage of splattering glass as it disappeared into the night.

12

A breaking dawn of pink mist swirled wistfully over the crest of rock as Siegfried, her lover, panto-mimed his search, vainly, endlessly through somber clouded marshes and wild mustard glens where na-ture unfurled in pastel oranges and vivid magenta. She watched, seizing her cue, the flutes and violins rising in trills, as she reached up her hands swanlike, chenéeing forward toward his lost lips. He did not see her. She bourréed into an arabesque. She was a phantom, an illusory substance shrouded in purple beams. Yet in the kingdom of death where no light would ever shine, tiny streaks of day caressed her arms, her legs. Siegfried, she called. Yet there were no words. There could never be any words.

Did he see her? Did he imagine that she still waited? Did he remember her eyes, her face? Sieg-fried!

As Miranda dreamed, her serpentlike hair curled against the pillow. She clutched onto the glorious circle of red light, the radiance of the moment part-ing her lips in smiling pleasure.

Then she felt his eyes. As the music swelled, his tempestuous gaze sought her out. She trembled inside, her hands in sleep reaching out, her legs free, dancing beside him, wrapping her feet around him, feeling his hands clasp her waist, spinning her as she breathed alive, the stagelights bending in magic waves as he hurled her whirling body up.

Such ecstasy took over her legs that she could not wait for the adagio. She leapt laughing toward the audience, her heart springing, as their faces warmed her movements. The solid wrists of men, the delicate fingers of ladies soared up to applaud. She was the most gifted, the most sublime of ballerinas and there was still more that she could do to enhance the wonder in their eyes.

She felt him embrace her. She half-turned, reached up, touched his cheek, took his face into her hands—then pretended a kiss, as she released him, backing away—back—back—letting him slide out of her memory into dark timelessness. As the stage was deluged by violet blue he sank into the mist, overcome, falling forever.

Miranda's twisted right leg yanked against the pulley, tears burning through her eyelids—oh no, I don't want it to end, it can't end—please! What had awakened her was a frightening sound whirring beside her bed. She awoke in a darkness more infinite and terrible, looking up at a figure so grotesque that her breath was sucked in.

Lying still, she was fascinated by it for a second. It was like nothing she had ever seen. Yet it should not have been there! That is what throttled through her as she stared up in disbelief!

Groaning, she tried to wrench away, to pull her leg, arching, curling back under her spine as icy perspiration shot through pockets beneath her breasts. *Oh, no*, she gasped, flung out of her dream into another deathlike swirl. The image clawed at her mind—she could not believe what she was seeing, there in the dark, silhouetted in the murky glow from the hallway lights—

She tried to turn over, to bury her face, but her body hung helpless, anchored to the pulley rope. *She had to look. She could not even cover her eyes.*

She imagined that she had rolled off the bed, had fallen onto the floor, tried to get up—yet she could not move. She lay there pinned, trapped by the unrelenting rope. She gaped at the enormous form towering, lifting the huge shape—the shape rising—rising—she whimpered, crying, holding back her breath, trying to roll, to slide away, but held firmly, helplessly by the pulley rope without the courage to scream. Anguish curdled inside her mouth as she felt fear, *more fear than was possible to feel.* Her head shot up, slamming into the steel back of the bed as the axe tore down with an earshattering crunch, splitting her leg in half.

She recoiled, seeing it fall, the foot, her foot bouncing against the opposite wall. She wailed like a child, trying to tumble, scrambling—she sobbed, screamed, praying for darkness, begging to plunge back lifeless toward death as she shook, her mouth pitifully foaming—then she crumpled over, grasping at the cold horrible stump oozing blood into the jagged sheets.

It was dawn. The early morning light stained the stark white walls with disjointed shadows. Relentlessly the two men labored in the hush of the tiny operating room. There were no closed-circuit television cameras, no tiers of rapt, pensive faces, no newspaper reporters lurking in the outer hallway. Besides the two men, there was just a scrub nurse with anxious eyes and an anesthesiologist keeping close watch over a portable transducer.

The verbal exchanges between the two men were totally without humor. They were doctors, dedicated to a task which involved constant discovery, a new world of medicine. Yet what faced them was a condition they had never before experienced. It had amazed both of them to such a degree that they had difficulty discussing it. It defied everything they knew.

Only one of the men, the darker, more agile of the two, had begun to suspect that something else was involved. On a deeper, more sensitive level he could not help but sense a significance to what appeared as so uncommon, so mystifying. He could no longer push away from his mind what he now felt in his heart, that some insidious element was overshadowing his consciousness. It frightened him, and yet he could not distinguish what it involved. What had happened to Miranda Reichert was not extraordinary, *it was impossible*.

At first he had convinced himself that the incident could have resulted from a tearing at the junction aggravated by an aneurism, unnoticed, which had dilated. A stronger vessel might have resisted it with ease, he tried to assure himself, but with twenty-four thousand beats a day surging through the artery, a rupture *just might* have taken place. But how did that explain the shattering of the rush rod? And the evidence that something extremely sharp had cut through the cross tissue?

He probed his brain for other answers. Yet he began to feel it, more and more. There were none. That is what caused his hand to sway ever so slightly, though he was certain no one noticed. There was a weakening in his fingers, something was blocking them. He was having trouble moving them forward. Of course he might have been imagining the effect of his fears. Yet why did he feel so incapable of performing this operation? Why did the thought of its success make him deathly afraid?

As soon as the duty nurses wheeled her in, he had hoisted Miranda Reichart's leg in a Hoffman apparatus, driving steel pins crossways into the broken shafts of the tibia so that the point where the two sections matched was visible through the dangling threads of blood vessels, torn nerves and slivers of tissue. Without waiting for the resident orthopedist, Christian had rejoined the leg himself. There was no time. But he kept worrying about the stiffness in his fingers; his mind whirled as he wondered how

Miranda's accident had happened. Had she freaked and yanked her leg off the pulley, hitting her ankle on the railing of the bed? Could that have caused the foot to fly off? He stared down at her face slumped against the table in shock. A brief image of the reporters asking questions, *Will she dance again? How soon? Did she really feel anything in her foot?* fluttered past him. He wished that he were not there. He wished that he had never set eyes on Miranda Reichert.

A pneumatic tourniquet inflated to five hundred millimeters of mercury was tightened onto her lower thigh. While Christian worked to save the artery, Bill hurriedly removed a vein from the dorsum of Miranda's other foot, placing a silk tie on the proximal portion to mark it so that they would know to reverse the vein, permitting the valves to open the opposite way. Betadine was then applied to maintain a sterile field.

It was as if he had never operated on Miranda's foot before. He was concerned about the posterior tibial nerve. Without it she would never again feel anything in her heel. Holding one hand against the other, Christian dissected down to where the break had occurred in order to graft the artery to the vein of the other foot. Then he stopped. His hand stopped. His fingers would not move.

He stared at Bill as he let the micro forceps holding the scalpel fall. Bill let out a curse, quickly grabbing them before they sank into Miranda's flesh. "What's the matter?" he growled.

"I don't know," Christian backed away as the walls peeled toward him, shimmering out of focus through the overhead lights. All he could see was the woman on the hospital floor crawling toward him—her face hideously bloated, erupting with scar tissue, a black tarlike substance hissing from her lips. He almost fainted—he had to run. "Where are you going!" Bill shouted.

Christian did not turn back as he fled through the open doors.

There was a man waiting in the hallway. Staggering dizzily through twisted shadows, Christian recognized Milton Reichert's grim face.

"Have you finished operating?" Reichert stared up, his eyes one great pleading expression.

"No," Christian shook his head, trying to get away.

"Well, what are you doing here! Why aren't you in there with my daughter!" The pleading look turned to one of menacing accusation as his echoing voice followed him down the hall.

"I can't . . ." Christian started replying weakly.

At that moment there was a scream—a naked nauseating scream that chilled both men; Milton Reichert's eyes turned white, Christian stood rooted. It was Miranda.

"We had to tie her down. We tried to finish the operation with her still conscious," Bill shook, spitting the words out through his teeth. "The anesthetic had no effect. I don't know . . . ." He pounded his fist into his knee as he sat there next to the locker in the micro surgery lab. "She kept screaming . . . oh God I—I never saw anything . . . anything . . . ." He shook his head. "I kept dousing the blood with a sponge—that's all I could do—she kept howling . . . I couldn't touch the foot. Finally we wrapped it in bandages—she kept howling . . . ."

Christian sat pale, peering into space, his body aching. "Nothing . . . ever happened like that before," he muttered. The memory of his dizziness was devouring his insides.

"Finally . . . finally . . . we quieted her," Bill went on. "She lay there *staring up*. Her eyes were dead. I never saw a face like that. All my life . . . she was enjoying the pain!"

"I'm sorry . . ." Christian tried to begin.

"You went rushing out—you—"

"I know." Christian nodded. "I don't know what happened. My hands—" He raised his fingers, staring up at them. But now they moved effortlessly. "I knew . . . if I stood there any longer . . . I felt . . ." He could not finish the phrase.

"The moment you left she started to scream—"

With that Bill rose from the bench. "I have to get some air." He started to leave.

"Where are you going?"

"To take a walk . . . somewhere . . . I've got to get out."

After Bill left the lab, Christian sat alone. His legs were still shaking as if he were powerless to control them. His head throbbed. Biting down hard he tried to quell the torrents of weakness. The thought of what had happened continued to make him shudder. As he got up to open his locker he spotted a piece of paper shoved next to the lock. It was an advertisement of some kind. There was a girl's picture and some writing.

He recognized Neville's face. Under it were bold letters: NEVILLE DECORMIER AT THE BUSHES, 23 WEST 73 ST. N.Y.C. SHOW TIME 10:00 P.M.

Across the bottom was a scribbled note: *Please come tonight. I'm afraid.*

13

"There's a three dollar cover and a five dollar minimum. For that you get two drinks." The morose-looking bartender in tight black jeans and an

ultracasual seaman's jersey leaned over the narrow
bar. It sounded so factual, so devoid of pleasantness,
that the voice could have been relating safety
instructions or directions to the men's lavatory. For
that moment Christian was irritated. He did not enjoy
feeling that he *had* to buy two drinks in order to hear
a girl sing, that otherwise he would be required to
leave the premises. Reluctantly he nodded, "I'll
have a rum and soda—not too much ice."

It was a tiny dark room with no more than fifteen
densely arranged tables, each of them lighted by a
solitary candle in a short glass lamp. The candles
flickered, restlessly casting a desolate gloom over
the walls and low beamed ceiling. The room was
filling slowly with people and he felt that perhaps he
was early, even though it was already past ten.
"What time does the show start?" he asked the
bartender.

"In about five minutes . . . or so . . ."

The rum and soda was pushed in front of him with
the already computed check. Christian reached for
the cold glass. He did not feel as if he wanted a
drink, yet he took a long sip experiencing the murky
taste of the rum swirling through his gums. He gazed
at the string of blinking Christmas tree lights carelessly surrounding the back mirror. It was not the
kind of place he would frequent, stuck away in the
back room of a residential hotel. There were paint-
ers' tarps with scaffolding and rolled carpets in the
hallway entrance. He wondered why Neville had
chosen to perform there.

But he suspected the answer. She was trying to
launch herself as a singer. She hated modeling, but
at this early stage in her career she had to sing
wherever she could, anyplace that people could come
and listen.

"You been here before?" the bartender asked, in
an offhand but decidedly prying manner. He was in

his late twenties, Christian guessed, and he looked like an actor. He had a stubby body and forced black eyes.

"No."

"Did you just move into the neighborhood? How did you hear about the place?"

"I came to see Neville."

"Yeah, she's good," the bartender smiled. "She's gonna be a big star. We have a lot of singers who come and go, but she's really got something."

"What is she doing here?" Christian was tempted to ask, but decided against it.

"She's great looking too," the bartender rambled on. "That's one of the reasons the guy who runs this place booked her. Her looks alone. You don't find many singers with—" He gestured, indicating the full extent of her curvaceousness. He hesitated. "Are you her boyfriend—or something like that?"

"No. Nothing like that."

"I didn't think so. She has this guy—he's like—got millions."

"Is he here?"

"Not yet. But he will be. He always leaves a big piece of change."

With that the bartender eased away. There was a waitress waiting for his services at the other end of the bar. Christian felt that the reference to the "big piece of change" was obviously intended to guide others along a similar pattern.

He took another sip of his rum and soda, beginning to feel extremely conspicuous sitting alone at the bar. Everyone else seemed to be in couples at the tables circling a small performing area, a piano and a microphone. He consoled himself with the fact that he did not have long to wait, only five more minutes . . . or so . . . It was the "or so" that bothered him. He wondered how many of the people there were agents and friends. How many had Neville ferreted out and begged to come hear her sing.

As he glanced to the rear of the room he saw a door open and an extremely distinguished-looking man with prematurely gray hair enter. He was slim, dressed in an impeccable brown suit and blue tie, with a strong, handsome face that was deeply lined, although he could have been no older than thirty-five. Accompanying him were two other men, tough looking, both dressed in dark innocuous sport jackets. They quickly slivered through the crowd, locating him a table close to the performing area.

As he sat down, the man's eyes glinted around at the seated couples, then toward the bar. They focused on Christian for a second, and as they did, he sensed that he saw a curious, almost amused expression gather at the corners of his mouth. Christian was certain who he was.

"That's him," the bartender murmured, wiping a bit of moisture from the top of the bar with a cocktail napkin.

"Do you know his name?" Christian asked.

"No," he shook his head. "But maybe someone else does." He started down the bar, but Christian waved, stopping him in time.

"Ladies and Gentlemen," a male voice was amplified over the speakers. "The Bushes introduces Miss Neville DeCormier."

There was a quick, sporadic shower of applause as she entered from the back wearing tight jean pants, a thin white silk blouse and a black bowtie. The fingers of the pianist who had crept out from behind the curtains raced into a rousing fanfare as she took the stage, smiling, the spotlights catching her eyes and her endless flowing blond hair.

Christian caught a glimpse of the silver-haired man sitting alone in quiet repose at the table, his two dark attendants lurking in the shadows behind him.

His aristocratic features had formed a smile. He was pleased.

Neville gripped the microphone. "Thank you. Thank you for coming. This is the first time I've been in the bushes." An eddy of laughter rustled through the room. "But of course I've been in the bushes before," she smiled, an embarrassed, shy smile. The audience immediately liked her.

"This is the third time I've performed in New York—for friends . . ." She went on—telling stories about where she grew up, how her parents urged her to come to New York, to leave home. "I wish I didn't have the feeling they were trying to tell me something." More spotty laughter from the audience of thirty or so. "Then I met this man . . . I was visiting my parents on vacation down in Florida . . . I was sitting by the pool playing my guitar . . . singing. He came up to me and asked if I would be interested in cutting a record. He said he was the president of a company in New York and he wanted to pay my way here. I mentioned his offer to my parents and they were amazed. To say the least." She laughed as the audience continued to warm to her coy, fleeting delivery. "But it turned out he was telling the truth. So here I am." With that she burst into a rendition of a soft, tender ballad, her eyes dancing over the faces of her listeners as the piano in the background subtly picked out the accompanying chords. Christian felt uncertain for a moment, he did not know how to react, then he joined the others, completely taken in by her voice, the nuances of mood that she gave to the words . . .

> *I've been waiting since morning*
> *And the bed isn't made . . .*
> *Yet I know that he'll walk*
> *through that door*
> *And say, "Jessie, it's time that we go . . ."*

Brisk tremors of excitement gathered inside him. He
wanted her to be good. He hardly knew her, yet he
felt extremely proud. She looked perfect . . . better
and better . . .

> *'Cause I know he's been searching*
> *For someone like me . . .*
> *Someone who loves the way he moves,*
> *Someone who wants him just as he is . . .*

The spell was so infectious, so intimate, that Christian forgot for a moment about the gray-haired man
poised at the table across from him. Then he felt
Neville's eyes turn. They glimpsed him sitting on
the bar stool. He wanted to smile, to say with his
facial expression that he loved watching her, but she
turned away.

> *I can't really tell him*
> *The way that I feel,*
> *I know that he'll laugh and say, "Jessie—*
> *I once wish'd it were so . . ."*

Christian wanted her at that moment more than
ever before. He wanted her to belong to him. She
finished the song—ending with a grand flourish—
glanced his way, hesitantly, glowing toward everyone looking up at her, then she stopped singing,
carried away by the immediate rush of applause.

Christian ordered his second drink from the now
quickly moving bartender and sat back to await more
of what her voice and sparkling eyes would create.

She began another song, then another, and as he
listened he stared across at Dana Michael Coburg
sitting forward in his chair, as taken in as everyone
else. Coburg's looks were striking and with all those
hundreds of millions he could understand how Neville might have found him irresistible. He seemed to
have the assuredness of someone who had exerted
absolute control over his environment all his life.

That's what Neville had been attracted to—his confidence, the strength in his eyes.

Each of her songs was varied, wonderful. Christian began to feel so close to her that it was as if each word she uttered was for him alone, telling him something about himself, about the loneliness of loving in a world where no one wished to love her back.

And then she was finished. She darted away as the small audience started to cheer. She hurried back once toward the piano, bowing, smiling, happily extending her arms out to all, to everyone, then moved off to the side, floating toward him. She passed—clutched his clapping hands—he felt a slip of paper dangle for a second off her fingers—he grasped it as he watched her disappear into the darkness beyond.

The spotlights descended back into gloom, bathing the room in an aura of false, tense reality. Christian opened the note. Written on it was an address.

The thought of meeting Christian played through her mind. He would be waiting for her. A subtle yearning had awakened; perhaps it was the excitement from performing—''coming down'' after reaching such a crescendo of emotional exposure, even if it was on the barren stage of a nightclub. She could feel him somewhere in that city, perhaps crossing the park in a cab—or already waiting in front of where she lived. She wanted to talk to him, to let it pour out—her frustrations, her fears about Bill. She badly needed to tell someone. But what could he do? They were both helpless. Unless Bill would listen. At that moment, despite everything, she needed to be with Christian. She had no one else. It was more than an attraction, it was an inkling that he would not run away.

The luxurious black limousine veered out from the

curb and was immediately caught up by a teeming swell of screeching taxicabs. The driver's suede gloved hand settled on the horn, urging the blustering wedges of traffic to allow him to creep by. Finally he pounded out a series of blasts as he awaited an opportunity to surge forward. But there was a truck blocking the street, a huge dark vehicle with no signs or markings identifying it.

"Would you like some champagne?" Coburg lifted a glass from the accordion rack, reaching with his other hand for the neck of the opened bottle of Tattinger.

"No," she said.

"Not thirsty?"

She shook her head. "You have some . . ."

Neville felt momentarily cut off from the world. She arched back into the fur-lined seat as Coburg leaned across, kissing her moist lips, gently enveloping each of her breasts with his arm. "You were wonderful," he said. "Ben Rice, the painter, is giving a party in his loft in Soho—I think you'll like it."

"I'm tired."

"What do you mean?"

"I'd rather not."

"Then we'll go to my place."

"I'd rather go home—please—" She stared up at him, observing the unsettling look in his steely eyes.

"Why home? *I don't understand.*"

"I don't—want to go anywhere. I'm just too tired," she sighed. "I'll take a short nap and we'll get together later."

"I still don't understand—" His hand touched her inner thigh, caressing it hungrily. "You can't be *that* tired."

"I just don't feel well, Dana." She smiled, attempting to make him believe her words.

He stared at her closely, scrutinizing her face, her unyielding expression. "There's nothing else?"

"What could there be?"

"I feel something. You're not telling me the whole truth."

"I am, darling." She reached up, smoothing his cheek, rushing through his gray sideburns with her fingers, kissing him warmly, as he grabbed her in sudden passion.

The limousine began to move, breaking away from the traffic toward the signal lights at the end of the block.

"My place." Coburg motioned to the driver.

"I don't want to go there—please . . ." she begged. "Not now—maybe later—please, Dana—just this once—I want to be by myself for a while."

"Look—I gave up my evening to see you perform —now I want you for a little while."

"I wouldn't be any fun . . ."

His jaw dropped. He didn't like it. He didn't believe her for a moment. "It's your brother."

"That's part of it—"

Coburg sat back, bristling with anger. "I'm getting tired of him. You know what happens when I get tired of someone."

"Why!" she suddenly wailed, fright filling her as she clung to him. "*Because I won't go home with you!*" She trembled all over. "Oh please . . ." she begged. "No . . ." She shook her head. "Please, Dana, he's my brother . . . I love him . . ."

Nine-eighty was one of the most elegant co-op apartment buildings on Fifth Avenue. Darkly modern, its twenty-two stories rose in tiers of tinted smoke-glass windows. In front, surrounded by islands of ferns and ivy, stood a wrought-iron sculpture of a fantastically shaped castle. A glittering overhead awning led into the lobby, bordered by stark gray pillars. Christian had waited for over an hour, having coffee in a restaurant on Madison Avenue. He had gone away, then returned. It was past two a.m. when he crossed the brown flecked carpet leading through the revolving door for the second time.

On duty inside were two doormen in formal blue uniforms with gold braid, one of them reading a newspaper, the other nervously pacing.

"Neville DeCormier," Christian said.

The doorman reading the newspaper rang up. After a moment of silence he turned, giving Christian a vacant, cold stare. "She still doesn't seem to be home."

Christian laughed to himself. He had taken her seriously, that was the joke. She had no intention of meeting him; he had misunderstood. As he walked slowly back out into the street he chuckled at how foolish it all was, the idea of seeing her later, or her meeting him. She was with Coburg—*the man she lived with.*

Yet she had given him the correct address. And no telephone number. That part was confusing.

He was about to cross Seventy-ninth Street and head down Fifth Avenue when he sensed something swish behind him, a presence moving out of the island of bushes to his left. Christian turned.

The man had wispy white hair and a snubby, purplish nose. He could have been in his eighties yet he had a vital, luminous face. A blue suit jacket, which must have been several sizes too large, with torn, ragged sleeves, hung loosely from his chest and shoulders. His soiled gray trousers were cinched up by a length of hemp rope knotted tightly against his stomach.

"Can you spare twenty-five cents?" the old man asked in a thick, hushed voice, almost as if he were embarrassed to utter the words.

Normally Christian might not have given him anything, but there was something about the old man's glistening blue eyes that was irresistible.

Christian dug into his pocket. "Here you are," he said, handing him a quarter.

"Thank you, sir . . . thank you . . ." the old man sputtered, as he moved back up the street with short, halting steps.

Christian turned away and started across the street. He had edged off the curb, following a green traffic signal, when he felt a rush of air, a sudden ear shattering thud, followed by a sagging rip as if a languid bag of water had splurted open.

Quickly Christian wheeled. What he saw was horrible.

An enormous stone building block, at least six feet in diameter, lay split open across the old man's face. His eyes had popped loose from their sockets. There was blood everywhere, streaming out of his ears and mouth onto his filthy white shirt. The thin, crunched legs sprawled loosely over the edge of the curb.

Christian backed away, looking up the side of the twenty-two stories toward the roof of the building. But he could see no one.

He hurried to the body, leaning over, hastily feeling for the battered wrist. There was no sign of a pulse.

The two doormen from Neville's building were rushing toward him. "I'll get the police!" one of them yelled, retreating, fleeing away, as the other one crowded over him.

At that instant Christian spied a limousine swerving into the driveway of the building. The door shoved open and under the overpowering shower of bright lights from the awning Neville leapt out. She went tearing inside as the black car shot around the driveway back out into the street.

Should he stay? Quickly Christian made up his mind. There was nothing he could do for the old man. Glancing away from the pathetic, lifeless fig-

ure, he rose and walked uncertainly toward the building entrance.

Neville's eyes burned as she stared at her face in
the mirror. The conversation with Dana had left her
weak from sobbing. She longed for a way out. Perhaps she should kill herself.

The impulse had suggested itself before. It was
always lurking somewhere back inside her brain—yet
she had no intention of ending her life. There had to
be another way of resolving her unhappiness, the
awful floating sense of fear.

As the door buzzer rang, the first thought that
entered her mind was that it was Dana. Despite her
entreaties he had come back for her. She felt her
body cringe, her nerves stab up through her skin as
she lifted the peephole and looked through it.

But it wasn't Dana. It was Christian!

"Wait—wait a minute!" she shouted, her thoughts
tumbling with joy. Hurrying into the bathroom she
slid off her clothing and threw on a violet silk robe.
It felt cool next to her perspiring skin. Quickly her
barefeet crossed the white fur floor rug. She opened
the door.

Immediately she noticed that Christian's eyes were
intense, scary looking. "What is it?" she murmured.

"Did you see what happened?"

"No . . ." She shook her head. "No . . . I didn't."

"An old man . . . I was just talking to him . . . a
huge block of cement fell off the roof . . . it hit him
. . ." He gestured, his hand shaking.

"That's horrible . . ." Reaching for his trembling
hand, she led him inside.

"I was just talking to him . . ." Christian repeated.

"I'm sorry . . . May I . . . may I fix you a drink?"

"No . . ." He shook his head. "Not right now
. . . I don't feel like it."

She watched him, longing for him, wanting him, as he slowly took it all in, the perfectly matched parquet floors, the paintings on the walls, her plush modern furniture, the oriental Ming vases. Then he gradually headed for the huge window looking out over the park. "It's great for watching sunsets," she remarked nervously.

He nodded.

"Sometimes I sit here having a glass of wine—"

"You live alone?" he asked finally, focusing the words as if her answer was very important to him.

"Yes."

"For how long?"

"Six months. It was a gift from Dana." She let that sink in a second, then added, "Won't you sit down." She gestured toward the lime green sofa curling around a coffee table piled high with magazines.

"Okay," he said, finding a spot beside a pile of pillows.

She grabbed a large stuffed cushion and sank at his feet. "Are you all right?"

"Yeah . . ." he nodded.

"Did you enjoy the show tonight?"

"It was okay . . . fun . . ."

"There were a few agents there . . . but it was mostly friends . . . you're sure you wouldn't like a drink?"

"All right," he sighed. "I'll have a scotch—no ice."

She rose quickly, effortlessly bending up from her knees, and walked toward a silver cart filled with bottles of gin, whisky, imported liqueurs. Fumbling for a glass, she filled it with a small amount of thick brown liquid. She sauntered back, handing it to him.

Sitting down again on the cushion, she watched him sip from the glass. There were deep tired lines beneath his dark eyes. His face kept changing, the long creases of his cheeks drew in as a look of restless dissatisfaction cramped his sensual mouth. He attracted her intensely. Yet he was different from any man she had ever been close to. His abrupt, almost primitive manner frightened her. Yet she wanted him.

"You look exhausted," she said.

"Yes . . . I guess so." He put down the drink, after taking a long sip. "It's been an awful day."

She reached forward and touched his knee, her fingers creased the edge of it, not exactly communicating affection, more curiosity, interest. His legs were taut, strong, stirring. It excited her to sense his muscles tighten. "Yet you came tonight. I appreciated it. Do you want another drink?" She started to leap up.

"No—" He grabbed her hand, yanking her down. "No . . . I've had enough."

She looked into his face for a lingering moment, wanting him to kiss her, but he hesitated. "Did you make love to him?"

His demanding interest startled her. "Why—why is it important?" she asked, breathless with fervor and excitement.

"Because I waited so long . . . I thought you weren't coming home."

She shook her head, slowly assembling her thoughts, her feelings. "He wanted me to," she said finally.

"Why didn't you?" His dark eyes burrowed through her. She wanted him to hold her—*desperately*.

Rising, she took his head in her hands, clasping him by the ears, staring deeply into his eyes. "I wanted to wait for you," she said. She felt his hand reach inside her silk robe, the tough skin of his fingers surge toward her vulnerable breasts.

Suddenly she held him. Her body quivered as she took him in, her arms reaching down, kissing him hard—her tongue spinning between his lips into his mouth—*this is what she wanted*—bringing her knee up, she reached down gently, grasping for the zipper of his pants—

At that instant the buzzer roared across her mind. She felt him stiffen, as the tension left him, the anticipation, the joy of wanting her. The buzzer sounded again. "I'll go," he muttered, leaping to his feet as if expecting an intruder . . . the police . . . someone about to ask him questions concerning the dead man on the street.

"Who is it!" he angrily yelled.

But there was no sound.

In annoyance he yanked open the door and stared down the shadowy golden papered hallway, softly illuminated by hidden banks of indirect lighting. The door of the apartment at the end was closed. There was a strange silence as if a presence, someone else was there. He felt the hairs move on the back of his neck as a stench overpowered him, putrid, obnoxious. His eyes watered.

Choking for breath, at the same instant trying not to breathe, he slammed the door.

"What was it?" Neville asked.

"I don't know," he shook his head, his mind racing. "There was . . . no one . . . nothing but a terrible smell . . . awful . . . like a dead animal."

She beckoned to him. Uneasily, he returned to the lime green sofa, looking drained.

"Are you sure you're all right?" she asked.

She watched him intently as he finally relaxed. "Now I am." With a shrug he desperately reached for her, the tension, the yearning suddenly overwhelming him as he whirled her over on the spacious couch.

Hungrily she clutched the zipper of his pants— forcing it down—touching inside—happily feeling the hardness, the strength of his body.

Gently, invitingly, she helped him slide off his

tight trousers, until she felt his bare, cold skin.

She wrapped her tongue inside his mouth as she felt him driving at her. She reached with her fingers to caress his thighs, feeling the hair rise along his back.

She trembled, laughing, giggling to herself with pleasure. She wanted so to take him inside her. "Darling, I love you," she whispered.

He kissed her gently, then warmly, her neck, her throat, caressing the nipples of her breasts with his tongue until she felt them grow so hard that they began to ache.

"I need you so . . ." she whispered.

He buried his face in her arms. "I had to ask you if you made love to him . . . I had to know . . ." he muttered, as if begging her forgiveness.

"I know . . ." she responded. " . . . I know. But it wasn't important. It was never important . . ."

His warm tongue touched her, began flicking away at parts of her body that she could barely remember existed, as his hand reached deeply along her thigh, reassuring the chill of her body with his fingers, his mouth, his tongue—as she held on, edging off the cliff into mad excitement. He was filled with such tenderness, such warmth, that she wanted to give him everything. More than she had given to anyone. Her fingers raced through his thick hair—wanting him not to stop—finally easing his mouth up to her lips, kissing him desperately, lying back, waiting, wanting to absorb all of his moody strength.

And then—sleekly—he was inside of her. She shuddered with rapture, grasping, clutching at him—it was too much! Better than she had ever known. Better—better than anyone.

"Oh God, I love you." She spun into him, sweeping across his body in soft waves, as she felt all of her strength collapse, then rise up, trembling with wonder, cool and warm at once.

Then he said it—what she had been waiting for—"I want you . . . you're so beautiful . . . I love you . . . I want . . . you . . . so much . . . so much . . ." He began to move inside her, resolving her feelings of pain, sorrow, frustration, fear, transferring her passion into pure movement, to allow her to run through his fingers, his arms—to permit her to experience everything—and she let go—she almost died—she felt so wild—as if she were on another planet, another world—somewhere out of that empty apartment —as she held him whimpering, shivering, struggling with joy to experience everything about him—his dark eyes were beautiful, his arms were beautiful, the long curving hair on his legs was beautiful, his neck and hands were beautiful—she wailed, absolutely overcome—perfectly, as he bound her so close to him at that moment, that she stared up. She was right. She had sensed it, she had known about him all the time. *He was wonderful.* Then she closed her eyes—experiencing the most exquisite pleasure possible.

14

She handed him a goblet half-filled with a murky, coppery liquid so unexpected, so foreign to his memory that it caused him to blink his eyes several times, forcing back the clouds of deep sleep until he was certain that it was—orange juice. Greedily he reached forward, sipping it in without questioning in his mind whether or not it had been poisoned, or worse, imbued with a fatal love potion which would cause him to slather like a dog, following her around on all fours, clinging at the wisps of her clothing, wanting to seduce her day, night, hourly, by the minute. But no spell was cast over him. He yawned and closed his eyes again, stretching back into a sumptuousness of pillows.

He wondered about people who fell in love, who followed after one woman, who could not stand to lose sight of her. He remembered Eskimo stories of husbands giving their wives to other men as a symbol of generosity. In America, a man believed that a woman was his, until death, his alone. To give her to make love to someone else would be unthinkable. It made him laugh as he considered it.

He opened his eyes feeling Neville beside him. Her face in the morning was absolutely beautiful. The makeup was gone, what little makeup she wore. Her long blond hair had split in half, a portion of it draping over each breast. Clad only in a pale-green silk kimono with the enormous figure of a dragon embroidered on the back, her bare feet sauntered across the hardwood floor. He reached toward her with one hand.

"Yes?" she said.

"I think you'd better get in here."

"Oh, you do?" she smiled, her eyes becoming huge. "I was there all night and all you did was sleep."

"I'm awake now."

"Is that a challenge?"

"No. A plea."

"But I'm not sleepy . . ."

"Neither am I . . ." He stretched out for her.

Quickly, she bounced in under the sheets and he took her in his arms, feeling warm against her body, excited by the thrill of her tingling wet skin.

"Did you take a shower?" he asked.

"Of course. And I cooked breakfast—bacon and eggs."

"No herring and cheese and strawberries?"

"That's what they eat where you come from."

"It's not bad. Much more satisfying."

"Then I read for a while . . ."

"What time is it?"

"It's about ten."

He propped himself up, frantically stunned by the thought. "You mean I've been sleeping while the rest of the world has gone to work?"

"Christian?"

"Yes," he muttered as he settled back, edging her toward the pillow on which his elbow was resting.

"Christian?"

"Yes."

"You're a beautiful man."

"That sounds strange."

"Didn't anyone ever tell you that?"

"Never."

"You're beautiful," she repeated, wiggling in close, kissing the outer edge of his lip, his eyes, as he closed them just in time, until he could not stand it any longer, as he pulled her down, feeling his way into her body, his mouth and tongue on her lingering nipples, reaching down, parting her knees, her thighs—but she stopped him. There was a look of genuine fear in her face.

"Are you still worried about Bill?" he said, slowly easing, letting her go.

She shivered. "I think about it all the time. I can't help it."

He took her worried face in his hands, not wanting her to be unhappy. As he traced the line of her face with his lips she nuzzled close to him. "You think I'm going to let him hurt anyone of yours?" he murmured.

"You don't know Dana—you don't know him! The phone rang at least a dozen times through the night—but I couldn't—I couldn't answer it—'' she blurted out fearfully.

"You don't have to take his calls anymore . . . I'm here. I won't let anything happen. Come on, sweetheart . . . come on, darling . . .'' His heart reached out for her, infinitely, bearing all his joy. For the first time he felt all-powerful, protective. "*I love you* . . . don't be afraid . . .''

Her expression changed. Smiling radiantly she gradually relaxed as he effortlessly lifted her up in his arms, cradling her to his chest, kissing the curving slope of her soft neck, finally, faintly, his lips brushing against the wisps of blond hair hidden behind her ear, as he smiled to himself.

As they walked through the revolving door into a haze of thick, smokelike sun, Christian, in squinting his eyes to avoid the impasse of awakening rays, noticed a heavyset, thick-shouldered, muscular man in a navy blazer and gray slacks standing beside the wrought-iron sculpture of the castle at the end of the driveway. The man seemed to be waiting for someone. He did not move, and even though there was nothing about him which suggested a premeditated, artificial pose, he seemed thoroughly out of place. It made no significant impression, however, until he and Neville had crossed Fifth Avenue and headed into Central Park. They had gone a hundred yards when Christian glanced back. The man was following behind them.

But although the man's presence had aroused Christian on a subconscious level, he was much more involved in Neville, their bodies occasionally touching, her hand reaching for his, holding on. Yet he could not help glancing back at the man, still following—his expressionless face, the heavy unsmiling eyes, the way he crept distractedly along. Could someone have hired him to follow them? Coburg?

Christian chuckled to himself at the thought of being monitered through the streets of New York City by vans with tape recorders and electronic "ears." But he said nothing to Neville. He was enjoying being with her in the openness where no one passing had a notion if the two of them were lovers or married or simply friends. Their only connection was invisible— what he felt about her—how much he desired her—the wonderful, free feeling that this seductive, voluptuous, blond lady wanted him. At times it seemed overwhelming, as was any involvement so new, uncertain, exciting, yet other thoughts filled him with a strange unexpected hunger so deeply mysterious that he was afraid to explore it. Perhaps it was loneliness— the solitary remoteness that he had lived with all his life.

The path leading beside the lake wound past gaudy, colorful carts vending fat salted pretzels and steaming trays of brown chestnuts—then twisted onward under the branches of eucalyptus trees where small sweat-shirted boys scrambled kicking a soccer ball. At the end of the path, opposite the park on the other side of the thoroughfare, erupted an ancient rockpile of unbelievably baroque buildings encrusted with fanatical leering gargoyles. Christian and Neville crossed the busy street and stopped at the foot of the towering steps. Above them, astride an iron horse, furiously flaring its nostrils, sat an enormous carved bulk of a man with several live pigeons fluttering and roosting on each of his dominant shoulders. The base of the statue was inscribed:

Theodore Roosevelt
1858–1919

On the curving walls surrounding the statue were chiseled epithets: *Rancher—Scholar—Explorer—Scientist—Conservationist—Naturalist.*

Christian pointed to a red banner stretched across the main entrance behind Theodore Roosevelt's head, heralding in massive block letters—*The Heritage of Greenland*. Something prompted him. "I want to go in," he said.

"Why?" she asked, at the same time eager to join him.

"I want to see it."

Tripping up the steps they passed through a set of steel doors into the cathedral lobby, deserted except for an information center bordered by rows of pamphlets and counters displaying replicas of ancient relics and artifacts. The woman behind the counter had yellowed oriental features.

"Which way is the Greenland exhibit?" Christian asked.

The woman pointed a wrinkled hand toward one end of the gaping cavern, then gestured with her finger down. "You go through the hall of mammals," she advised in a clinging raspy voice.

Christian glanced over his shoulder as they headed toward where the woman had directed. The man was gone—wholly imaginary—no one was following them. All of it was anxiousness caused, he was certain, by the events of the past twenty-four hours . . . Miranda Reichert, his experience in the operating room. Yet he felt uneasy as he led Neville across the lobby.

Through more steel doors they descended a flight of stairs which led into a series of gigantic chambers dimly lighted by overbearing open-mouthed pillars. There were vivid murals on the walls depicting lost civilizations of antiquity—Egyptians, Greeks, Babylonians. The spacious black floors echoed his footsteps as they entered the hall of mammals. He turned a corner. A sixteen-hundred-pound grizzly bear lunged from a luminous glass display. They hurried past a myriad of buffalo shapes, mountain lions, crouching cougars, huge horned sheep until they came face to face with two Greenlanders grasping large circular drums, beating them with thin sticks. A painted plaque explained that the two men were settling a quarrel by singing songs of derision, taking turns, one singing, accompanying himself on the drum, while the other feigned indifference. From overhead speakers, Eskimo voices chanted.

> *Ke! Ke! Keq! Shugunra* . . .
> *Ke! Ke! Keq!*

Neville was joyous, laughing delightedly at the spectacle, brushing back her tawny hair, speechless. Finally she asked, "Do they fight?"

"No. They dance, they sing—they act out what they feel, what angers them about each other."

"You mean—Eskimos *never* fight?"

"They are the most peaceful people on earth—nothing is considered more repulsive than aggression or violence. They have never even fought a war."

Behind the exhibit were displays of stone kettles suspended over blubber cooking lamps, scoops for removing ice from holes cut for fishing and large skin nets. Christian stopped before a curved white bone instrument which he pointed to. It was a snowknife, used for building snowhouses. "That's used by the northern people."

She hugged him a second, silently. "What kind of a hut did you live in?"

Christian pointed to a plaster of Paris model beneath a round domelike top made of rock, with harpoons stuck along the ice walls. Near it was hung a pair of wooden goggles and a salmon spear with jagged bone teeth. The memories came back. "I used to love to fish . . . late at night on the fjord with the sun burning up from the water. My mother would cook the fish while I sat overcome with hunger—staring at the fire."

"What happened to your parents?"

"They both died," he replied, unwilling to go on. *It had begun to bother him . . . it deeply bothered him . . . the place was like a crypt. The walls were too heavy, too filled with memories.* The Eskimo chanting throbbed from hidden speakers—*Ke! Ke! Inguvork! Ke! Ke!*

Along the opposite side of the dark glowing cavern were hundreds of ceremonial masks, feathered, with red eyes and jagged smiles, round with grotesque, sharply pointed features.

"They're horrifying!" Neville murmured.

"Yes, I always thought so."

"What do they mean?"

"The Eskimo hunters believe that they must appease the souls of the animals so they can hunt them. I always thought that the animals could not be that ignorant. But it was magic . . ."

"Magic?" Neville's eyes fluttered.

"To live as an Eskimo is to inhabit a world controlled by spirits. My grandfather could talk with them. He was a shaman—"

"A what?"

"He was known as *angagkog*. You would probably call him a witch doctor. I remember a ceremony when I was a little boy. The sweet female singing—the deafening flapping and rattling and swishing noises—then everything became silent. In came the terrible monster *a jumaq*. It had black arms and whomever it touched would turn black and die. It went through the village with heavy steps roaring *Amo! Amo!* Everyone fled for fear that the monster would touch them. I felt my grandfather clasp my hand as I stood there, rooted, not moving. At last when the commotion subsided—my grandfather smiled down at me—his eyes were wonderful—I felt more confidence than I had ever known before or since. He said, 'Lanuk, you see how the spirits protect us.' "

"Lanuk?" Neville peered at him, consumed with interest.

"That was my name once," Christian said, his face transfixed by thoughts dimly remembered and those forgotten. "I never knew what it meant," he added.

Nearby there were more sculptures, boats and caribou fashioned of ivory, sandstone and wood—and a young woman, wearing a puffed-out yellow Indian dress, arranging necklaces and clusters of shells in a display case. She had high cheekbones and the front of her long hair was cut in severe black bangs. She turned slightly and Christian glimpsed her piercing blue eyes. As their eyes met she instantly drew back.

Christian edged Neville toward the display case. "Look at this." He pointed to the ribbons of beaded jewelry.

"The colors are wonderful," Neville replied.

Christian glanced up quickly at the young woman watching him. She seemed haggard looking, her eyes wild and darting, as if she had recently undergone some intense emotional crisis. There was an expression of stricken terror on her face. "You're the one that it wants," she suddenly blurted out.

Christian stared at her, taken aback. "What?"

"You're from the Netsilik tribe . . ."

"How—how can you tell?" he stammered.

"I knew." The young woman's bronze features trembled. At that moment Christian sensed a feeling between them, a dark, terrible feeling, as if they were the only two people in the room, as if she were about to tell him something more—something that no one else knew. Yet he did not recognize her; he was certain that he had never met her in his life. "I'm sorry," she suddenly apologized. With a quick movement the young woman slammed shut the top of the glass case and stalked out of the gallery.

"What did she mean?" Neville stared up at him.

Christian shook his head. "I don't know."

Neville clutched his arm playfully. "She seemed to know you."

"No." He shook his head uneasily, stunned by the experience.

Neville persisted, warmly trying to charm him. "Perhaps you met her at a party."

Reassuringly Christian put his arm around her, at last kissing her, feeling her give way into him.

At the end of the hall two gray doors were marked, *The Berserker Exhibit.*

"What's a *Berserker*?" Neville asked.

"I don't know," Christian said. Yet a memory came back to him—the sound of the word—*Berserker*. He *had* heard it before. But where?

Unevenly, the room seemed to sway in sections, filtering with light—as the objects on the walls, in the display cases, the faces, the eyes, the mouths, formed one great weaving mask, colorless, strange, phosphorescently consuming all place and time in an arid semblance of rituals lost, paganly decadent—as at that point, that imperceptible moment, there was a bluish, transitory alteration between life and death—a gap when all breathing stopped—when there was no longer the world which Christian and Neville knew as familiar. Then, unheralded by the faintest premonition, they walked through the two gray doors into *The Berserker Exhibit.* As Christian entered the small dark chamber something stirred within him. Ancient drawings in purples and dark browns and flowing blazing reds painted on huge animal skins sprawled against the curving walls. It was a chamber of death—hideous—the way the colors flowed. The human bodies strewn across the landscape of ice and snow had broken bleeding arms, their stomachs torn open, their eyes popping out in terror as if some abominable force had surprised them, plunging them into spiritual agony—more than a depiction of slaughter—but a repulsive rendering of carnage so vile, so ritualistic—though there was something else—*something beyond* which seized him, causing him to stiffen—*he had seen it before! Through the grass he glimpsed the bleeding bodies— the flapping skins—he raced into the hut—No! No!*

Neville held his hand, sensing his fright, "What is it?" she asked.

He did not want to see—he was shaking—the room led into a murky corner from which a shadowy figure loomed—a gigantic form on a pedestal wrapped in a bloody sheet. *The thing was alive!*

The figure watched, unmoving, its eyes scrutinizing him in triumph—seeing Christian's face—yet another face beyond—the brown wrinkled features of its dreaded foe—the face of the shaman. "*You've come at last*"—Christian heard its voice within him—the strange savage moan—"*I've waited.*" The eyes of the figure burned into him—"*What I've planned is working.*" Trembling, Christian gaped at the ominous face—as its voice tore through him. "*I will not stop. You are almost mine . . .*"

"We've got to get out!" Christian shouted in a frenzy.

"Why?" Neville's eyes opened wide, startled by the change in his voice.

"We've got to—"

"But why?"

He grabbed her hand, practically running, leading her, pulling her back through the halls of crouching, lunging beasts, past the pillars of burning light into the dark muralled chambers—the eyes of the figure following him up the stairs—its terrible voice—"You will die. I have you . . ."

He had to get out!

When they reached the street Christian hugged her to him, attempting to thrust back the image which had taken over his mind.

"What's the matter?" she asked in alarm.

"I don't want you to live alone," he blurted out. "Not anymore—"

"What do you mean?"

He could not begin to think, to reason, as the horror overtook him. He had seen it—it was too late—

The shuddering reality of several double trailer trucks roared past. "You can't. You've got to believe me!"

"I don't know what you mean!"

"I'll get you a dog . . . I can't be there every night . . . I have to be at the hospital . . ." he muttered, trembling, pure thoughts rushing out, aware that he was not making any sense, as spinning nausea overtook him, then a feeling of utter wordless dread so incomprehensible that he had no strength to control it.

Her face stared, wanting him to say more, "But—but I don't want a dog . . ."

A sharp autumn wind blew off the river, blistering the sterile red brick building as the scrambled tiers of smokestacks on its roof emitted a fine black ash billowing uptown toward Harlem. The constant barking of thousands of dogs could be heard a block away and as one drew closer certain dogs seemed to be whining in panic.

Through the doors beyond the cheery reception area with its red, yellow and green balloons, golden ribbons and idealized cat faces painted in a frieze on the concrete wall, was a ramp leading to a cell-like room.

On the wall beside the door to the room was taped a poster with the beaming face of a fox terrier puppy, its eyes melting with affection, and the words, *If you think they're dumb then you're just not thinking.* Alone within the room, Tom Zelinsky, tall, thin looking, in his late thirties, with curly wedges of black hair and amber spectacles, swung a steel cage containing a white Samoyed into the decompression chamber. The dog gaped at him with a startled, frightened look as Zelinsky slammed shut the door, isolating the animal inside the iron belly. The alert white ears perked up as Zelinsky flicked a lighted blue switch. He glanced away to avoid seeing the dog's black button eyes turning glassy as the air was sucked from its insides. A minute went by. Zelinsky flicked off the blue switch, yanked back the door, dragged the cage from the machine and opened it, flinging the Samoyed onto the pile of lifeless shapes in the center of the floor. Rapidly he replaced the Samoyed's cage with another, lifting it from a rack along the wall. It contained a scratching, whimpering sleek black Labrador. The Labrador yelped, frantically roving back and forth, looking for a way to escape as Zelinsky repeated the lethal process.

In seconds the Labrador's eyes tightly shut, its legs and paws trembled with energy, its twisted body lay cradled in a deformed heap at the bottom of the cage.

By skipping lunch, Zelinsky had put to death two hundred dogs since he arrived for work that morning. Unfortunately, the steel cages were cold, sending shivering chills up his spine each time he grabbed hold of the iron bars. If only he had listened to his wife and put on a wool cardigan before he left the house. He still had three hundred dogs to go.

He was driving himself too hard, but the volume of animals pouring into the shelter had become awesome. Mostly they were strays, but cruelty cases were on the rise. When the intercom flashed, Zelinsky picked up the phone. "Yes."

"Did you get to that silver husky yet?" It was Rick Peterson's voice calling from the front desk. Now he had to think . . . Zelinsky glanced over the crates of furry bodies—not that it was necessary. He was almost certain that the dog was still in adoption room twelve. "No. I didn't get to it."

"Can you come down for a moment, Tom?"

Zelinsky wiped the combination of sweat and animal saliva from his hands with a flowered yellow towel hanging from a tile rack near the sink and left the room. Striding down the ramp toward the lobby he saw a man and woman standing by the front desk. The man had black hair and blazing dark eyes. He wore a gray overcoat. The woman was blond and extremely curvaceous.

"Yes?"

"We'd like that silver husky," the black-haired man said.

"Fine—sure," Zelinsky smiled, reaching over the desk for a preadoption form. He handed it to him and watched as the man filled it in. Name—*Christian Bangsted*. Occupation—*Surgeon, Bellevue Hospital*. To the question, "Why do you want a pet?" the black ballpoint pen quickly furnished the words—*As a watchdog*. As the man finished writing, Zelinsky pointed toward the typed framed agreement at the bottom of the page:

> All shelter pets must be neutered so that they cannot reproduce. You must sign a legally binding contract agreeing to have this performed. Failure to have your pet spayed or neutered will result in the shelter reclaiming your pet. A shelter representative may at any time visit with you and your pet. If at any time the shelter representative feels that the animal is not receiving adequate care, the animal may be reclaimed.

"That's okay," the man agreed.

Within minutes Zelinsky was leading the couple through the grated gates into a long antiseptic hallway past a series of green doors, finally into adoption room twelve. His nostrils were assaulted by the stench of urine as he was greeted by the immediate barking and craving for affection of the eighteen dogs inhabiting the small room. Enclosed in a narrow three-foot cage, the silver husky leapt up eagerly, its eyes shining hopefully as the black-haired man crossed the wet floor, reaching forward to pet him. When their eyes met, Zelinsky sensed an unusual emotion pass between the man and the dog, almost as if they knew each other. A card attached to the cage read:

Name: "Nima"
Husky
Housebroken
Good with children
Adoption fee—tax deductible

Zelinsky opened the door of the cage releasing the dog as the man bent down, petting it. The dog was playful, leaping up into his arms as the man patted his neck and snout.

"This one's lucky," Zelinsky remarked. "He was scheduled for today."

"Scheduled?" the woman asked.

Zelinsky was having difficulty averting his eyes from her long, magnificent legs, exposed by a fetching split skirt. "To be put away. By law we only have to keep them alive for forty-eight hours."

"That's cruel."

Zelinsky frowned irritably. "Look lady, we get the end result of the irresponsibility out there. We have feelings. It's depressing. But what do you expect us to do?"

"There must be people who want dogs."

"We pick up a hundred thousand a year. At the most only a thousand or so—like this one—" he pointed to the husky—"ever get adopted."

"It's still—cruel," she repeated.

"Aren't we all victims of something?" Zelinsky smiled.

15

Christian spent a long time in the shower.

Even though it was past midnight, he let the hot electric beads drain down his arms, his legs, the back of his neck, the muscles pulling across his spine, until the images and sounds of the hospital became deadened somewhere back inside his brain. He relaxed. He opened his eyes and stared at the mirrored walls fogging up as a result of the shower's steam, and he was glad suddenly that he was home. Christian closed his eyes again, and threw back his head for a final burst of soothing warmth.

He would sleep well. He was becoming so relaxed, standing in the mellow spray, that he could experience his feelings trail off into soft tingles down his hands and fingers.

He would let the water warm him. Then he would sleep.

It was quieter at night. He had the feeling that he was the only person in the world still up.

Certainly the only one in his building taking a shower.

He screwed tight both handles, the hot water first, then quickly the cold. When the water stopped, he stood shivering a second, naked.

Grabbing for the purple sheet towel hanging on the door hook, he wrapped it around him.

He rubbed the towel against his body furiously until he felt the blood surging through him beneath the skin. Then he shook his head wildly and wiped his black silken hair dry.

He glanced at himself in the mirror. He no longer looked as if he were an Eskimo. His full, sensuous lips at times bore a hunted look that made him appear more unsure of himself than he was. But at this moment his dark eyes and thick curving black eyebrows gave him a defiant expression. Perhaps he was Italian, or Russian. Perhaps he had lived in Brooklyn or Queens all of his life. Perhaps his name was Joe Miller and he played softball on Saturday afternoons and drank beer with the guys or watched television with his girl friend.

Perhaps he did all of those things.

He turned off the light in the bathroom, pulling the towel around him one last time and then letting it drop to his ankles.

He pushed open the door and saw across the bedroom that Neville was asleep or perhaps dozing, with her head back, her eyes closed. The only light in the room was from the tiny pinspot above her dresser.

He switched it off.

Neville's breathing was so silent that for a moment Christian had to listen to imagine that she was still there. He stretched out next to her, his naked legs wrapping themselves in the rolling folds of white sheets which covered her perfect body.

Then he leaned down and felt her knees. Reaching beneath the sheets he discovered the pulsating warmth of her white skin, the soft blond hairs on the inside of her thighs. With a sudden burst of excitement he swooped down and kissed her belly. He felt her stir, her fingers reach out, curling around the back of his neck just beneath the hairline.

Should he awaken her? She was very tired, sleeping, dead to the world. If he awakened her she might be too groggy, half here, half somewhere else. It bothered him for a long moment, before he decided to.

He came up with his tongue under her heaving breasts, parting them with his face and nose, kissing her delicate violet nipples, one and then the other, then repeating it again, faster, each time with a quick lick of his tongue, until he felt her legs stir, her knees come up slowly . . .

He reached down and touched the pocket of warmth between her thighs—then her eyes opened.

They were azure. Even in the darkness he could see their color in his mind's eyes. He could see her blond hair, long and matted all over the pillow, floating against his cheeks. He breathed it in.

Her body was all perfume. Her tongue touched his lips, flicking across them hesitantly and he knew that even though she was still half-asleep, she was begging for him to come to her.

Yes, he would come.

"I love you, darling," she whispered.

With that he sank his lips and mouth against hers and suddenly his body went wild.

The sheets were gone and they were in each other's arms and she was clawing at his back, ripping at his hair as he forced the thickness of his cock into the warm recesses of her excitement rippling beneath him. The warm pocket between her legs yearned open, taking him in slowly, then with a lurch as he felt his penis throb forward. She gasped, thrilled.

Oh Neville, he sung to himself until his ears were ringing with pain and pleasure. His feet turned out into the widest corners of the bed. He began humping her like crazy. Her ankles, long and extended, caressed the cheeks of his ass, as she pulled him down deeper with her toes.

She began to breathe heavily. Her fingers tore at him, inflicting tiny wounds of pain all over his body, until he almost swung and hit her to stop her from ripping him with her fingernails, but instead he drove deeper into her, breathing wildly, his arms and body all over her, rolling her against the sheets, faster and faster, until it seemed almost as if she was about to die with excitement.

Oh Neville, he sung again as his tongue felt for the fullness of her lips, then leapt deep into her mouth. She responded with her whole body quivering and shivering and lurching toward him, as he stayed inside of her, plunging deeper until he was met by all of her warmth and joy and magnificence.

He came inside of her again and again.

Finally, he sank down, and was quiet all over.

He felt guilty for a moment afterward. He could not give her any more. He had given her everything but he knew that she felt cheated. She needed so much more than he did.

She needed more of him that moment and he was forced to go through the motions now of caressing and kissing her when he felt so little left.

Finally he turned over and lay on his back.

She clung to him like a child. He took her into his arms. Tenderly he breathed into her ear. He kissed the back of her neck, the edge of her mouth, then her lips.

Deep inside of him he had begun to love her, to count on her. He was no longer merely fascinated by her wonderful looks, the long golden hair, the soft white skin of her body. Perhaps it was not love; he had never been in love. But it was perfect there, just the two of them in each other's arms.

He saw through the dim darkness the shape of the dog.

Nima was standing near the bed panting, waiting to be taken out.

Christian slowly removed his arms from under Neville's head and pulled himself up. He did not feel like walking Nima to the park at that hour of the night. But at the same time he knew the dog expected it.

Christian glanced at his watch. It was one-fifteen.

Rising up out of the sheets, he replaced them again over Neville's silent body, over her legs and back up to her neck. Then he draped the comforter across her feet.

Quietly he slipped into his blue Adidas and pulled on his jeans. He reached for the gray workshirt that he remembered having draped over a chair by the bed. Because of his late night walks with Nima he was growing accustomed to dressing in the dark.

He crossed the room and turned the latch on the door.

Pulling back the bar which held the lock, he slid it into position, easing the door open. Nima slipped out first. Christian followed, lugging the door shut behind him.

He did not put Nima on a leash. Instead he would carry the long leather strap in his hand just in case a policeman should challenge him. But at that hour of the morning he doubted that anyone would challenge him.

Descending in the elevator, he strode through the lobby past the two doormen. Nima began to whimper anxiously. The dog nuzzled its snout against his leg. Its gray eyes stared up into his.

"Okay, Nima . . . okay." Christian gave him a pat on the flanks and then trotted after him into the driveway.

Fifth Avenue was a musty glow of overhead streetlamps. Christian noticed that there were two or three cabs heading toward him in the distance. But there was no reason to wait for the red light to change.

Crossing against the light, he entered the darkness of the park. He passed a pile of broken park benches, green litter cans, a children's playground with orange and yellow slides, and signs posted—*No Dogs Allowed*.

The dog ran ahead smelling the grass, the shrubs, disappearing and reappearing in and out behind bushes which squatted along the fence and walls. Nima finally vanished between the shapes of several dark rock formations beyond.

The park seemed totally unpeopled and yet Christian knew that in another area, only a short distance away, there were people waiting to make liaisons in the blackness. The city at night, a voiceless hum, as quiet as the city ever got, it penetrated him as he kept his eye on Nima's flashing fur.

Several of the streetlamps were burned out along the walkway. He headed up the incline into the broad grassy area near the Shakespeare Theater.

At that point the husky tore across the baseball fields, leaping into the air, its silver fur glistening in the moonlight.

Christian laughed. Suddenly he felt as if he were a child. He was no longer in New York but back in Greenland, as the dog, *his* dog, its iridescent fur flying past him, growled playfully.

The dog raced away from him, then around him in wide circles, ever narrowing, just missing his legs, then away again with a quick dart.

Christian shouted, "Nima! Nima!"

Then Christian took after him, waving his arms and hands. Nima pranced frantically, leaping up and down as Christian caught snatches of his ears and head, giving him a playful slap, then ignoring him as the dog vied for his attention, cutting in front of him, jumping up with both his paws to brush his arms.

In the distance, the lights of the midtown buildings glowed. It was an awesome sight and Christian never failed to be impressed by the contrast of the city, poised as if it were a wall of glass and light surrounding everything.

Yet as he rounded the path past the baseball diamonds and the fenced-in basketball courts he felt alone in the darkness.

It seemed impossible in a city that size to be alone, yet it was a feeling that often overcame him late at night, a sense of isolation, of having no roots at all.

He had come from another world. In most ways he had changed and yet part of him stayed back there among the wind and the ice, the floes of white in the distance, the seals swimming in the bright sunlight while the rest of the world was pitch dark.

He welcomed being alone. Nima sensed it also, walking beside him now, stopping when he stopped, moving forward slightly, as if pacing his steps.

Christian petted the dog across the ears.

It was at that instant, near the bridge leading to the jogging path, that Nima began to snarl.

The dog's ears cocked; its body pitted suddenly forward as if a knife had been stuck into its chest. Nima had fixated on a clump of dark bushes.

The bushes moved. They swayed at first, then shook with a frenetic zigzag.

For a moment Christian felt a chill of terror in his throat. Was there someone waiting for him in the darkness?

The dog shot forward.

"Nima!" Christian shouted. He reached out, quickly grabbing the chain collar.

Nima tried to yank free; he pulled, almost breaking loose, growling angrily. But with each lunge Christian yanked him back.

Christian sensed something. He could not be certain what it was, but the bushes continued to sway as if a wave of wind crossed over them.

There was a scent so foul he almost vomited. *It was the same stench that had filled Neville's hallway.* Then he saw it. In the bushes, the gray outline of something enormous.

Within twenty feet of where he stood, it watched him from the blackness. Then as Christian held on to the dog's collar, the strange scent formed into a cloudy mist.

Suddenly it stood up on its hind legs—four massive red eyes burned down. Then it leapt at him.

Christian screamed, his hand to his face, defending himself.

As he fell back, he let go of the chain collar. He felt the dog tear from his fingers. "Nima!" he almost shouted.

But the thing—the thing was on top of him.

He was overwhelmed by its sickening hot breath—the slime of its skin—

Christian buried his face in his arms.

He heard a sudden howl, like a human scream, a scream of pain. Then a burst of terrible ripping.

There was another howl, a sharp shrill baleful moan. It was the dog.

Christian's eyes were filled with blood. They jiggled with frenzy. He shuddered, unable to see, as the horror choked up into his chest.

16

As he became aware of the gray light piercing through the window he felt Neville stir. She tossed, then gripped the pillow, uttering a plaintive, soft crying sound, as she reached across the emptiness of the pale yellow sheet, wanting desperately to cling to him.

But he was not there. Not by choice, but because his rippling nerve endings would no longer allow

him to lie waiting for her arms to locate him under
the rumpled down comforter. He sat rigidly alone on
the end of the bed, his legs stiff, his body immobile,
staring into the endless opening darkness flashing as
if it were an infernal camera's iris, his brain winging
ahead, but racing chaotically nowhere, his narrowed
eyes half-asleep, half-awake, attempting to experience whatever was left of his mind, his intense
cavernous grief.

Yet he could no longer feel pain or dread or
agony, only numbness.

There was a recurrent throbbing—he had listened
to it through the night, acknowledging that it was the
raw hum of the city in his ears. The cabs, horns
honking, millions of voices, sighs, sobs, restless,
echoing out of a gigantic volcano of emotion, trapped
into one voice, wordless, high-pitched, hysterical.
There was no silence left, in all the world. There
was only the immutable shriek of panic.

Yet through it all he listened to his breathing
which ushered forth in heavy deep gasps. Only his
breathing made the throbbing meaningful. It distinguished him from a table, a lamp, a chair.

He was afraid, wrought with terror, overwhelmed
by a trembling weakening sensation. The fear mounted.
He was no longer able to function, to finish
thoughts left hanging in his mind. His hands shook,
at times uncontrollably. He could feel himself hurtling.

He wrapped the chain leash tightly around his
wrist, then gently unwrapped it, repeating the action
without feeling the coldness of the metal or the way
it creased his skin. The chain leash symbolized everything. Yet it meant nothing.

He could barely think, remember, and that, at
least, was a relief to his tired senses. He did not
want to remember. He wanted to sit and feel and not
know where he was.

Neville stirred again. He felt so remote from her, so cut off from any recognition of an existence apart from his own, that he was actually threatened by her bodily presence.

He had seen death. Helpless, uncompromising slaughter—the mutilated bodies of women, men, children wheeled into an operating room. But none of it had seemed so empty, so sad, as the finality which had overcome the animal he had adopted, the dog scheduled for extermination—whose end had been put off a few hours only to be accomplished in the most brutal manner possible.

Nima. A nice name for a dog. Somebody's dog. Perhaps a little boy who had always dreamed of having a silver-haired husky with deep-set blue eyes to run with, to feel laughter welling up, rolling down a hill of soft white snow. He was sorry that the dog had died, that the dog's insides were strewn across the trees and bushes. He was sorry that he could no longer feel the dog next to him. He was sorry that he could not express true sorrow. The tears that sank and flowed so deep inside him made him feel rigid and cold.

There was something he had not faced, did not want to think about, had avoided locating in his mind's eye. Yet it haunted his dreams.

What would he tell her?

"Christian?" It was Neville's soft voice awakening.

Should he turn so that she could see his face? So that she could ask him—

"What's the matter?" she whispered.

He shook his head. He avoided looking at her. He did not want her to see his eyes. Instead he got up and walked to the window. Beneath him lay a white wet garden with bare forked tree limbs jutting up, mashed against rows of hollow-eyed windows rising beside a red brick wall. He would have liked to have stood there forever, not to have had to face her, to have to explore the worst part of what he now knew existed. In the distance a church bell rang. It reminded him of the village at Umanak the mornings before he had to leave for school. He recalled running along the hard-packed dirt streets bordered by embankments of rock piled against the raised doorsteps of small, oddly shaped wooden houses—a stern-faced Danish schoolmaster viewing him through harsh wire-rimmed spectacles—"Christian, what have you prepared? A poem? A speech?"

"Where's Nima?" Neville asked.

The sound of those two words made him spin, as if ready to engage at last in a battle with death. *He would confront it.* He *would* tell her.

"What is it?" There was fear in her eyes, suddenly reaching out. Shreds of blond hair had fallen back over her ears. She looked so irresistible that he leapt over, grabbing her, hiding her beneath him, clutching her hands as he felt the awful terror rush through him.

He did not speak for several moments. He could not speak. Suddenly she seemed more to him than a lover, a woman that he wanted to possess. Those feelings belonged to another person, not him anymore. He felt so empty—

"I—I—took him for a walk . . ." He shuddered as her hands reached up to hold him, to bring him down to her neck, her breasts. "There was something—something in the bushes . . ." Pain flooded his eyes as he reached for an image. "I don't know what it was. It leapt out . . ."

She was startled, afraid, yearning for more, desiring to know everything. "What—what happened to Nima?" she asked.

With a hardness, an intense interest, she held him. Something prompted him to yank it all out of his mind—push it away—*forget it* before it was too late.

In a few more minutes he would leave her, he would return to work at the hospital. Then tonight, very late, he would come back wanting more than anything to rediscover the tenderness, the beauty of her body; he would lose himself once more in her dazzling flesh. *Block everything else out. Why not?* He smoothed a lock of her golden hair from her cheek, away from her mouth. He wanted to kiss her passionately, to make love to her with all his strength, to hold her, caress her. Yet he continued to stare into those vaporous green eyes, afraid to speak.

He felt naked in Gene Woodruff's tight, compact, white office—unready to discuss the internal administrative conflicts confronting the department. Christian's head still reeled, his insides churned from exhaustion and nausea; even a cold shower had not managed to revive him. Yet Gene insisted they talk *that morning*. He had set the meeting for ten a.m.

When Christian arrived Bill was already pensively waiting. He glanced up at him inquisitively.

Christian's impression of Gene had changed considerably since he had first sat, less than a year before, listening to him heatedly relate Bellevue Hospital's practices and procedures, adding his own acerbic opinions about all of it. Gene was in his late forties, well dressed, almost dapper. Yet the observation one would draw from looking at the deep lines in his mature, aging face, the anxious-to-pin-everything-down glare of his red puffy eyes, was that he drank too much.

There was no doubt that he was deeply troubled. He explained that his position as head of the Micro Surgery Department had been severely threatened, yet he wished to avoid going into detail. Christian toyed with the idea that Milton Reichert, in a moment of rage, might have written a damning letter to the Board of Trustees . . .

"There's too much focus—too much attention—"

"What do you mean, Gene, I don't understand," Bill interrupted.

"It's everywhere—in the newspapers—on TV. The press has gotten the idea that we're the only people at this hospital practicing surgery. And I get the feeling that some of us have begun to believe the same thing." Gene coughed. Beneath the faded, thinning hair, imbedded beyond the prematurely dissipated features, his harsh eyes looked Christian over, anticipating a response, a disclaimer, an angry defense. But Christian could not summon the energy to argue. He kept seeing the face of the dog—the dark hovering force lunging at him from the bushes . . . He choked inside, trembling all over as he sat, listening to voices—unable to make sense of the words . . .

Bill scowled. "What do you want us to do, Gene?"

"Let the air out of the bag a little—that's all."

"How? Should we change our names? Do you want us to walk around the halls in disguise?"

"The interview you gave the other day—" Gene peered at Christian—"was picked up in a news article headlined, 'Bellevue Surgeon Says Miranda Will Not Walk.' "

"I didn't say that,'' Christian snapped bitterly.

"What did you say?"

"I stated that Miranda had imagined that she was experiencing a sensation in her foot—when it was only a phantom sensation."

"Why did you say anything?"

"I shouldn't have," Christian agreed solemnly.

"Don't you see where that kind of a remark puts me?"

"He didn't say that Miranda wouldn't walk—he told the truth. Didn't you just hear what he said?" Bill countered testily.

"But he must have implied it."

"Are you fucking kidding!" Bill shouted. "I mean—what is this?"

"Look—I'm not against you guys!"

"Well you sure as hell sound like it! Someone rattles your cage a little with a phony newspaper headline, so it's everyone for himself—"

"Look, Bill, goddamn it!" The veins in Gene's neck were expanding. "The point is—that we're in big trouble."

"You're in trouble," Bill snorted, "we're not."

"Goddamn you, I'm gonna punch you in the fuckin' mouth. We're the darlings of the media. They can twist anything we say—there's no fucking way we can clear ourselves."

"Why should we *have* to clear ourselves?" Bill snarled.

"Because *we have jobs here*. It's a sensitive situation—and it's becoming a pain in the ass!"

Bill shifted uncomfortably. "I feel like I'm back in school getting chewed out for smoking in the can."

Gene angrily jostled himself up from behind the desk, rose a few inches readjusting the cushion under him, then sat back down. "A man was brought into emergency last night—from a car crash."

"I know . . . I know . . ." Bill nodded impatiently.

"The right leg had been amputated—"

"I know all about it—" Bill butted in.

Gene hastened to finish. "But there were also multiple rib fractures. Yet he was rushed to micro surgery. Everyone forgot about the patient. Why wasn't he first treated internally? He died from loss of blood in the chest cavity because all that was on everyone's mind was sewing his fucking leg back on!"

"That's not the first time that kind of thing's happened," Bill covered.

"Oh really? So you advise that we should just forget about it?"

"What are you trying to say, Gene? That we should hide what we do? Feel ashamed?"

"You know, Bill, you're a goddamned egomaniac!"

"Oh yeah? Because I won't knuckle under—quiver and shake—like you?"

"Look—look—" Christian cut in. "What are we talking about?"

"He's trying to blame *us*," Bill stabbed back obstinately.

"I'm not."

"Then what is it you're saying?"

"I want no more interviews. Say nothing. You got that? All we need is a headline, 'Surgeons Let Patients Die.' "

"Then we're out of business," Bill chortled sarcastically.

"C'mon, guys," Gene pleaded, tensely unhappy.

"All right—okay—" Bill quickly sobered. "As long as we're all on the same side. Whatever side that is."

"Do you agree, Christian?" Gene focused on him.

"Whatever you say."

Christian got up quickly without a further word and headed into the white snaking hallway. Before he had taken several steps through the current of residents and nurses circulating in both directions, Bill caught up with him. "Gene's scared."

Christian nodded silently. The morning sunlight filtered through the plate glass windows above as he headed toward the street.

"I have never seen him so shook up."

"He works too hard."

"Like a coffee?" Bill offered.

"No, not now. I don't feel like it."

They passed through the automatic doors which parted leading into the outside courtyard. A brisk wind fluttered up through their white linen jackets. Christian stopped on the porch, taking in a deep breath of the air flowing from First Avenue, mingled with carbon monoxide fumes chugging from the herds of automobiles roaring past.

"I haven't seen you around much," Bill finally remarked. "You been shacking up with some chick?"

"Kind of." Christian winced.

"Someone I know?"

"Yeah. You know her."

"Which nurse is it?"

"She's not a nurse."

"Dr. Ferguson—in the biology lab?"

Christian shook his head.

"And I know her . . ." Bill's thoughts were racing, attempting to picture the face of every female resident on staff. "Eunice Robbins in X-ray?" The idea obviously astounded him, but he blurted it out anyway.

Christian hesitated, then looked him straight in the eye. "I've been seeing your sister."

Bill tensed up. He stared, absolutely amazed. "What do you mean? You mean—Neville?"

"How many sisters do you have?"

"But—but what about Coburg?"

"What about him?"

"Jesus Christ!" Bill exclaimed, delighted.

"What could she see in me—that's what you're thinking, right?"

"I mean—" Bill could hardly say it—"you and Neville—are in love?"

"I'm sure you and I can still be friends." Christian grinned.

Bill suddenly roared with laughter as he pounded Christian reassuringly on the shoulder. "That's great! That's wonderful!" he enthused.

"Our only worry is you."

"What do you mean?"

"Coburg. How hard are you going to push him? Are you going to force him to hire some thug to smash your brains in?"

"Look—" Bill's eyes threatened. "After what that son of a bitch did to Neville—"

"What did he do? He used his influence to help her career. Set her up in an apartment. Bought her beautiful clothes."

"As long as she agreed to do anything he wanted— *anytime he wanted to fuck her*—"

Christian felt anger rise inside him, yet he tried to shrug it off. "You must think a lot of your sister," he jabbed back.

"She's a kid, for Chrissake."

"No." Christian shook his head. "She's a woman. A little frightened . . . that's all."

"You don't know her that well."

"I love her."

Bill scrutinized him carefully. Finally he muttered, "Does she feel the same about you?"

"I think so."

"And you think Coburg's going to sit back and let it all happen?"

"He has no choice."

"Look—uh—we're not in Greenland—part of some primitive culture where you pick a woman and fight for her in hand-to-hand combat—winner take all."

Bill's face was distressed, his short-cut hair disheveled by the wind. Christian smiled as he gazed at him. "We'll be okay, Bill. Don't worry. Let Neville and me handle it."

Around dinnertime Christian had phoned from the residents' quarters wanting more than anything to hear Neville's clear throaty voice, eager to picture those soft green eyes, full lips—her warm seductive body, her breasts trembling near the receiver—he wanted to embrace them, to hold her, filling her with love, intensely. It bothered him that she was not home, but he chided himself, laughing self-consciously. He let the phone ring at least a dozen times. He was becoming suspicious, demanding. He phoned back twenty minutes later. It was an unusually warm evening. She could have strolled down Madison Avenue—gone shopping for groceries. He wanted passionately to hear her voice. Perhaps she was lost in a nearby bookstore, perusing a row of best-sellers— or at the little German bakery with the piping hot tarts in the window, the one with the steps leading down.

When he phoned again at eleven there was still no answer. As his head sank into the pillows, the close corners of the tiny room forced in toward his eyes. He would feel happier in a few more hours. He would hold her against him.

He closed his eyes . . . feeling the cold . . . the emptiness . . .

He clung to her image . . . *Neville* . . . *Neville* . . .

What had he found in her? Physical beauty, a sophisticated woman older than her years, someone who could be tender, magnificently responsive, someone who wanted him? What could he give her? All the warmth he felt, the fathomless joy that she kindled, that she could reach and quietly touch within him.

Could there be more than that between a man and woman? More than a oneness that defied the perils, the fears of becoming someone else . . .

Yet he wanted more. He wanted to be with her, to share more than her bed. He wanted to walk with her on a long beach and kiss her eyes in the moonlight. For the first time in his life someone was that important; she was everything he ever wanted. As he relaxed against the sheets she was with him . . . he could feel her next to him . . . curling up within his arm . . .

Neville . . . he could see her face . . .

Almost immediately there was impenetrable darkness. With a switchlike flick, a shutter snapping, he lay somewhere inside his head—falling deeply, heavily, blotting out the sadness, the dog's face . . . the figure . . . *the figure leaping at him.* He shuddered . . . searching for her lips . . . fiercely wanting . . . everything . . . about her . . .

There were broken flowers—he absorbed their violent pink colors—the parched grass beaten down all around. Above the heraldic sky screamed white light, forming the face of a yellow god—a death mask of stark virility, crowned with a blazing iron helmet from which jagged white hair tumbled. Christian swayed at the edge of the void, the chasm—the mists took in his lungs, his arms—his breath holding back inside him. Then the thundering began. A world of stillness shuddered with a roar similar to that of the earth splitting apart. Warmed by the sun's heat, the crystalline glacier began to calve. Mighty crags tore loose from the ice cap, toppling and crashing into the sea. Flocks of sea-eagles, snowy owls, falcons and grouse soared to their nests at the edge of the tundra. There were fields of white snow and seals dying—their mushroomed eyes bulging near where hulking caribou grazed, resolving into a chilling panoply creased by dark, shadowy, wolflike shapes. He stared fearfully over the yellow falls of ice, wrenched by yet another roar from the mountainous glacier overhanging the dark shore.

Then he saw the ship.

It was made of ice, translucent, its long body chiseled into a swerving prow. Without oars it floated through the mists, gliding openly past the rocky shores which parted from where the fjord was frozen at the edges.

It was a perfect ship, obviously fashioned by human hands, yet it seemed deserted, unearthly.

On the barren land was a half circle of primitive huts, clustered, ominous, made of stone and bearskins with trails of smoking ash creeping through slit roofs. Christian had never been there—he was certain—not even in another dream. It was not an Eskimo village—it seemed so remote—yet he remembered the familiar violet sky of southern Greenland, the tremulous burgeoning ice, the blistering single shafts of sharp blinding wind.

It was freezing cold, yet he felt nothing, so insulated was he, as if he were a spectre, a shadow ebbing at the base of the glacier, fitfully spying the approaching smooth carved ship sliding toward the shore. The icy vessel reminded him of a drawing he had found among ancient portraits in a book long before . . .

There were huge blond men crouched beside the huts, heavily bearded, their cheeks burnished by the sun, their eyes a blue glaze. They wore dark furry helmets, wild-looking men with thick woolen hair, their shoulders and forearms massive. Lying at their feet were circular war shields, curved axes, worn, jagged swords . . .

Their voices threatened to drown out the wind as they laughed, snorting and poking at each other.

The pale ship drew nearer. It rested, as if it were on the crest of foundering. Several of the helmeted men glanced at it inquisitively, strangely removed, willing to accept it as a harmless omen, yet ill at ease, for a moment doubting what they seemed to sense.

At that second the sea was alive with flaying hordes armed with wooden spears and stone knives—hearty brown-faced men with slit eyes, yellow skin, hoarsely shrieking, plunging from the sides of the ship. The band of helmeted warriors outside the huts leapt to their feet, taken by surprise. In another instant blue flames poured up inside the stone huts.

There were screams, tortured howls of trapped men attempting to get out, being baked alive by the merciless fires. The helmeted warriors were in panic, their eyes rolling, thrashing about for their thick axes, their circular shields. Shouts of wonder, of fury, filled their lungs, as the brown-faced figures from the ship savagely attacked.

Cries of rage pitched forth across the ice as the whole world rocked. Axes and clubs hurtled, each sinking with unnerving force. Bodies spun, flew. Hatred came together in that hour, resorting to desperate, desolate whimpers—hands clutching hands—legs sliding—grasping—wailing chokes—the awful evidence of agony.

There was blood washed against the snow, mutilated torsos and screaming eyes torn out of heads reeling, cut off, rolling toward the water—dozens of them, hundreds. The slaughter raged, as Christian gaped at the graceful figures of the fur-covered, slit-eyed men consuming the blond helmeted faces. It was abominable to visualize what followed—

The splitting in half of bodies, curled wooden spears diabolically gouging through walls of flesh, screams of pain—turmoil—shimmering terror—

The brown-faced invaders ran amuck, their knives ripping, shearing the heads from the blond men—until there remained one man—an enormous giant, frightening-looking—beating back the valleys of slit-eyed attackers—with each lunge of his stone axe crumpling scores of bodies to their knees—blood shot in rivers from necks, from pathetic twisted faces.

The huge giant towered above them, his face an ugly wound of vengeance. *And then something unthinkable happened!* His body convulsed as if in a fit—his enormous frame tightened, trembling, suddenly overcome by a black shroud of coarse fur and talons and spearing blood-soaked nails. *Christian watched, panic-stricken, as the figure was transformed* into a howling inferno of violence. The human face dissolved—a low groan ushered from his jaws.

The slit-eyed men sank back—afraid to believe, to move—gasping in terror—

It was hideous! Horrible! Never on the face of the earth had anyone witnessed anything like it!

The figure of the man was gone. In its place loomed a grotesque four-eyed animal—unlike any animal ever created. It roared derisively, sloping away past the brown-faced men, held back—afraid to follow. The creature plunged into the freezing waters of the fjord—swam toward the opposite shore—finally emerging victorious—shaking water from its heaving black fur.

There was more darkness. More death. *Christian was haunted by the presence of the leering beast.* Through the crawling, half-butchered bodies he attempted to look away—

A flash of heat tore at his face. A burst of light exploded up through his flesh until he was alone in a room. A dark familiar room. He saw blond hair—the face of a woman. As he recognized her, a terrible dread overtook him.

The soft pink flowered sheets parted. She stared into his eyes—fearfully screaming, twisting, as she rolled off the edge of the bed.

Christian backed away, sensing another presence— he wheeled—the thick smell was nauseating. He moved to his left as the shadowy form plunged past him onto the defenseless woman's body—

The beast and woman rolled together on the floor—she howled, her arms reaching up to beat it back—screaming, until her eyes were gone—Christian could do nothing—

The shimmering force was sickening. It tore apart her legs, deeply sliding into her, its ugly black hair rising in slicks from its body. She pounded at it, wailing, gouging at its fur, as it forced her apart, pulling back her ankles, snapping off her foot—

Blood squished everywhere, splattered across her bed. Christian felt it shower against him—her kidneys—her heart—her lungs torn out, flying—

"Neville!" he shouted, helplessly. Unable to move, he watched the growling figure churn at her flesh, tearing at her beautiful breasts—then it ripped off her head!

Christian choked awake—streaks of saliva on his pillow covered his mouth. His face burned as if it had been singed by flames. He staggered, one foot on the floor, rising in pain, his body shaking—afraid of the vision—*terrified.* As he vomited, his room in the residents' quarters shot in against his eyes. He yelled, screaming for help.

He had to get out of there—to save—*Neville.* Oh God! Neville!

He raced, falling forward toward the door, his shoes off, grabbing them as he crawled into the hallway, pulling them on, not bothering with the laces. But his legs wouldn't move—he fell—he forced himself up—

He had to hurry—to run—

Tearing down the four flights of concrete stairs—no elevator—*he didn't have time—*

Pushing open the metal doors—into the TV room—out through the glass doors down the corridor—into the courtyard. He fled toward the street.

"Taxi!" he screamed, horror pouring from his eyes. "Taxi!" And then it was there—yellow—with a blazing "on duty" light—

He leapt inside. "Nine-eighty Fifth Avenue!"

The cab broke forward up the east side. The street was dark, pitch dark. There were cylinders of smoke-stacks hugging the river—empty gas stations, park-ing garages—lights of stores and buildings—*he had* to find her—please—it wasn't too late! *It couldn't be!*

The cab stopped for a red light. "You've got to get there—fast!" he screamed at the bearded man slumped over the wheel.

The driver whined, his crinkled expression staring back, "But I can't—"

"It's a matter of life and death!"

"Look—I'll get a ticket."

"Goddamn it, please—*please*—I'll pay you—" Christian shrieked.

The cab shot across the intersection against the light. The driver, head down, floored the accelerator, missing several screeching autos as two pedestrians leapt out of the way.

Christian choked up inside, grabbing for the back of the seat. "Don't kill anybody!" he yelled.

"You wanta get there or not, goddamn it!" The driver bit down in rage as if something inside him had been unleashed—had suddenly *gone wild.*

The cab bore through the blackness, at each intersection challenging vehicles about to lurch forward cutting them off. It sped past the whipping flags of the United Nations—bars and restaurants packed with people—bookstores and all-night coffee shops. The driver stripped through red light after red light, the speed of the cab increasing as he jockeyed the wheel back and forth crazily.

The night became a jolting black blur, a ribbon of uncertain shapes—marquees, fluorescent signs run together—headlights stirring, reaching out at them, then veering, halting, as if aware that the street belonged to the bearded man in the front seat who was no longer afraid—of anything.

He seemed to sense that no one would cut him off, and that made the experience more frightening—that no laws applied, there were no qualms of conscience—

Rifling across the intersection of Fifty-seventh Street—flying through overcoated crowds trailing from movie theaters—under the dark bridge shoving toward Queens—past chic clothing stores, ice cream parlors—past *Friday's, Maxwell's Plum,* Sloan Kettering Clinic—the wide street showering them on all sides with darting trucks—a man on a bicycle just ahead—*in front of them,* stopping—

The cab's brakes slammed on—locked—Christian was pounded back into the seat—the cab spun halfway around—then the gas roared, the pedal jammed down heavily underfoot as they crunched forward—maneuvering—fighting again for the empty corners—hitting them the moment the signals turned red.

Block after block riddled the windshield. Across Seventy-second Street, past delicatessens and hardware stores—the bleak night absorbing them deeper—as Christian felt the gripping tension in his face—*he had to get there!*

Down Seventy-ninth—wheeling, slicing around the corner—five—six blocks to Fifth Avenue—

But what if he had imagined it! He hoped he had! He wanted to believe he had!

The street was jammed, tied up with cars—but the driver, with one hand stridently blaring his horn, stroked forward—finally shooting in and out past a bus across Park Avenue—moving faster than before—as the modern corner building flashed into view. He skidded up the driveway, slamming down the brakes with all his strength.

Christian shoved a twenty dollar bill at him—leaping out through the doorway of the building—past the glass shields—past the doorman—

"I've got to get up there—DeCormier—" His mind was maddened. The elevator doors opened, he rushed in, the doorman following.

"What is it—what is it!" The doorman floundered.

"Is she up there?" Christian demanded, knowing the answer—*trying to picture her*—*waiting*—*wanting him*—

"She came in about twenty minutes ago. Why? What happened?" Frenzy had taken over the door-man's eyes, the same fear Christian held back.

"She's alone?"

"Yes."

The doors opened on *eight*. Christian tore down the hallway—grabbed the doorknob to the apartment —but it was locked. He had to force it—slamming against the door with his shoulder—"You've got to get me a key," he pleaded helplessly.

The doorman's face was ashen. "Okay—okay—" he slurred quickly, racing back toward the elevator, slipping inside just as the doors began to close.

Christian waited, wanting more than anything to see her perfect lips—her eyes . . . but the vision savagely riveted him—the dream. He rushed at the door, hurtled against it with all his might. Kicked it, pounding wildly with his fists and shoulders— ferociously, desperately trying to tear loose the lock—but it was too solid. There were other people— disturbed—staring out through half opening doors. "What are you doing? What are you up to?" a man shouted at him from the end of the hallway.

Christian crashed into the door. It gave—it almost flew open—

The doorman appeared—racing—out of breath— sliding the key in—

Christian leapt into the living room—

And then he saw the walls! An awful gush of sorrow filled his heart. The walls—*the ugly blood-stained walls*—the paws, the tracks so revolting, vile—clawmarks! *His dream roared back!*

He fell into the bedroom—retching—

The flowered pink sheets were foaming with blood—but the room was bare, empty. No Neville—no one. Except for a grotesque thing lurking, covered by one edge of the top sheet. He tore it back, revealing a putrid chunk of black fur floating in mucuslike slime.

"Bill—"

The sleepy voice crept over the receiver. "Yeah . . ."

"It's Christian—" He cradled the mouthpiece up closely to his lips. "I was just at Neville's apartment—she's gone."

"What do you mean?"

"There's blood—all over the walls—the bed—"

Christian felt the sudden deadness, the unbelievably cold silence on the other end of the line. It lasted seconds before Bill let out a roar—*"That son of a bitch!"*

"What do you mean?" Christian responded in alarm.

"I'll get him!" Bill shrieked.

The line went dead as Christian huddled in the narrow phone booth.

17

Leland Dawkins was fifty-eight years old. Having retired from the New York Police Department with a sergeant's pension twelve years before, he looked forward to retiring again. This time he planned to relocate. Finally he would move with his brother to Fort Lauderdale, away from the grueling winters of Manhattan. Together they had purchased a small condominium four blocks from the beach.

As he perched forward on the green stool, all alone

in the massive lobby, he glanced through his thick black-rimmed glasses at the sign-in sheet illuminated by a single fluorescent tube on the desk in front of him. Only two people had gone upstairs since midnight and one of them had left within twenty minutes. The other person was still up there. His signature was a scribble, almost unreadable, yet it unmistakably belonged to Dana Michael Coburg.

Dawkins yawned, carefully pivoting the rim of his cap to the front peak of his salt and pepper gray hair, straightening his red tie, adjusting his brown uniform jacket, the buttons of his starched white shirt. From force of habit his fingers felt to make certain that the brass numbers *3812* were still tightly fastened to his left lapel. Once one of the numerals had broken off in his locker and he had been criticized for not noticing it. It was the little things which confused one's existence. Not having taken enough time to shave before appearing on the job, a wrinkled shirt, a mustard stain which could not be completely washed away in the men's lavatory—everyone noticed, or seemed to. Their eyes flickered down, centering on that one area, conveying uneasiness, suspicion.

Across the black marble floors giant pillars showered banks of light against the dark murky murals peopled with huge symbolic figures depicting the progress of man. In front of him the row of red and black telephones sat silently, while all around, the empty shops strung along the edges of the arcade, the newspaper stand, the separate entrances to three banks awaited the morning crowds.

He thumbed through the Rolodex, reviewing the names of the various firms, their personnel. He knew most of them by sight, but there were constantly new faces. Perhaps he was too involved to notice the revolving doors in front of him sway open. When he looked up a tall young man hovered over him.

"Yes, sir?"

"Coburg International."

"Who are you seeing?"

"Mr. Coburg."

"I'll call up."

Dawkins grabbed for one of the red phones. He was already dialing when he looked into the dark barrel of a revolver.

The young man ordered him up.

Dawkins rose as the weapon waved for him to move from behind the desk as rapidly as possible.

Within seconds they entered an elevator. Inside the wood-paneled chamber Dawkins caught a side glimpse of the man's features. The lips and cheeks were as cold as steel, his eyes stared menacingly.

When he entered the lobby Christian was trembling —still overcome by the tension, the gnawing dullness of loss.

He had left Neville's bedroom exactly as he had found it, except for the object, more a presence than an object. The police would be unable to relate it to anything living.

There was no guard at the front desk. It bothered him as he headed for the huge wall directory. Next to the listing for Coburg International was the floor number. He moved toward the somber bank of elevators. Under his arm he carried the hideous shape, wrapped in a pink flowered pillowcase splattered with blood.

The elevator doors drifted open and he got on. The doors snapped shut after a silent moment. Rising, as the elevator swept skyward, he remembered Bill's voice on the phone. There had been more than a note of stunned horror. He felt, he grimly guessed the thought which had entered Bill's mind. It was two a.m. Could Coburg still be up there?

He called Bill back five minutes after their con-

versation and there was no answer. Would Bill have
run out to find Coburg?

He hated him. Frenzy seizing Bill's mind might
have caused him to suspect anything.

The door opened onto the sixty-seventh floor. From
the glass-walled office at the end of the dark submerged hallway, dim lights burned. Christian raced
forward, catching the sound of a voice raised in
anger.

*"You fucking son of a bitch—you're going to die!
This time . . ."*

It was Bill.

Christian tore through the waiting room toward
the back office. Through the open wood-paneled
door he glimpsed the security guard hunched against
the side wall. Bill was jamming a revolver into
Coburg's face.

"Wait!" Christian roared.

Bill lurched back, whirled, pointing the gun at
him. "What is it?" he shuddered, poised to fire.

"It wasn't Coburg—I saw it."

Bill stared at him, stunned.

"I saw it happen—" Christian hurled the blood-
stained parcel onto Coburg's desk. "Part of it's in
there—"

The eyes of the two men drew back.

"What do you mean?" Bill muttered.

"Open it."

Bill resolutely clenched the revolver, not to be put
off from the course of action he had chosen. His
eyes reeled as he focused on the caked, ugly brown
bloodstains—his hand reached for the pillowcase. At
that second a shot shattered the atmosphere—two
more shots—followed by a savage volley.

Bill went down, holding his throat, blood scurrying from his neck and head. As Coburg laughed.

Christian spun, seeing the two uniformed figures
with rifles crouched at the door. They were ready to

fire again. But Bill's body quivered against the red oriental rug, his face distorted in spasms of agony. Christian bent over—the bullets had entered Bill's forehead and the soft area beneath his left ear, shearing open his spine. "We've got to get him out of here!" he shouted, demanding angrily.

"Let him die," Coburg smiled. "Don't touch him." He brusquely motioned Christian back.

Christian turned, staring at the murderous faces of the security guards, blank, unnatural faces—aiming their rifles *at him.* "*I'll kill you—*" He leapt, hurling himself at Coburg as the room went black.

There was vicious movement—men running toward him—then a low intense growl.

There were screams—blistering gunshots ringing through glass—guards shouting—a vile ripping sound—more shots through sounds of roaring, chewing—*he heard raging torment as the guards ran for the hallway*—startled—beside themselves, fleeing, shouting to one another, yelling for help—then he glimpsed something on the floor, something moving—*enormous and black*—as a quick sudden fire broke through his brain.

The light of dawn was beautiful—encrusted with rays of red and purple melting into streams of ravishing, flowing colors. From the sixty-seventh floor it appeared as if running rivers of paint had been poured against the open sky. The window he faced was gone. In its place a blank air mass loomed. Cold whipping wind swirled in on him, forcing him to roll over onto his right shoulder. A sharp jolt bolted through it. His neck burned horribly, his eyes blurred, part of his ear was submerged in a wet, cementlike stickiness. His first thought was that he had been shot. He remembered the pain—the black deadness. It so agonized him as his eyes scrutinized the forms scattered across the office that he began to shiver. It was then that he sensed his shirt was wringing with blood.

There was blood everywhere—globs of it—the entire office had been gutted, demolished beyond any rational description. Coburg's body lay nearby, a sight so ghastly that Christian had to look away. All that remained of the security guards were jagged clots of lacerated flesh—chunks of brain tissue—a foot—the piece of a jaw—layers of colorless intestines in putrid patterns wound through chair legs—more carnage than he could have imagined in a hundred gruesome nightmares.

Bill lay cold, lifeless, on the floor beside the desk, his eyes frozen, pitifully staring. *Poor Bill.* He could still hear Bill's voice, his remark that morning, which seemed days, weeks ago, his head thrown back in a cocky laughing jeer—"You and Neville—*that's great! That's wonderful!*"

Loneliness overtook him. He had lost the two people who had become closer to him than anyone. *He loved her so*—he finally admitted it. He had wanted her—that was all.

How far had he really come from Greenland—from the massacre of his village that grim frozen morning?

As Christian got to his knees, he felt all life ebb from his body—he could barely stand.

He grabbed for the desk, dizzily swaying, glimpsing the bloodstained pillowcase in the spot he had left it, torn open, revealing its morbid contents, the awful thing he had found on Neville's bed.

Navarana sat rigidly forward, staring at the television set in front of her. On the screen the newscaster's grave eyes resembled chips of veinless granite as he intoned, "And now to Tom Starling at the midtown offices of Dana Michael Coburg . . . Tom?"

The camera cut to the interior of a building. It

dollied down a hallway jammed tight with reporters and police. The deep nasal voice of a reporter was picked up suddenly by an off-camera microphone—"Grim . . . sadistic . . . torn limbs scattered across the carpeted floor . . . a bloody torso . . . bits of flesh . . ."

The scenes of Coburg's office clung to her insides as Navarana's blue eyes became riveted. Having just gotten out of bed, clad only in pale blue panties, she sat shivering as she listened to the reporter's voice droning across her living room—"What was once the office of Dana Michael Coburg appears to have been ravaged by some superhuman force . . . furniture broken . . . windows shattered . . . doors ripped out of the walls . . . a bloodbath of fatal destruction . . ."

Navarana could not take her eyes off the television screen. As she watched, her high cheekbones and short-cut black bangs froze her slender face into an expression of increasing apprehension. She was frightened, incredibly frightened by the images of merciless carnage flashing in front of her. They reminded her of another scene, a darkened cave caked with human flesh . . .

The bodies of two small children.

She began to sob, quietly, bitterly.

Again the voice of the newscaster broke in—"Dana Michael Coburg had inherited one of the world's largest personal fortunes . . . the details of his brutal murder, and the murder of four others in his offices this morning, remain a mystery. To add to the mystery is the disappearance of one of Coburg's female friends, model Neville DeCormier . . ."

A photograph of a woman's face—sweeping blond hair, soft, perfect features—flashed across the screen. Navarana gasped—she had seen that face before.

"Police a few hours earlier found the wall of Miss DeCormier's luxurious Fifth Avenue apartment

smeared with blood . . . and what appeared to be the
tracks of a huge animal . . .''

Navarana's bronze features became deathly still.
She sank forward to the edge of the sofa breathing
painfully, as if something were stuck in her chest.
Her blue eyes watered with terror. She reached forward flicking the dial to improve the focus as the
camera closed in on a massive dark impression.

*"One of the other victims found in Coburg's office
was a micro surgeon at Bellevue Hospital—Dr. William DeCormier—who was identified as the brother
of model Neville DeCormier. Meredith Knowles of
the Channel Four newsteam attempted to interview a
close friend—Dr. Christian Bangsted—the same doctor who was interviewed on this program a few
weeks ago following the tragic accident involving
nineteen-year-old ballerina Miranda Reichert . . .''*

The television screen filled with reporters as a
man in a white coat, with black hair and heavy
eyebrows, emerged through two doors. He appeared
surprised, shaken.

Immediately Navarana recognized who it was.

"Dr. Bangsted—'' The reporter shoved the microphone toward his face. He attempted to avoid it, to
back away.

*"Can you tell us your feelings about the tragic
death of Dr. DeCormier?''*

As the cameras followed him, the doctor pulled
away, his face set in a hollow, tortured expression.

The cameras continued to trail him through the
hallways as the reporter's voice carried over—
*"Obviously too overwrought, Dr. Bangsted is unable
to give us a comment about the murders . . . we now
switch you back to the Channel Four newsroom.''*

Navarana shuddered with anguish. She knew what
was coming.

There was no way to stop it. No way in the world.

PART THREE
November

18

Christian always had trouble talking to the thin, bony-faced guard at the front desk of the morgue. Haitian, with a strident, staccato speech pattern and incredibly black eyes desperate to be understood, he invariably turned away after he spoke, with a glance of arrogant dismissal as if it were not important what anyone else had to offer, even though it was absolutely essential that what he was getting at was grasped completely. And that was usually difficult. His attempts at English were spit out in phrases, quick, abrupt, jumping from subject to subject, cautioning, often guarded, sometimes bewilderingly antagonistic.

His name was Henry and he was in his early twenties, Christian guessed. He worked days, Monday through Friday. That he had gotten a job as a supervisor at the front desk dealing directly with the public was astonishing. No one could ever determine exactly what he was saying, and after a while it had become quite a joke around the hospital. But he had been hired by the city and it was obviously a position without much of a future. He seemed offhand, careless about everything except his principal duties. His major concern seemed to be to fill in the five-by-seven-inch slips of paper fastened in a sheaf to a clipboard on the admitting office wall.

Each hour during the eight hours he was on duty he checked the temperature in the cooling chambers, noting his findings next to the date and time. It was essential that the refrigeration level remain between thirty-five and forty-two degrees Fahrenheit; otherwise, as he once chaotically explained, "The corpse . . . begin . . . to swell." It was apparent that Henry did not mean "swell," but Christian made no attempt to correct him. Their relationship tended to be abnormally delicate as it was, and he was careful not to cause him embarrassment. He needed Henry's help.

Eventually all the unclaimed bodies in Manhattan found their way through the rear entrance into the basement of Bellevue Hospital. The City Morgue was the most prolific source of supply to medical schools and dissection classes throughout the state. "Corpses . . . constant disappear," Henry had recently complained. "Security . . . more tight." In return for Henry's constant cooperation, Christian felt it necessary to supply him every few days with a fresh carton of cigarettes.

It could have been a humorous situation if what was involved had not been so harrowing. From Missing Persons, Christian had learned that several unidentified females had been delivered the night before. With sinking deep eyes and momentous self-importance, Henry shoved the *Funeral Directors Receipt Book* at him. "More last night . . . come in than usual . . ." he confided. There were five entries, each with a serial number, approximate date of death, time received, approximate age, color and religion. The last five columns were blank. Under each heading specifying the name of deceased, in black ink, were the handwritten notations *XF*.

Christian jotted down the serial numbers on a slip of paper. Beside the receipt book were additional bound volumes—*Autopsy Reports* and a thick black book labeled *Babies 1977 on*. It contained entries for all the unclaimed dead babies brought in during the past two years.

"You want to see . . . you check the numbers yourself?" Henry gestured erratically.

"I'll find them," Christian assured him. For over a week he had kept a constant vigil, searching for Neville. But her body had not turned up. It was a pointless ritual, almost as if by finding it he would be able to guarantee to himself that she was gone forever. Continuing to look for her unsuccessfully kept his hopes alive. If he were industrious he might have sought out the morgues in Queens, Brooklyn and the Bronx as well. But the thought of such an undertaking seemed even more disturbing than what he was doing. It filled his days to look for her, to search for her still, lifeless form in the cold concrete rooms beneath the hospital, waiting for her to appear, but constantly dreading the possibility.

Henry watched him closely as he moved past him. "You be back . . ."

"In a few minutes," Christian agreed. He wondered what would happen if he did not come back. Would Henry draw his revolver and begin stalking him through the corridors?

The stark walls, the stuccoed ceilings were the same color—grayish white. As Christian entered the zigzag of connected rooms he noticed that the black hoses used for washing clots of blood and scum from the stone floor were draped over chrome nozzles along the wall. There were two banks of silver steel doors, twenty or so in a row, four deep, looking as if they were meat freezers in a large Manhattan restaurant. Each door was approximately two feet high by three feet wide, numbered in black.

He pulled open the one marked *twenty-eight*. The stiff, naked, waxlike, female body within the narrow shaft was wrapped in a white plastic shroud which crinkled as he touched it. He pulled it back. The plastic liner stuck to his fingers until finally he had to tear it loose. The woman's bloated stomach was green, a murky, froggy green. Her face had hardened, her jaw stiff and jagged with atrophy, her eyes cold slits. She was at least in her forties, Christian guessed. He felt relieved that he did not recognize her.

He rewrapped the body with the white plastic covering and shoved the pallet back into the chamber, slamming shut the steel door.

The next number was thirty-four . . . red-haired, luminous yellow skin. There was a savage knife wound circling one of her breasts. Her matted black hair was coiled in tiny curls around her neck and the long line of her mouth was slung open. Her stomach had been sewed up the middle.

He headed for fifty-three . . . thin, scrawny, emaciated, hair partially fallen out, her eyelids a sickening brown . . .

After a quick glance he shoved the pallet back in.

As he opened each of the doors on the list, he rolled back the long pallets, experiencing a feeling of tense expectancy. He knew that he would eventually find her, he was certain of it. But what would he do? How would he react?

He tried to remember her face.

When he got to seventy-three the chamber was empty.

Had it held Neville's body? Has she been taken to autopsy? The thought rushed at him. He pounded shut the steel door, hastening down the cold passageway past a pile of tiny, simply nailed wooden boxes. Immediately he recognized what they were—coffins for babies. He entered a brightly lighted room filled with students performing autopsies.

The corpse nearest to him had dark hairy skin with blood trickling out a wound in her side. Checking the other bodies lying on the row of tables, he saw that the one on the end was that of a female—*with blond hair, her face turned away.*

He raced for it, skirting a string of mops and glass cases filled with chemicals, noticing the two young men sloping a long pipe with a brown rubber hose, bending it back and stroking it down deeply through a gash into her naked stomach.

Christian confronted her face. There was a horrible rip at her throat revealing the bones of the neck and shoulders and the torn vessels leading into her chest. It was not Neville, but the woman was young, her lifeless body trembling eerily as the embalming fluid poured into it.

"Still not her, huh?" One of the young men peered at him, smiling.

Christian shook his head.

"I'll keep a lookout—she's blond—young—"

Christian nodded.

"We don't get too many like that. She'll be easy to spot."

Christian remembered that the student's name was Jeffrey. He had light, threadlike brown hair. He was from Farmingdale University. "I'll give you my number," Christian offered.

"Naw . . . I'll only lose it." He gestured, holding up his rubber glove-covered hands. "I'll get to you through the switchboard."

Christian left the embalming room. The deodorant used in the morgue was so effective that there was *no smell of any kind*. He suspected that it somehow deadened the olfactory nerves. Perhaps Henry had been correct all along. Perhaps he had really meant to use the word "swell."

Christian headed down the hallway, passing through the admitting office, past Henry, out toward the bank of elevators. There was one waiting, the doors open. He entered, his horrible morning chore completed.

He was glad it was over. He needed to get away from the hospital, to walk in the sunlight, down a street, with men and women jostling about him. He had seen too much death, he had begun to accept it as the most stirring part of his conscious life. It had cornered him with an unrelenting fascination. Yet when he walked out of the elevator into the huge waiting room in the lobby he could not help but gape at the faces, the forms, the shapes of the people he saw. For them it was only a matter of time . . . each of their days were numbered. The steel numbered doors waited.

He was becoming morbid. Yet what really distinguished them from the stiff arched bodies below? A twitch of the facial muscles, a shifting of the eyes, a control over their bodily movements—and of course their dreams, their sorrows, the momentum which each of them had concocted to fill their lives.

He felt someone watching him. It was an unsettling sensation that he had been aware of for days . . .

He glanced across the sea of faces, then focused on one face—a young woman with tanned skin and long black hair cut against her forehead in bangs. He recognized her from somewhere. Quickly he headed across the lobby, but she was already out the exit—running—

He chased her into the street, finally halting as he saw her escaping uptown in a cab.

For several moments he stood rigidly before the pale sandstone and brown brick facade thinking about Neville. It was as if she simply had moved, gone away, without leaving an address where she could be located. Yet the image of her face caused his mind to wander aimlessly, then jump ahead crazily. He was unable to relax, to sleep except in snatches, to think clearly for an extended period of time. He was troubled, beside himself; the emotions in his mind jumbled up until his head ached. It was as if part of him had died, unable to come back to life since that morning he had awakened on the carpeted floor of Coburg's office.

He missed her. He missed the longing that he had once experienced, all the while knowing that she would come to him. It was as if she were golden, perfect, more beautiful than anyone he had ever known.

She had seemed all-knowing—she knew all about him, how to please him, to make him happy. In the short time they had been together wrapped in each other's arms, the passionate moments, the long, tender, searching exchanges of feelings, of understanding, of him wanting her and her wanting him desperately—wanting to hold everything else out—wanting only to belong to each other—it was more than his memory could recapture, could grasp. All dreams of other women were gone.

He remembered her green eyes. The evening they had met at the Top of the Sixes. Her lithe, sensuous figure—the full wonder of her warm clinging thighs—her soft lips that took him in—the feeling of her hair, long and loose in his fingers—the night he heard her sing—the way her voice had curled up through him—she was breathless, aware, she would not let him go.

He had not experienced such feelings before—with anyone. She came into him as if she were a wave of magnificent pleasure—poised—wondering all about him. There was nothing he could not tell her, he let go, wanting, reaching for her in the darkness—the cool sheets spreading as he reached down toward her subtle heaving nipples—kissing—caressing them . . .

I love you, he had said. Feeling at the same time that the words were not enough. He could have been saying them to someone else. *But he meant them.*

The two of them were not opposites—each of them were the same person, after the same feeling, the same trembling joy. It was almost too much! He said it again and again and again, wanting it to mean more, wanting her desperately to understand that he would never mean it the same way to anyone else.

You're wonderful . . . you're everything I want, she said. Yes, he believed her. At that second they had forged a pact of complete confidence in each other. It would not happen again. Ever.

He gazed up. Twenty-five stories of large rectangular picture windows gaped out over Central Park. The modernness of Neville's apartment building made the building's huge shape seem hollow, empty of anyone in it who mattered—as if it were a shell, bringing forth the memory of those few hours they had been together, when he had truly loved someone for the first time. It angered him that so much of his life had been robbed, stolen away. Once more, he was alone. He had left a world that for him no longer existed, a plane of shadows and violet streaking shafts of sunlight. Friends, family, all gone. There was no one who mattered.

His life was hollow. The moments were becoming repeated patterns, bits of thoughts, vague surges of wished-for feelings. He felt so empty.

But he would no longer search for her in the morgue—he decided at that moment. Instead he would try to imagine she was with him, still alive, waiting for him. It made no sense. It was almost laughable—a painful expedient. He knew she was gone. He had lost her.

With his head down he moved sadly, experiencing little more than his numb bewilderment, through the swollen traffic of Fifth Avenue, the bustling lanes of buses and taxicabs, alongside the bent glass panes of the Metropolitan Museum of Art, finally into Central Park, down a garbage can lined pathway. He passed by a fence-rimmed playground where children gaily danced on a teeter-totter as a herd of blue-gray pigeons rushed toward a crust of bread on the sparse lawn. Above, a needle-shaped monument towered through the treetops, its slab sides pockmarked with ancient hieroglyphics, practically obliterated by centuries of wind and rain.

It was so long ago and yet he could still remember his grandfather speaking to him. He had died when Christian was very young, but he could picture the old man's face worn by the savage weather, his frail matted hair turned white, his eyes radiant and burning.

His mother had explained that his grandfather bore within him a shining fire so that he could see in the dark, both literally and mystically. Remote from other men, fasting, constantly at the state of exhaustion, his duty was to protect the tribe from all evils, especially those creatures of the night, confused by the moon, who prowled endlessly.

Then one day his grandfather died—he was not immortal. He left the tribe unprotected.

Immediately Christian wanted to be the shaman, to take his grandfather's place, but his mother patiently told him that a man could not become a shaman of his own free will; it was the *sila*, or the spirits themselves, who through dreams appointed the chosen one.

He was disappointed. He felt that his grandfather would have wanted him to be as he was—a leader—with all the powers of the spirits at his command. Yet in time his ambitions faded as his father guided him to become a seal hunter. It was not as interesting as becoming the shaman—but, as his father reminded him, the world was becoming more modern and there was less and less need for men with spiritual powers.

His father had lied to him. He had known it even then, which was probably why he had always disliked hunting seals.

It seemed ironic that just as his grandfather had

been a witch doctor, he had become a modern doctor. He wondered what the old man would have said if he could have observed him stitch a foot back onto an ankle through a nylon maze of micro sutures.

Christian moved on. He hardly ever reflected on the past. It seemed so remote, so primitive. It was as if on the day he had discovered his village massacred he had cut it all away and become someone else, another person, critical, hastily retreating from the Eskimo ways. He had no link with the past. He did not want one.

The place where the dog had died was near a crumbling stone bridge connecting to the cinder jogging path which circled the reservoir. It was a hidden, lonely area, surrounded by arched, sinister-looking bushes, slightly out of the way—a patch of broken decaying branches and dead hollow trees which appeared as if some obscure force had violently ripped a swath through them. He sensed the presence of evil. But perhaps it was only his memory. Torn grass and slick oily mud oozed up against his feet. A heavy sulfuric atmosphere parched his nostrils. He hated the place, it revolted him. He despised it. It made his flesh crawl.

He thought of the dog. *The thing tearing out at him—its hot breath searing across his face.* He began to tremble.

A wet wind blasted across Central Park, sweeping the yellow leaves into spinning flurries which shone in the cold afternoon air. There was an invisible rustle of shrubbery, subtle, frightening. Christian climbed the crest toward the jogging path and looked through the metal hurricane fence at the reservoir.

The waters of the reservoir were slimy green, surrounded by rocky crags—a shimmering expanse over a mile in length in the midst of towering buildings, glistening penthouse windows and the roar, the

ever-present screeching choke, of lurching brakes
and traffic horns.

It was larger than any city lake, cut off, isolated
from the inhabitants of Manhattan, patrolled by warning signs and spiked wire higher than most men
could climb. Yet on the surface of the glimmering
sheltered water white gulls floated interspersed with
flocks of green-faced mallards and snow-flecked silver widgeons. Amazingly the air seemed to be devoid of automobile exhaust fumes, although less
than a block away the Metropolitan Museum towered over Fifth Avenue, which spewed forth an endless succession of yellow taxicabs.

He stopped at a water fountain, swilling his mouth
with warm liquid. He felt increasingly tense, beside
himself, as he remembered the statue of Theodore
Roosevelt.

The wind whipped against him as he hurried across
the grass. He had to find an answer—*there had to be
an answer*.

When he got to the Museum of Natural History he
leapt up the steps through the vaultlike entrance. The
information center bordered by rows of pamphlets
was exactly the same. The same oriental woman
waited stiffly behind the counter. He hastened across
the lobby, through another set of steel doors. Down
into the basement he tore, through the gigantic chambers dimly lighted by arcs of open-mouth pillars,
past the vivid murals of Egypt, Greece, Babylonia.
His footsteps clicked across the spacious black floors
as he entered the hall of mammals. The sixteen-hundred-pound grizzly lunged from the luminous glass
display. He rushed past the herds of buffalo, mountain lions, crouching cougars and huge horned sheep,
as all the while one memory burned inside his
brain—the paintings, the huge animal skins dipped
in purples and blazing tides of red—the human bodies strewn across a landscape of ice and snow—

broken bleeding arms, stomachs cut open, eyes roaring out in terror—*exactly as in his dream!*

He thought that he heard the Eskimo voices, chanting—

> *Ke! Ke! Keq! Shugunra . . .*
> *Ke! Ke! Keq!*

Then he remembered—he had been no more than eight or nine—his grandfather's voice—that incredibly strange word—he had heard it *for the first time*—Berserker.

What had his grandfather meant?

Perhaps he had taken a wrong turn. The two Greenlanders with their thin sticks and large circular drums—where were they? He plunged into the series of rooms beyond. There were display cases filled with golden ornaments from Peru, artifacts of the Incan civilization, copper eating bowls, spoons, dark stone figures . . .

He stood defeated, his arms loosely hanging. He tried to focus . . . to remember . . .

The murky corner—the horrible figure emerging—a gigantic form on a pedestal wrapped in a bloody sheet—

He rushed back through the hall of mammals, the animals moving in snatches all around him, his mind spinning. He ran back through the gigantic chambers—the empty glowing radiance—the walls raging with lifelike armies marching and ancient royal processions—up the stairs he tore until he reached the woman at the desk.

"Where is the exhibit?" he blurted. "Greenland—the *Berserker* exhibit—it was here a few days ago."

The oriental woman's narrow yellow eyes stared at him. She gave a brief shrug. "You must ask at the office."

"Where is it?"

"Perhaps someone in anthropology . . ."

"It's important," Christian insisted. "My name is Christian Bangsted. I'm a surgeon at Bellevue Hospital." Hurriedly he delved into his coat pocket, his hand emerging with a plastic identification card.

She studied his posed picture, matching it with his name, the technical information printed on the card which identified his position at the hospital. She fumbled for a white building directory, paged through it, finally picking up the phone, dialing quickly. She hesitated a second . . .

"Dr. Rasmussen? This is the information desk in the lobby. There's someone here looking for information about the *Berserker* exhibit . . ." She hesitated again, finally handing Christian the phone. "It's Dr. Rasmussen," she prodded.

"Dr. Rasmussen," Christian said.

"Hello—" The man's voice sounded weary with age and ruffled. "What is it?"

"I wonder if I might see you for a moment. It's extremely important."

The voice on the phone paused, as if concerned about the time factor, before finally reaching a conclusion. "All right."

Christian hung up the phone.

The oriental woman pointed across the cavernous lobby. "You go to the fifth floor . . . the Seventy-seventh Street elevator. Section eight . . . room twenty-four . . ."

Christian hurried in the direction she pointed. Up a short bank of stairs to a hallway brightened with light—past a series of sculptured African heads—into an elevator. The elevator doors closed. As he rose he noticed the array of colored posters on the elevator walls:

Gold of El Dorado
The Heritage of Columbia
Tickets Available Second Floor

The elevator let him off on five. The sides of the hallway were lined with stoic white lockers and floor-to-ceiling glass display cases filled with exact, towering rows of thousands of small, labeled boxes. He hastened down the long empty corridor. It gave him a dismal feeling, as if he were alone in a huge vault. Finally he came to a painted sign with an arrow—*Section 8*.

He took an angular turn, prodding by more glass cases filled with drawers of clay pottery, stone idols, animal fossils and human skulls. He heard the sound of a typewriter in the distance as he approached a dead end. The white door to room twenty-four was labeled *Dr. N. W. Rasmussen*.

He turned the knob of the door and entered a narrow, brightly illuminated office with two high fluorescent banks burning down on a row of tables and desks. Across the green and yellow flecked tile floor, amidst bookshelves jammed with thick heavy maroon volumes, sat a dignified-looking white-haired man who appeared to be in his eighties. He had extremely pale skin and wore a light tweed jacket, starched white shirt, pinched wire-rimmed glasses and an old-fashioned dark green paisley tie. Beside him, next to his desk, apparently about to leave, stood an attractive woman in a leopardskin coat with whom he had obviously been engaged in deep conversation.

"Dr. Rasmussen?" Christian broke in.

The white-haired man nodded, gesturing for Christian to enter, to sit down. Then he turned back toward the young woman, kissing her tenderly on the lips. "Tell your husband I'll speak to him tomorrow," he murmured, under his breath.

The woman quietly expressed something to him of great intimacy and touched his cheek.

The white-haired man responded. "It was wonderful seeing you again," he said.

The woman smiled and left the office, shutting the door firmly behind her, as Christian sat forward. Finally he spoke. He saw Rasmussen begin to turn away, as if dismissing the importance of his presence.

"I hope I'm not disturbing you."

The tight spectacles and wrinkling brow turned, focusing on him. "Well, you are. I have a lecture I am arranging and I'm very busy."

"I won't take much of your time . . ."

"Who are you?" Rasmussen fired at him pointedly.

"Christian Bangsted. I'm a doctor . . . at Bellevue."

"What do you want?"

"I'm looking for the exhibit from Greenland. The *Berserker* exhibit."

"It was dismantled two days ago."

"Where is it?"

"In the basement. In packing cases."

"Is it possible to see it?"

"No. I'm sorry." Rasmussen shook his head. Once again he began to turn away, to become involved in any one of the infinite number of projects that seemed to clutter his office. There were stacks of unbound sheets of white paper and dozens of worn-looking volumes lying open, interspersed with tables of printed reports and several pine filing boxes.

"It's extremely important," Christian persisted.

With that the white-haired man turned. His face conveyed a sense of anxiety. "I told you it's impossible."

"I thought if I could just look at some of the cases—"

"They're simple wooden cases hammered together with three inch nails." He hesitated, attempting to fathom Christian's purpose. Finally he inquired, "Why is it important?"

"I'm interested in the culture of Greenland," Christian hedged, carefully picking his words. "I'm *from* Greenland. I'm an Eskimo . . . from the Netsilik tribe."

Rasmussen, for the first time, appeared intrigued. He sank down behind his desk, the eyes behind the spectacles drifting a second. "What interests you so much about the exhibit?"

"The *Berserker*," Christian quickly responded.

Rasmussen snorted as a smile took hold of his drawn, aging face. "Perhaps you should read the old Norse ballads."

"Where would I find them?"

"In most any good library. I may have a copy . . ." He turned to glance at the bookshelf over his shoulder. "I suggest the *Kvids* of Helga Hundingsbana. In fact, here it is." He withdrew a dusty brown volume with a torn blank cover. Opening it, he gestured for Christian to begin reading in the middle of the first page—a stanza of verse—

> *May the blade bite,*
> *Which thou brandishest*
> *Only on thyself, when it*
> *Chimes on thy head—*
> *Then avenged will be*
> *The death of Helgi,*
> *When thou, as a wolf,*
> *Wanderest in the woods,*
> *Knowing no fortune*
> *Nor any pleasure,*
> *Having no meat,*
> *Save rivings of corpses.*

"Very lyrical." Rasmussen cocked a dry smile. "Hidden in all kinds of embroidery and symbolism."

"But in relation to the *Berserker* exhibit—" Christian kept him in a steady gaze. "What impressed me were the paintings—the animal skins—the battle—"

"Yes, I thought so," Rasmussen nodded, closing the book.

"All those human bodies and faces being massacred—the stomachs torn open, those eyes—*it seemed so real*. What do they mean?"

"Nothing," Rasmussen retorted flatly. "Merely primitive art. There is no evidence that there was ever a confrontation between the Eskimos—who were then called Skraelings—and the Vikings. I myself excavated the Viking settlement of Narssaq near Eric's Fjord. I dug there myself. There's nothing that indicates such an incident occurred. But it has grown up as quite a myth," he smiled icily.

"What was the *Berserker?*"

"The bogeyman." Rasmussen chuckled, laughing for the first time.

"What do you mean?"

"The dark one—the fiendish spawn of the Viking god Odin." Rasmussen rolled his head back, his eyes sparkling with mirth. "It all began with Odin."

"Odin?"

"In Norse myth he was the supreme deity. He inspired the *Berserker* with special powers."

"What kind of powers?"

"Well . . . part of it comes down to us as legend, part myth. Where one begins and the other ends . . ." He shrugged. "It was an old Norse custom for certain warriors to dress in the skins of the beasts they killed in order to strike terror in the hearts of their foes. It is a fact that in one thousand A.D., the *Berserkers* were the most feared warriors in all of Europe, the most terrifying of the Viking invaders. They fought without armor and nothing could harm them. But they were subject to diabolical possession."

Rasmussen was warming to his subject. His brown eyes deepened. "They took part in demonic rituals and wore the skins of ferocious beasts. But it was their fits of rage—howling, foaming at the mouth and ravening for blood and slaughter . . . it was said that their frenzy reached such a pitch that they were transformed into wild beasts themselves.''

"Is that all you know about them?''

"There are other legends. It is said that they possessed superhuman powers. They bloodied their shields and dyed their bodies black and chose moonless nights for their battles. The terrifying shadow of such a fiendish army inspired mortal panic in the hearts of their enemies. It was believed that if a warrior were killed in battle in this state, he remained a *Berserker* forever. There was only one way they could be destroyed.''

"How was that?''

"By cutting off their heads and setting fire to their bodies.'' Rasmussen grinned, amused.

"Did they travel to Greenland?''

Rasmussen coughed and sputtered a moment. "Well, of course, no one knows for sure. As a result of their unnatural acts, certain Vikings were exiled from Iceland in the year 1037. There is evidence that these peoples did settle in Greenland for a short time. Perhaps some of them were *Berserkers*.''

"Is there any way to pin it down?''

"There are stories.''

"What kind of stories?''

"Well, now you're into a different field—I suggest that you talk to Navarana.''

"Navarana?''

"Navarana Rosing-Porsild.''

"Who is she?''

"She designed the *Berserker* exhibit.''

"Is she here?''

"No longer. She quit her job a week ago. She lives in Litchfield, Connecticut—off an old road— Cuttings Road, I believe it's called. But you'll have to write to her. For some reason her phone has been disconnected.''

Christian began to rise, feeling that the discussion was ending.

"There's one thing I should mention to you—" Rasmussen eyed him.

"What's that?"

"She's a very emotional girl—*lovely though* . . ." Rasmussen smiled, a streak of autumn light from the window reflecting on the bald spot near the back of his head.

19

It takes a lot, yeah, yeah, yeah—
To keep real love alive . . .
So when you get all crazy and wild
There's still the price to be paid!

The sky exploded into a mountain of glistening hail, hurtling down in showering white streams of screaming clumps and pelting fragments as the rented Monza careened frantically from one side of the road to the other, grinding recklessly across the thin gravel surface. Christian clutched the wheel as a roar of rock music bellowed from the car radio.

Give me one more moment that's mine—
Then try—try—try to give it away . . .
Try try try . . .
Oh try try try . . .
Yeah try try try
To keep me away . . .

He cradled a paper cup of once steaming coffee, now cold and bitter, beneath his chin, angry with himself for not taking along a map, for relying on vague descriptions culled from uncertain gas station attendants who conceded that he was somewhere in western Connecticut, but who too often seemed uncertain as to exactly where.

He had been driving continuously for two hours when he entered an area of wooden posts on the side of the road, telephone poles with black wires, stone walls, thin-branched trees, red barns and mailboxes with names scrawled across them.

The wooden houses were white in Litchfield, bordered by meandering weed-choked streams in dark pastures, cows in fenced-in farmlands and signs: *Fresh eggs, potatoes, apple cider.*

Smoke rose from chimneys over crawling barren hills. It was wintry and desolate. When the hail stopped, flecks of snow in the air mixed with blustery bits of rain. He passed a lot piled with rows of fresh-milled wood and a sign nakedly hoisted beside the road:

> Rufus E. Martinson
> Native Lumber Sales Yard

A bent-over, scrawny-faced man in a green woolen cap with a plastic visor warily watched him as he lowered the window. "Do you know where I can find Cuttings Road!" Christian shouted across the field.

"Down there . . . 'bout a mile . . ." The figure gestured with a mitten-covered thumb.

"Thanks. Thanks a lot." Christian flicked the button on the door beside him, automatically rolling up the window. He drove on apprehensively.

Perhaps he should have taken Rasmussen's suggestion and written a letter, but there was no time.

He felt a desperate urgency to make direct contact, to find her himself.

Throwing out the cold coffee, he drove a short distance until he approached a heavily wooded area guarded by a large posted notice:

Game Refuge
Closed Area
No Hunting. Keep Dogs Out.

As the car climbed a hill, he caught a glimpse of a large lake—a desolate point of jutting rock—before he came to a private road with a chain gate.

The road had been freshly oiled, and the stench of tar assaulted his nostrils. He parked the Monza in a clump of yellow leaves and got out. Taking his blue canvas bag from the back seat, he slung it over his shoulder. A wave of cool damp air flew against him as he zipped up his tan fur jacket. He climbed over the chain gate and began to walk.

There were other signs—*Private Road—Keep Out—No Trespassing*—but he ignored them.

He walked approximately half a mile inland to where the trees and underbrush became most dense and the road narrowed, then broke off, dividing in half. He stayed on the portion closest to the lake, which he glimpsed from time to time looking down the embankment through the pale sparse tree limbs. And then he spotted the wooden house, private and alone in a field of tall grass, with a slope behind it leading down suddenly to the water. It was an old house with sunken framed windows, an arch, pointed roof, and a soot-stained brick chimney through which gray smoke rose. He hoped to find the woman there, despite the fact that there was no mailbox, no sign of identification. He wondered what she would be like and what Rasmussen had meant by the comment that she was "very emotional."

He stepped up on the porch, hesitated a second, then pounded on the screen door. Although there was no response he sensed that someone was inside. He pounded again, finally shouting, "Hello! Is anybody here!"

There were sounds on the other side of the door, rustling movements. The door swung open.

Her tan face was cut off at the forehead by a crow's wing of short black hair, silken, shining, but it was her piercing blue eyes that practically knocked him over. The impression of her dark features was sultry, elegant, yet there was an unbelievable wildness about her. He was inflamed by her high cheekbones, the way her eyes seemed to hang there, searching him, her lips moist, sensuous.

"I remember you," he suddenly murmured. "*I met you* at the museum! You've been following me!"

She did not seem surprised. Instead she smiled. Then she spoke in a clear, rich voice, in an Eskimo dialect he could not identify. "*Oqoloqati qinairuma galaur pavkit . . .*" Breathing heavily, she seductively licked her lips.

He shook his head. "I don't understand." But he was afraid to look deeper into those blazing blue eyes. Something warned him not to—as they filled with soft tears. "Why were you following me?" he muttered.

"I have waited for you," she said. There was a jade-green feather in her hair and she wore a sleek leather ceremonial robe covered with imprints of crimson butterflies and golden flowers. "I dreamed about you," she said as she reached for him. "*You are the shaman of our people.*"

He drew his hand away, shaken, as if it involved more than he was ready to handle. *She's mad—crazy,* he thought. But at the same time he knew she wasn't. His awareness that she was perfectly sane yanked at him as he reluctantly entered the house.

"What do you mean?" he finally forced out.

She sank before him, touching his legs, fondling him, staring up into his eyes as if begging him to command her. Suddenly she clasped his knees, rocking toward him—"*You've come at last.*"

He felt he was dreaming, he had to be dreaming . . .

"Are you Navarana?" he asked, unable to absorb what was happening, kneeling down toward her, clutching her hands.

She nodded without taking her eyes from him, obviously desiring him with all her heart.

"There was no other way to reach you. Dr. Rasmussen told me I'd find you here . . ."

"Dr. Rasmussen is a fool," she snapped menacingly.

"Why do you say that?"

"He would not believe anything I told him."

"What did you tell him?"

"About the horror . . . the destruction . . . the terrible things that were happening. But you know what they are . . ." She clung to him desperately. "I'm frightened," she said.

Yet there was a peace about her that was awesome, pure. For the first time in days he felt the grip of worry loosen. Perhaps it was helped by the cleanness of the air, the living freshness of the surrounding trees. He felt light-headed, almost unafraid.

"I don't understand . . . all of this . . ." He ran his hand through her soft exotic hair, taken in by the spectacular luxuriousness of her costume, the smoldering primitive feeling in the atmosphere. He basked in the joy of suddenly being wanted, feeling himself an object of desire in the eyes of someone so splendid. The timbered ceilinged room seemed larger than the entire house. Lurking over the thick fur rugs, the mazes of sandstone sculptures, of ivory formations, ceremonial masks and painted animal skins, was the sweet scent of perfumed incense, or perhaps hundreds of unseen crushed blossoms. A fire crackled in a huge rock fireplace, two massive logs flaming and flaring up a towering flue.

"I recognized you the moment I saw you," she said, her lips inches from his mouth. "I prayed for you to come . . . I prayed that you might find me . . ." There was such tenderness in her eyes, such mounting sincerity, that he was taken completely off guard. Her sweeping brown cheeks, her red-lipped mouth and ravishing blue eyes made the way she held her head seem even more regal. She could have been a chieftain's daughter. She reached her arms out—"Don't be afraid. Let me hold you."

He felt queasy, as if he had been drinking heavily. His eyes blurred as she embraced him.

Then it all rolled out of him—the story of his life—his father's death—the savage destruction of his village—he let it pour forth, wanting her desperately to know, as if in that desolate wooded house there was one person in all the world who might give him the answer he was looking for.

Perhaps she was insensitive, playing a morbid trick on him. How could she have any knowledge about what he was saying? He tried to hold back his pain, his feelings—but they tore loose.

He told her about his love for Neville—about the dream—the horrible sordid nightmare—rushing to find her through the streets of Manhattan—

He opened the blue canvas bag and let it slide out onto the floor—the sickening object he had found on Neville's bed—the chunk of black fur covered with gray slime as if it had been ripped away by someone fighting for their life.

"The *Berserker*," she said, her lips icy and smooth.

"What is it?"

"The most *inhuman* . . ." Her lips suddenly were precluded by awful silence.

"Why is it here—*now?*" He immediately wondered why he had used the word *now.*

"Because of you," she replied. "For a thousand years the shamans held it back. But now we have become *civilized*—the tribes have no more shamans. It's loose—it cannot be stopped . . . *but you must stop it.*"

"*How?* I don't understand . . . I don't." He shook his head, bewildered.

She gave him a long, lonely look. "Don't worry about that now." Her fingers trembled across the back of his neck, gently caressing him, kissing him so softly, so warmly, that he finally relaxed.

At first, Christian suspected that the water would be too cold for swimming—but she urged him to the edge of the lake. Laughingly, she mocked his hesitation, stripping the feather from her black hair and pulling the leather robe up over her tantalizing almond shoulders. Her naked body glistened magnificently as she dove into a swirling gray pool between a pair of gargantuan rocks. Tearing off his thick plaid shirt he plunged in beside her, shivering frantically. But she clasped his hand tightly until he relaxed, letting the water ooze over his taut muscles.

Her wet hair cascaded behind her ears as her lips caressed his neck. "It's wonderful, isn't it?" she said, her long beautifully shaped legs fluttering beside him, enwrapping him playfully.

She darted away laughing as he chased her, scooping at the surface. He grabbed her foot, spinning her around. She fought him off. As they found a series of deep pools she curled up against him, her lips straining for his mouth.

They dove and swam and splashed—his mind reeling with pleasure. He felt himself attracted to her warmth, her understanding. It was as if he were home—in a misty, half-real environment where he

could be himself. As they slid through the quiet
water he was happy for the first time in days. She
nuzzled against him, her puzzling blue eyes luminous,
intently searching his face. "I love you," she whispered.

He grabbed her shoulders, hugging her close.

Finally he could stand it no longer. He pulled
himself out of the water, back up on the shore,
gasping for dry air. He shuddered as she threw him a
towel, wrapping it around him, forcing back the
chill.

"We should do this every day," he sputtered,
reaching for her. She whirled away.

Laughing, she tore for the house, her naked body
snaking through the tall grass. He raced her up the
path, slipping, falling, his wet feet creasing the mud,
the towel whipping against his legs. She flung open
the screen door and threw herself down next to the
fire. As he entered she turned away from him, staring down, her hands firmly on her knees. He sank
on a pillow within close range of the protective
flames. Then he reached for her.

"You didn't expect this, did you?" she grinned.

"Not with a name like Navarana Rosing-Porsild."

"Are you hungry?" she cut in.

He pinned her shoulders down, sliding over her
long legs. "How did you know?" He kissed her full
lips, smoothing down her sliding wet hair. "You're
so wise," he murmured.

Darkness dissolved the tree branches near the windows. Yet the calmness conveyed no hint of a wind.
Christian imagined that outside there were hordes of
stars glittering over them.

"I'm frightened," Navarana said, nuzzling up next
to him.

"But I'm here," he comforted her.

"I know . . . I know . . ."

"Then what are you afraid of?"

"I haven't told you everything," she warned, trembling in his arms.

"About the *Berserker?*"

"Yes."

"What more is there?"

He felt her body tighten as if she were reluctant to let him know.

"Can't we escape it?" he asked finally, wishing there was nothing, nothing in the world that would interrupt what he was experiencing. He reached down for her warm thighs, cradling them under him, kissing her lips. "You're absolutely wonderful . . . *wonderful . . .*" he said.

Her hands came up, caressing his face. Her alluring blue eyes restlessly searched him. "I'm so sorry," she said at last.

"What do you mean?"

"I feel so sorry . . . for you."

"But I'm all right."

"No . . . No . . ." She clung to him disconsolately.

"What do you mean?"

"Its purpose is to destroy you."

"But why?"

"I must tell you everything."

"All right . . ."

"When the invaders came—there was no way to stop them. Our people would not fight . . ."

He grasped her tightly as the flames licked selfishly at the tottering logs beside them. It all seemed so far away—tales of darkness—of hovering terror. He listened reluctantly, wanting to blot it all out, to squeeze it once and for all out of his mind.

"Finally our people turned to the shaman for help. We built a boat made of ice . . ." she went on. "Each day the invaders saw the ice boat moving toward them through the water—but it was empty and they laughed as it broke into pieces near the mouth of the fjord. But one day our men were in the boat—with knives and spears. The shaman caused a fire to rise up in the huts, burning many of the invaders to death before they could escape—''

"Wait," he stopped her. "I saw it happen. I saw it . . ."

"Our people attacked the invaders . . . killing them. But one escaped . . . a warrior of such ferociousness . . . before the eyes of our men he turned into a beast . . ."

"I know . . ." Christian murmured.

She whimpered with unutterable terror. *"He's come back. He's here with us now."*

A shroud of menace took hold of Christian's heart. He thought of Neville—the dark growling thing in Coburg's office—for the first time *he believed.* "Don't worry . . . don't be afraid . . ." he consoled her.

Outside, there seemed more than intense blackness— *a rustling in the trees*—something moving toward the house—through the bushes—the tall grass—giving off a reeking stench—

At that same second Christian felt an object scurry, brushing by his fingers. He could have instantly dismissed it, flicking it aside—

He glanced out of the corner of his eye at a tiny brown creature, baring its teeth, rising toward his thumb.

He leapt up with a scream, grabbing a log by the brick grating, slamming it at the revolting mound of fur—as his eyes focused on other shapes rushing at him from distant corners of the room, sickening figures with flashing yellow eyes.

"It's come . . ." Navarana wailed, hideously beside herself, running into the kitchen, as Christian fought off the creatures—*the wooden floor was alive with them—they crawled across his bare feet—he leapt back—*

The house was swarming—Navarana stumbled to-

ward him. "I saved this for you," she screamed.
Her eyes rolled as she held a silver-linked chain
connected to a dark stone, thrusting it at him. "Wear
it, *oh God* . . ." She sank down. He grabbed her as
the furry mounds covered her body—he managed to
yank her free—

There was a sudden wave of pounding which
shook the house. The fire sputtered, went out—

"Into the cellar!" she wailed. She grabbed for the
floor, pulling up a portion hooked to a chain, revealing wooden steps leading down. "Hurry—" she
motioned. He obeyed, reaching for her. "You go
first!" she directed, overcome, hysterical.

Quickly, he started down the stairs, the tiny vile
shapes leaping onto his shoulders, their teeth ripping
at his throat. He beat them off—*then he looked
up—as at that second she slammed the section of
floor closed on top of him!*

He pitched off balance, rolling forward down the
stairs into a pit of slime. The darkness overwhelmed
him. He reached up—up the stairs—pounding on
the floor—trying to get out—desperately!

Then above him he heard a cry, a soft female
voice, a plaintive moan—as a thousand beady eyes
greeted him, surrounding his legs, his arms, his
face, scurrying by his hands. He braced himself—
shuddering.

Inches from his face was a metal grating imbedded
high in the cellar wall. Trapped, Christian stared
through it, listening to Navarana's horrible cries. A
black oily substance swam down her naked body,
stark, ugly against the smoke-drenched sky. She
yanked in torment at the tightening leather thongs
slicing into her wrists, her athletic thighs squirming to
break free. "Pl—please—oh—h—ha—ha—G—G—
God! Please—h—h—help—" she choked.

Her eyes bleared with panic. The torn nipples of

her breasts, her ruptured lips, her discolored throat were shoved forward by an iron hook clawing at her neck.

If it were possible Christian would have fought his way out of the cellar, would have torn down the walls to get at her. A cold wave of nausea ripped through his veins. He could not bare to watch, yet the sight drew him, sickening him with revulsion.

A sudden fall of sparks splattered against his face as the blazing fire roared toward the tops of the dark trees. He stared out through the cellar grating, pinned on every side by insidious shadows—intense, flickering eyes poised to attack.

Yet what held them back?

He kept his body absolutely still, peering into the night only a few feet away from the fitful conflagration.

Navarana drove against the cruel thongs, her wrists streaming with blood, her shoulders bent between two towering limbs.

As the shape appeared—enormous.

Its huge hands reached down and lifted a faggot from the fire. Navarana turned in torment, sobbing, as the thing shoved it up between her legs. She howled, *catching fire*—horribly twisting—screaming into the dark.

He felt the sun cut in at him, warming the wet slime slipping from his fingers. The creatures had vanished—their terrible eyes had retreated from the light. He had watched them as they scurried through slits in the stone foundation. He looked about the cellar, toward the wooden stairs.

Painfully he forced himself to move, his body stiff, bent, aching. He grabbed for the edge of the stairs, working his way up, straining at the floor above him, pushing at it with all his strength.

But it would not give.

He trembled, overcome with fury. Angrily, he slammed his shoulder into the wooden boards, again and again, lifting, driving with his knees to jockey them loose. Finally, he felt the boarded section squeak up. Slowly it lifted free, allowing him to crawl from his cramped prison.

The house was torn apart—wooden masks, pieces of broken sandstone relics, smashed ivory sculptures lay strewn across the floor. Yet a piece of a log still smoldered in the stone fireplace—reminding him of a tall slender girl with almond skin.

His knees buckled, he was barely able to walk. Yellow sweat dripped from his hair as he forced himself across the wooden floor. His bare feet were cut, torn open, his arms and legs swollen with tiny infected sores.

It made him sick to remember. He wished he had no memory left.

He threw himself at the screen door, practically yanking it off its hinges. His mind roared with hate as he rolled helplessly down the grassy path. Slowly he regained his balance, steadying himself, trying to stand.

The remains of the fire were clumped in broken arched chunks. There was one chunk—a charred torso. It lay near a growth of weeds, covered with grotesque black bubbles, *the white bones exposed—Navarana's chest bones*.

He howled tearing at the weeds. Suddenly he was a madman, jumping, wailing. He would fulfill his own curse now. He screamed, baring his teeth—picking up the white bones—hurling them into the air.

20

At the end of a trail of fluorescent purple arrows flashed a revolving red signboard—

Gold—Instant Cash

Near the bleak, crowded corner a tall gaunt man shivering in a thin black windbreaker hawked six-foot-long sausage-shaped yellow balloons. "Five for a dollar!" he shouted over and over in the same monotonous falsetto—"Five for a dollar!" Between Fifth and Sixth Avenues truck horns blared up and down the street, abruptly halted in traffic behind a stalled fire engine. Their wails were punctuated by the constant sound of leather soles on the narrow sidewalks, clipping past the seemingly endless row of tiny shops; gem exchanges and gaudy emporiums, competing side by side for attention, their windows sparkling with ovals, heartshapes and starbursts of diamonds, sapphires and rubies in every setting possible. Painted, dark-lettered prices positioned behind each item ranged from one hundred and ninety-five dollars for a tiny set of diamond-studded earrings into the thousands and tens of thousands for bracelets, lockets, necklaces dripping with tear-shaped emeralds, drinking cups, silver encrusted chalices, ornate bands of woven platinum, crosses, medallions. There were painted signs, signs everywhere—*We Buy Diamonds and Old Jewelry—Top Prices Paid—Diamond Cutting—Importing—Expert Appraisals*—a staggering glut of improvisational advertising.

The sidewalks were flooded with people talking in diverse languages—packs of heavily bearded men in long black overcoats, their white collars opened at the throat, brushed against tourists and uncertain sightseers peering at cuts and carat weights with bewildered, longing eyes. It was a carnival, Las Vegas, the flea market in Tangiers, all melted into one frenetic conclave.

In the center of it stood the austere firm of *Leon Fishman, Lapidary and Pearl Exports,* a stark, neon-lighted showroom where frozen-faced salesmen with arms crossed stood waiting behind counters as prospective customers milled in and out gaping at velvet-lined beds laden with glittering jewels. The proprietor, Leon Fishman, prided himself on knowing more about the gem business than anyone on Forty-seventh Street. He had tired, overworked eyes and heavily cheeked jowls, a white-haired balding little man, dressed in a nondescript gray suit, gray vest and gray tie loosened about his perspiring throat. He was extremely busy, but then he was always extremely busy. He fitted the magnifier in front of his eyes and stared intently at the dull blue gem. He shrugged, scratching his head, unable to make up his mind. Finally he glanced up at the dark-haired young man wearing a heavy cocoa-colored turtleneck sweater, faded jeans and battered green sneakers. There was a look of desperation about the young man's face—deep-set lines flowed in grooves under his brown eyes as if he had not slept in days. He was obviously troubled by something, beset by nervousness. Perhaps he was a chain smoker or on drugs. It was a shame. He was a handsome-looking man. To waste one's precious youth was unforgivable.

Fishman winced, agitated. ''I've never seen a stone like it.''

''What do you mean?''

''It's real—whatever it is. Wait here a moment.''

Fishman shuffled through the shifting crowds toward the back of the noisy showroom, clasping the silver-linked chain in his fist. Abe Fabricant, his closest friend and partner of thirty-one years, would know the answer.

Abe sat behind the appraisal counter, his head bent low over several plastic bags filled with gold trinkets, weighing them in his fingers. "Abe—will you take a look for a moment?"

Abe's ruddy face peered up. "You notice I'm very busy," he grunted.

"I've never seen anything like this," Fishman insisted.

Abe glimpsed the heavy blue stone fixed to the silver chain clutched in Fishman's hand. He stared closer, blinking for a moment. "It's chrysoprase," he concluded.

"It can't be," Fishman shook his head. "Chryso-prase is green."

"Almost always," Abe rasped, breathing heavily. "Except I saw a piece like that once." Under the overhead neon glow the smooth blue stone appeared lifeless, dead. "It comes from the coldest region of the arctic."

Fishman turned to notice that the young man had followed him and was standing near his shoulder. "You heard him?" Fishman asked.

"Yes," the young man nodded. "Is that all you know about it?"

"Where did you get it?"

The young man did not seem to enjoy the question. The muscles of his long cheeks hardened. "It was given to me . . . by someone . . ."

Abe studied the stone carefully through his jeweler's lens. Finally he gazed up. "It's an ancient amulet. The setting is perhaps three—maybe four thousand years old." He shook his head. "It's amazing, isn't it? There isn't even a market for such a thing . . ."

Les Margolis drew the Bogen high-impedence microphone to his lips. *"Attention please—"* His authoritative voice boomed through the halls, relayed by speakers buried in banks of plaster above the high, dimly lighted ceilings. *"Attention please—the American Museum of Natural History will close in ten minutes."*

He rose from the desk, clamping his walkie-talkie to his belt, and moved militarily through the series of glass panels dividing his space from those of the others in his office. With hair slicked-back, his abrupt black mustache and a look of perpetual worry on his face, the whites of his eyes bulging forward made him appear every inch the head of building security. The fact that the museum was closing so late bothered him—it was not normal procedure. It threw him off balance. "Why nine p.m.?" he had angrily complained to Ron Dorndorf, one of the directors. But Ron had brushed him off, explaining that it was a temporary measure, due to extreme interest in some of the special exhibits.

Still, it bothered Les. There had been evidence of recurring break-ins. And then the week before the burglar alarm had been unaccountably left off and a basement window was found open. Since then Margolis had worked strenuously to impose tight security in the building.

The museum's ten floors were not patrolled at night by seven guards, in addition to a twenty-four-hour closed-circuit television camera system which had just been installed in each area. It was relatively foolproof, but there was always the chance that somebody might slip through.

At closing time the lavatories were searched. Two trained female guards checked the Women's and two male guards checked the Men's. The only doors left open from the inside were the fire and emergency exits.

Checking his watch Margolis entered the long connecting exhibit halls, hurrying through *Meteorites and Minerals* into *Small Mammals, North American Indians* and the compelling darkness of the *Northwest Coast Indians*. He passed by an attractive young brunette with a beaded bag over her shoulder.

"Miss—you'll have to leave the museum."

"Is it closing?"

"Didn't you hear the announcement over the speaker system?"

"No," she replied vacantly.

"It's three minutes to nine," he snapped. "Wouldn't want to lock you in." He watched as her steps quickened. He smiled to himself. Most everyone was amiable; they obeyed.

Margolis clutched the walkie-talkie under his chin. "Phil—are you there?"

A voice crackled back. "Section twenty-two is closed off."

"What about sections nineteen and thirty-one?"

"I'm getting to them, Les."

The sudden sound of a series of huge hall doors banging shut made Margolis feel secure—his men were in control.

He zigzagged through two more hallways, hurrying several visitors along, back out to the main entrance, watching the lights begin to flick off.

Christian had heard the echoing voice over the loudspeaker announcing that the museum was closing. He listened to the receding footsteps on the tile floor, the sounds of people passing by on their way out of the building. More voices. Then the huge doors locked with a volley of resounding slams. He waited several minutes. He checked his watch. It was nine forty-five.

There were obviously watchmen left on duty, but hopefully they were stationed in the hallways outside. It was a chance—but he had to get down into the museum's basement.

Perhaps there was nothing for him to see—little more than he had observed the day he had come with Neville. But he felt—he sensed—*something*.

With a long narrow screwdriver he jimmied the lock from the inside, carefully edging back the sliding cylinder. Silently the door to the tiny closet marked *Fire Hose Inside* slipped open.

He had checked several locked closets before choosing this one. Then he had watched, attempting to appear as casual as possible, waiting for a gap when the corridor emptied of visitors, before hastily working his way in. Once he was huddled inside, he suspected that the guards, as part of their routine, might open each of the locked doors, but they did not open his.

As he crept out of the closet, he hesitated. It was pitch dark in the huge gallery, causing him to feel a stirring trepidation. He flicked the switch on the handle of the two-cell industrial flashlight. An eerie bath of light played over the long row of gigantic African idols carved out of wood crouched on both sides of him. Near his hand was a glass case filled with odd slinking shapes. He turned away, unsteadied by the silence, reluctant to break it, even with the sound of his own footsteps.

He walked gently, consciously flat-footed, as if he had moccasins on. He held down the glow of the flashlight as much as he possibly could. Passing several enormous shapes, he felt monstrous glass eyes glare at him through the gloom. It was still early, yet it seemed as if it were the middle of the night.

An enormous grizzly stared down at him, its hulking arms extended, its blazing yellow eyes surrounded by cavernous black pockets. At night the museum felt like a haunted castle surrounded by a moat—a bizarre exhibit in a carnival of uncertain horrors. He flashed the light away from the grizzly's eyes toward the rear of the gallery. There were two gray iron doors marked *Not Open to the Public*. He moved quietly toward them. When he got there he gave the doors a heavy shove. They clicked open, revealing a flight of stairs leading down.

He wondered how many floors lay beneath the dark gallery, how many disconnected rooms and murky corridors. Step by step he proceeded cautiously into what appeared to be a temporary exhibit area. The dense chamber flowed zigzag into empty hallways with low ceilings and overhead heating pipes emitting long subterranean shafts of steam. He was not used to wearing jewelry around his neck and the silver chain with the dull blue stone throbbed heavily against his chest. He had vowed to abide by Navarana's wish, to wear it—yet the chain chilled his shoulders with a peculiarly intense inner cold, its sharp edges rubbing the back of his neck raw.

He made his way through more iron doors—rooms within rooms—cluttered, uncompleted displays—hundreds of them—made up of human skulls—carcasses of animals—teeth, jawbones, matted hair—glowing banks of Indian beads, painted bowls, primitive musical instruments—pits of loose earth—cases erupting with artifacts—plastic bags of topsoil, steel pipes, ladders, brooms, open electrical floor plugs, paintbrushes, blocks of wood—and then a harpoon, used for killing seals. He sensed that he was heading in the right direction.

With his flashlight burning across the blackness he passed through another set of iron doors, leading down a flight of stone steps past cages and drill presses, electrical saws, a gravel floor covered with endless boxes—*and a row of wooden crates*.

He was overcome with anxious energy. He beamed the light over several nearby workbenches, before spotting a tool to work with—a claw hammer.

Clutching the hammer he sank the claw into one of the crates, bending back the top of the boards, tearing at them, ripping at the nails. The crate was packed with the ancient drawings in purples and dark browns and flowing reds painted on huge animal skins. Twisted broken bodies lay strewn across a landscape of ice and snow. He slammed back the boards, blocking out the images.

Quickly he began tearing at the largest crate in the room. He ripped back several boards. It appeared to contain a figure on a pedestal—covered by a white sheet. The sheet fell away.

He recoiled—almost dropping the flashlight—suddenly imprisoned by the unnaturalness of the grim, unforeseen presence—horrible—a shape so grotesquely formed that he sank back. He had to force himself to gape at its twisted ugliness. The body might have belonged to a wolf or a bear—yet it had no feet. The flesh of its legs wound hideously into talons. But the claws *were human fingers.* He knew—he felt its humanity. He could sense its cold eyes grinding into him though the stone face was missing, broken away. He pictured the vile features—he had seen them *in his dreams*.

The four hellish eyes blasted out of sinking fissures—from the jagged mouth squirmed a scaly floating tongue . . .

He noticed something which made his flesh turn icy cold. Cruelly gouging into the chipped remains of its throat was the outline of a necklace—a chain, grasping at a single stone.

It was an exact replica of the amulet he was wearing.

His heart raced. He had to get away, to get out of there. Suddenly he heard the sound of the guards—doors crashing open—voices—they had discovered him.

He dropped the hammer, starting to run—but where? Down a passageway into blankness—more darkness. He reached out, grasping, feeling another set of doors, beaming the flashlight furiously down a flight of stairs—*the sounds were right behind him*. He leapt, hurtling into an underground parking area, gasping for breath. Then he spotted a sign—*Exit*. He raced under a yellow gate—his footsteps echoing against the tomblike walls—up a cobblestone drive which coiled into the street.

As the roaring traffic of Columbus Avenue grabbed him in he spun across it—horns blaring—a truck barely missing him—brakes pounding to a stop, squealing. He ran toward the river—finally halting, unable to run any farther—huddling in a doorway—wanting the image of the thing to go away.

Rasmussen's words impelled him forward.

". . . their frenzy reached such a pitch that they were transformed into wild beasts . . . There was only one way they could be destroyed . . . by cutting off their heads and setting fire to their bodies . . ."

Unfortunately Christian could not get away from the hospital until late afternoon. It was past five when he raced into the subway. He headed downtown repeating Rasmussen's words again and again in his mind, until he had lost himself in a daze of anger and passionate contempt for the thing he had set out to kill . . . but perhaps *kill* was not the correct word. Could there be a mortal, fatal resolution to anything so evil and monstrous? Wasn't he dealing in legend—blind myth—a literary supposition in an old Norse ballad? This was the present—the actual world— *the events that were happening to him were* real. Yet it had to be stopped. He had watched too many others die—the thing had gone on murdering—Navarana had warned that its purpose was to destroy him.

But she had shielded him, let *herself* be annihilated. Why had she resigned herself to a brutal, humiliating end, and at the same time *feared for his existence?*

It could have destroyed him many times. Yet it had systematically eliminated those people who were part of his life, as if it were chopping away his arms, his legs, until he was isolated . . .

Was its purpose to destroy everyone that he loved? His parents, his village, the one woman he still yearned for desperately? *Neville.* So perfect, so beautiful—her image even now hidden from his thought by a terrifying, guilt-ridden shroud. *Neville* . . . who loved him . . .

He was troubled inside, battered by fears, threads of vague understanding, a creeping indefiniteness. What was the creature's hideous plan?

To lead him on forever? To drive him insane? Until suicide was his only escape? The thing had haunted him all his life, as if challenging him, threatening him to stand before it—to face it—to recognize it for what it was . . .

But what was it?

Yet the presence of the thing had sought him out . . .

But perhaps . . . perhaps that was it . . .

Perhaps he, Christian Bangsted, could not die? He smiled for a second, staring across at the bored, jaded, expressionless faces of the other passengers on the subway train. Perhaps that was why the thing could not affect him? He was immortal. Sardonic laughter welled up inside him—he was the only one still alive *because he could not be killed!*

His eyes watered. His throat burned. It was the

silver chain gripping at his lungs, tearing at his chest.

Staring down at the blue amulet, he cradled it in his hands. What meaning did it have? Where did it come from? What man or beast had it belonged to?

He rose slowly, almost afraid to move, as the train came to a stop. The doors parted, his feet touched the station platform, moving against his will. He climbed the steps, painfully, resolutely, bound to accomplish an insane, incomprehensible act. Yet what choice had he left?

The sky was somber, turning darker. He felt a chill, an unsettling premonition. Canal Street was a clawing series of ramps leading into the Holland Tunnel—yet further on, heading east, the boulevard expanded, bounded on both sides by warehouses stocked with bookbinding machinery, printing presses, auto parts. Racks of used clothing were jammed along the sidewalk, hemmed in by junk shops displaying boxes of canvas shoes and razor blades. An L-shaped store specializing in burglar alarms was wedged next to a surplus outlet, its windows flooded with men's work clothes, while out front sat piles of belt buckles and cowhide belts for three dollars each. Further along Christian passed cardtables spilling over with assorted radio parts, a stack of old Bunny Berigan recordings, junk furniture, worn western saddles, rolls of plastic and tin, pins, chains, watches, aircraft fittings, hot rod supplies, generators, hoses, tubing, matting, light bulbs, blankets. In Denmark it would have been called *loppermarked*, the flea market.

Christian reached the corner of Canal and Thompson Streets, a large store spilling out into the sidewalk—*Canal Hardware*. He entered the narrow aisles teeming with darting customers. A short, stocky man plowed past him yelling, ''Somebody want to pay? You want to pay?''

Christian threaded his way up to the counter where

he was confronted by a serious, gray-haired salesman, a set of wire-rimmed eyeglasses bobbing from
his ears. "Yeah?" he greeted him, unsmilingly.

"You have axes?"

"Behind the counter." He pointed.

"A two-headed axe?"

"Yeah, I got axes. Get in line." He gestured
toward the end of a row of a dozen people waiting
restlessly.

Christian took his place in line, overcome by the
feeling of unrelieved congestion. The commotion in
the store was incredible. Across the ceiling hung
buckets, steel ladders, racks of handsaws, thick iron
pipes, grappling hooks, snow shovels . . .

He glanced at his watch. It was almost six.

Gradually the line of people receded until the
same serious-faced, gray-haired man came out from
behind the counter, nudging him. "Come on. I'll
show you what we got."

Christian followed him behind a maze of counters
and glass display cases. Toward the back of the
store, on the floor, under a shelf, was a long thin
handle mounted to an enormous axe blade. "This is
the biggest we got," the salesman gestured.

"How long's the handle?"

"Forty inches."

"I also need a portable blowtorch and kerosene."

"Try Feder's on Renwick Street—down toward
the river. We don't handle that kind of stuff." The
salesman lifted the axe toward the counter. "Thirty-
eight bucks," he muttered.

Christian handed him two twenties. As he waited
for change, he ran his finger along the blade's edge.
He was satisfied. It could cut through anything.
When the salesman returned, Christian had it wrapped
in brown paper.

His one thought was the blowtorch and the kerosene as he headed back along Canal Street through

makeshift stands bulging with a panorama of tiny items—two-inch Italian marble bases for twenty-nine cents each—smoke detectors, two for a dollar seventy-five—spools labeled "*very* strong thread," two for twenty-five cents—waterproof laundry bags, ninety-nine cents—bags of red rubber balls, twenty-nine cents a pack—until he was tired of looking.

He hurried, starting to run across the thoroughfare jutting toward uptown, the headlights of automobiles and taxicabs jostling in and out past him. It was almost dark. The receding sun was a blue violet haze etching the sober black piers against a clouded amber sky. A young boy with deep Italian eyes rode by him on a bicycle. "Bet I got more money than you do," he giggled.

"I hope you do," Christian shouted back at him.

A short distance beyond the traffic's roar was Renwick Street, filthy, cluttered, tucked behind several large buildings in a spread-out section of warehouses and trucking companies. It seemed no more than two blocks long, barren, deserted, lined with empty parking lots and loading platforms, except for one small storefront with an unlighted sign—*Feder's*.

He headed up the sidewalk, hastening toward it. And then he stopped. A chain fence blocked the plate glass door, wrapping itself around two small front windows. From its base hung several large padlocks. There was no one inside. As Christian stared into the gloom he dropped the axe, angrily cursing at himself. He was too late. If only he had known about the place he could have headed there first . . . but how could he have known? He could have telephoned every hardware store in the area during lunch, or when he had that half-hour break at two o'clock . . .

He was weary of self-recrimination, his thoughts were filled with it. He would return in the morning.

In the distance he heard a church bell chiming. It

was six. The abrupt, empty street floated with murky shadows, lighted by a single glowing streetlight. A wet icy wind shearing off the Hudson River, one block away, whipped across the vacant parking lots and deserted loading platforms, gathering dust and debris, flinging it against his face and eyes until they smarted unmercifully. The weather had turned freezing cold. He was shivering. He listened to the wind bellow in and out between the skeletal buildings as he buried himself deeply in the folds of his jacket. Then he heard something which made his head spin.

It came from Canal Street—rising mercurially out of the patched, uneven darkness—an uncertain, blank outline—grimly racing at him—machinelike—

It made a sound. A muffled hushed wrenching —the whirring momentum of a plummeting object— closing in—

Christian stiffened, unprepared to experience *what he suddenly saw*. His body cringed in disbelief, his head rolled backward. He grabbed pathetically for the axe, then let it slide, slipping loosely from his stiffened hands, helpless to summon the strength in his fingers, to hold on. It was gigantic—a soot-covered shadow crowned with a monstrous helmet, waving something in its arms, something massive— coming at him—without a face—*without eyes*. "Jesus Christ!" Christian screamed, hurling himself backward. He felt what it was. *He knew*. He tried to scurry to his right, to make his feet budge, to break loose from the awful chill stabbing through his knees. The thing was almost on top of him—pounding— coming for him. He was afraid he'd fall—he'd fall in front of it—trying to get up—unable to control his legs—his feet—howling—whirling. There was a bar at the end of the street—he raced—pitching forward, toward the end of the block—forgetting himself— forgetting everything—as he felt the axe climbing above his head—the helmet rising—the facelessness

—the horror. "Oh no!" he screamed—"Oh no!" Stumbling across the broken sidewalk—"Please!"— feeling the blackness surround him—screaming.

He tore inside the bar—falling forward—plunging against the tables along the side wall, the green leather stools. He spotted the bartender, thin-faced, pale, red-haired, in a brown cardigan, arranging bottles. *"Get out!"* Christian shouted. *"Get out the back!"* He pointed fearfully, as the thing crashed through the door behind him.

Christian hurtled across a shuffleboard table—a pinball machine blinking with a scantily clad girl—the thing ripping it back—the jukebox relentlessly roaring—*You gotta give me love—give me love—give me love*—a color television blaring at the thickening pastel darkness.

Christian dove for the leather booths in back— pounding off balance into an ice machine—as out of the corner of his eye he saw the bartender, frozen, unmoving, staring up at the mighty axe—the blade sinking in a thrusting swoop—lipping up into a bloody slush of splattering brain tissue—the bartender's face gone—his head—the loose quivering ganglia of his ripped-open shoulders wobbling horribly.

Out of his mind, Christian rocketed through the rear door—enveloped in a hollow black alley— feeding him into a courtyard—a water tower—huge trash bins—more loading platforms—running hopelessly—pulled into the distance—toward the winding shape of a ladder. He tore for it—across wet cobblestones—sliding forward—skidding—his ankles splintering—as the wind racked his clothing—he grabbed for the bottom rung—leaping up—sensing the axe inches away from the back of his neck—

He clung to the ladder's sides—climbing— shimmying higher, higher—afraid to look back— sensing the axe whirling up at him—he hurled himself onto the roof—rolling—pitching across a narrow steel grating. He tried to grasp onto the edge, then he looked up—

Triumphantly the figure towered over him—its helmet glittering—spikes shooting from its skull—it lifted the monstrous stone axe—

Christian let go—sweeping at the air—slipping off the roof's edge—falling—his body crumpling inside—

The darkness clutched him in half—he choked, spitting—gagging—his eyes shut tight—as he felt something touch his shoulder—he curled—ready to die—shuddering with grief—

"Are you all right!" The deafening roar of the truck's pounding pistons rumbled beside his ear.

Christian blinked open his eyes, on guard, prepared to resist the slide of the descending axe—the giant helmeted shadow hovering over his brain. But instead he found himself staring into the grizzled, ruddy face of a man in a short visored cap, chewing on a cigar. "I'm alive!" The thought jarred him awake. "What happened!" The man leaned over, one foot stirruped on the edge of a long chrome bumper, illuminated by two massive headlights.

Christian lifted himself up, began to crawl to his knees, feeling the wet cobblestones tearing at his trousers, his back and thighs pressing with pain.

"Your head's bleeding." The beefy truck driver handed him a blue bandana. Christian clutched it, struggling to his feet, dragging it across the wet stickiness foaming from his forehead. He *was* bleeding . . . but he could move . . . he could walk.

"I'll be okay."

"Are you sure? I'll drop you off at St. Vincent's Emergency . . ."

"No . . . no . . ." Christian gestured, shushing him away, as he staggered forward across the courtyard. "Thanks . . . thanks a lot . . ."

He glimpsed the big truck driver finally shrug, climbing back into the cab. With a shifting of gears, backing up, he slowly turned, then roared off, bouncing into the night.

Christian stared across the darkness—lost inside.

21

The headache would not end. It seemed as if a hand were clutching the two bones above his eyes, twisting them, stretching the nerves around his sinuses until the top of his skull yearned to split loose from his scalp.

He kept his eyes closed. His one relief was darkness, deadness, in an attempt to hold back the steady incessant throbbing as his mind wandered, about to burst through his temples. The pain had spread down his neck, until he could only balance his chin on top of the propped-up pillow and lie motionless, his arms thrust upward against the sheet.

In the next room someone was playing a loud stereo—heavy rock disco rattled at the walls. He cowered under the blankets, glimpsing the clock. It was three a.m. He would not be on call for several hours, yet he had headed for the residents' quarters to rest. But he could not rest—he could not blot out the images of the flames—*Navarana's face*.

Fever had taken over his brain. His head pounded as he felt the bite marks of the tiny animals covering his body—the white walls, the closeness of the cramped room circling him, the white desk pushed in toward his face—*the thing—the axe rising*—

The phone rang—once—twice. He hesitated. Who wanted him now? In a stumbling daze he grabbed for the receiver toppling it off its cradle—

"Yes—"

Christian dropped the receiver, his feet tearing for the door, his knees jabbing across the lobby, pounding into the open street, Gene after him, yelling, "Hey, where are you going!" as he raced across a bank of surging trucks, their horns blaring. He swept out in front, rushing beyond their grasping headlights into the city's desolate darkness, his heart pounding, taking a shortcut, cutting across midtown, feeling her voice within him, "Darling—oh God, *hurry!*" Between Second and Third Avenues he plummeted across a vacant lot, through grass and weeds, over the top of an underground garage, hurling himself, zigzagging, slivering the blocks in half, jutting forward, running with all his might, his feet, his legs grinding, hopping over pipes and construction, along thoroughfares sawed up the center by barricades of piercing yellow lights, a siren wailing toward him. He flew through a pile of dank sewage, an alley behind a restaurant smelling of Indian spices and Turkish cuisine, another alley blocked by parked cars, down a deserted fenced-off street stacked high with black plastic bags of garbage. He raced across a schoolyard into a series of modern steel and glass shopping plazas, medical offices, health spas—the ghostly glare of street after street streaming through his brain as he ran up Lexington Avenue, his mind alive, swirling with dread, hope, horror. He had to get there, *he had to*. A sensuous blond in a black fur coat, waiting to hail a cab, gasped at him, reminding him of the exotic woman he loved, alone, waiting for him in the darkness. She was *alive!* Faster, *faster,* wanting to get there more than anything, afraid of being too late, of once again *losing her*, his eyes watered, blurred. He ran as if tearing through passages of a maze, the shapes of the buildings constricted, drawn in, bulging against the overhead glow. He passed all-night delis and cafeterias and pizza shops—automobiles raced past as he tore across bro-

ken, twisted, chopped-up, sunken shafts of sidewalk
—his leg muscles jerking his flesh, streaking with
pain, his eardrums roaring, sweat streaming through
his clothes—block after block over to Park Avenue,
Madison, Fifth, feeling his feet go, his legs stripped
bare by the exertion, the explosive darkness, steam
pouring up through the streets, strips of shredded
newspaper blowing around blackened corners.

He entered the park at Fifty-ninth Street, his mind
rolling, becoming mushy, running under trees,
stringlike, skeletal, as slimy mud mingling with occasional traces of grass shot sliding up from under
his shoes. The lamps along the walkways were burned
out, casting great foreboding hollows, yet the lights
of the city's buildings continued to crowd around
him—coldly distant—a vast checkerboard of rising,
luminous slots riddled with blazing red and yellow
beacons. He tore through the park until the total
effect raged at his mind, spectacular, as if he were
encased by a city from afar, held back, boxed in by it,
removed from its beating pulse as the wind wallowed
through the careening trees. Out of breath, his driving
feet yanked him forward, leading him toward the
cinder path and the mysterious darkness beyond.
Wheezing with pain he had to stop, hobbling forward.

Finally he got to the reservoir. As he climbed the
crest of the path sloping over a low hill, he stood
before the huge stretch of calm coal-black water. A
tall metal fence blocked him from its shores. Above
floated a full moon, silver *Limoge*, radiating a ghostly
phosphorescence across the starless sky.

He cursed angrily—*where was she?*

His thoughts were becoming uncontrollable, wild.
Suddenly he sobbed deep from within as he saw her
in his mind . . . Neville . . . waiting for him . . . *he
needed her at that moment more than anything in the
world*. He needed her voice . . . the closeness of her
skin . . .

Yet where was she?

He began chanting crazily to himself, the words forcing themselves out—

Inua . . . Inua tarneq . . . tamalrut . . . ja . . .
Aja-ja . . . aja . . . ja-ja . . .
Hoi . . . Hoi . . . aja . . . ja . . . aja . . . ja . . . ja . . .

Old words . . . archaic, meaningless sounds . . . a rhythm of dull monotonous memories. He shut his eyes to blot out the sudden rush of dizziness, letting his mind drift, focusing on images—shadowy faces of men, women, children—they passed through him, clad in fur collars, gutskin jackets, sealskins— appearing fearful, in agonized frenzy—their voices calling to him . . .

Then in the distance he heard a low murderous growl, hushed, emerging out of the spidery bushes.

At first what appeared to be tearing toward him along the moonlit cinder path was the awesome outline of a figure in a steel helmet waving a huge lethal axe, but as it got closer it was no longer that. It was running on all fours.

Christian braced himself, fear attacking his lungs, grabbing at his heart. The massive brutish claws were pounding. *Coming for him!* The chain with the amulet felt heavy around his neck as he peered up desperately. He saw a giant falcon—he could see it clearly—descending frantically against the wintry sky. As he watched, it swelled, becoming enormous, its black wings flapping like huge spiny shades shutting off the light from the moon. Yet it radiated a light of its own, drawing down toward him, a cool red fire, shuddering across the heavens, its sparks billowing against the black clouds, as it let out a terrible wail.

A sudden shock of lightning encompassed the reservoir, followed by a cascading downpour of burning hot rain. It enshrouded him, blistering his arms and neck. The falcon screamed, clapping its wings in a frenzy, its huge body bursting with light, as if incinerating, becoming jewellike, suddenly blazing as if it were encrusted with millions of fragmented diamonds heaving in oceans of violent colors. Its opalescent beak and hollow emerald eyes drove through Christian's soul.

He shuddered violently as he felt his face go dead—he saw himself reflected in the falcon's eyes. A moment of deep feeling, of compassion, passed between them. He knew why it had come. The spirit of his tribe had brought it to him.

The skin on his legs and arms curled up through his clothing—his ribs violently churned—his shoulders slumped over until he could no longer stand upright—

He lurched forward, slathering at the caked slimy mud. He felt his skull slide back as if it had been torn out of his flesh. His ears, his chin, his nose crawled—alive—expanding grotesquely—flowing pulpy—as his lips split across the jabbing razor edge of his sawing teeth. Green bile bled down his tongue. He whimpered in torment.

And then he noticed his feet—his hands—jutting out in scaly talons. He felt coarse, heaving fur encasing his chest, his legs, his body. He glanced up, rasping—as the *Berserker* leapt for his throat. Christian arose—the tenseness of his enormous jaws and spiked teeth sinking into the creature's flesh—tearing—leaping—feeling the force of madness in his veins—of uncontrollable rage. *He would kill it—he had the power*. He tore at the creature's neckbone—his mouth foaming with fur—his claws ripping into the gristle, clawing at its infernal eyes—as the beast shuddered—stunned—hulking backward in surprise.

Christian sprang at it—his talons ripping open its shoulder—savagely riddling its throat with his immense jagged teeth. He forced it down—the savage arms swinging at him—trying to defend itself. He rolled it across the ground, howling with fury. He would rip it to pieces! White saliva floating from its mouth covered the creature's eyes—it struck out vainly—*Christian's claws tore at its face, then yanked open its heart*—a black pusslike substance gushed forth. Yet the *Berserker* rose up—breaking away—hurling Christian back. With a sudden burst it roared up the side of the iron fence, springing across the dark void into the waters below.

Christian snarled in triumph, his nostrils foaming with blood, as through the slits of his blazing eyes he watched the creature sink beneath the waves. Looking up he saw the glowing colors rising toward the black clouds, the shape of the falcon unfurling its wings, the emerald eyes darkening, becoming opaque, lifeless, the faceted diamonds rolling from its feathers, falling in sheets toward the bowels of the lake as the mighty figure rose, conquering the wind, its beak pointing upward.

As Christian watched the giant falcon soaring, leaving him alone, he noticed his legs—his arms. The claws, the coarse fur, had disappeared. He was himself again. His heart stopped pounding. As the trees surrounding the reservoir shuddered in the darkness, the wind grew silent. He wanted to rest. To forget everything.

"Christian . . ."

It was Neville. His heart throbbed with joy. She was in the water.

Christian's foot notched through a hole in the fence as her voice cried out to him—"Help—help me—hurry—please hurry!"

Anxiously he began vaulting the fence. He rolled over the top of the metal spikes, letting himself go, hurtling into the black depths of the lake.

He rose in seconds to the surface—swiftly swimming toward the spot where he had heard her voice. "Where are you?" he anxiously shouted.

"I'm here," she called to him. "Over here—I'm so frightened—"

Inklike beads of water swooped along his legs, his arms, as he rifled forward toward the center of the reservoir, suddenly feeling extremely weakened by his human body. The water froze his hands, yet he could not stop. "Where?"

"I'm over here—over here."

He thrashed through the blackness, searching desperately, until the cold tore through his muscles and he could move no farther. Then he felt her—swimming next to him.

He turned, reaching out wildly, rushing against her, finding her, pulling her into his arms—"Oh darling," she trembled, as her naked body wrapped around him in wild embrace. *"I miss you I love you I want you!"*

"Neville . . ."

"I must have you—" She clutched him in a viselike grip.

He reached down, stretching his hand along her magnificent thigh, grasping her, clutching her shivering breasts to him. Her lips moved across his mouth, kissing him passionately. He responded, longing for her—his heart pounded—and then he felt her hands—not hands—*talons*.

Reeling in panic, he tried to pull away—as he saw her eyes—no longer green as he remembered—*as he wanted them to be*—but dark, red, monstrous—

Immediately she pounced—her strength was incredible—yanking him forward—ripping at his shoulders with massive dark claws as he spun—trying to slip loose. *But she held him powerless*, swooping him down to the bottom of the lake.

He choked in panic—the quick swirl of water increasing in his lungs—bursting. *He had to get loose*. His face filling with foam—his lips gurgling—he grabbed for the heavy chain—the amulet—as he glimpsed through her face *the horrible expression beyond*. He unclasped the chain. She saw it—yanking away—fleeing—but he followed her—the blue stone glowed in his hands—until he was on top of her—grasping her long blond hair, embracing her, *releasing the chain*—letting it coil around her neck.

As the chain adhered, she spun in astonishment, wildly, her hands flinging up to remove it. The blue stone caught fire—the silver links steaming—glowing white hot—gouging through the layers of her throat. Her head flipped back. She tried to tear the chain loose, plunging, anguished, ripping at the links, desperate to scrape them off—but as if they had a life of their own they fiercely bit in—sizzling—

He watched her face turn ashen, then coal black. Her sensuous body curled, corrupting into a putrid stinking mass—sinking—disappearing—

Christian thrashed to the surface—his head pounding desperately to breathe—every nerve ending and muscle fiber twisting to snap loose from his body. Above, the moon shone, sheltering down.

He swam for the shore—slashing forward in increasing agony—finally freeing himself from the water—rolling across the end of the rocky bank. Tears of bitterness, of unhappy emptiness, scoured his insides. He pulled himself up—climbing—clinging—lifting his knees to the top of the metal fence—then he fell over onto the deserted cinder path.

"Mother—Father—" he murmured. "*Mother! Father!*" he shouted. "Is this what you brought me into the world to see!"

He hunched over, wet, sobbing, a sharp wind creasing his shoulders, causing him to shiver unmercifully—he stared around him at the lights of the city—the vague, elusive promise of other lives, other dreams.

Free.